CONSTITUTION

CONSTITUTION

Book One of the Legacy Fleet Series

Nick Webb

www.nickwebbwrites.com

Summary: The year is 2650. 75 years ago, an alien fleet attacked Earth, without warning, without mercy. We were not prepared. Hundreds of millions perished. Dozens of cities burned. We nearly lost everything. Then, the aliens abruptly left. We rebuilt. We armed ourselves. We swore: never again. But the aliens never came back. Until now. With overwhelming force the aliens have returned, striking deep into our territory, sending Earth into a panic. Our new technology is useless. Our new ships burn like straw. All our careful preparations are wasted. Now, only one man, one crew, and the oldest starship in the fleet stand between the Earth and certain destruction: *ISS Constitution*

Text set in Garamond

Designed by Nick Webb

Cover art by Tom Edwards

http://tomedwardsdmuga.blogspot.co.uk

ISBN-10: 151476993X
ISBN-13: 978-1514769935

Printed in the United States of America

For Jenny, L., and C.

CHAPTER ONE

Sector 521, 10 lightyears outside United Earth Space
Bridge, ISS Kerouac

"Sensors are picking up a meta-space discrepancy, Captain. Narrowing the receiver band to confirm. Probably just a ghost signal. Distortion from a gravitationally-lensed supernova signal or something like that."

The captain of the *ISS Kerouac* sipped his morning coffee and nodded. "We should just rechristen the ship *ISS Ghosthunter* and make it official."

The sensor officer chuckled. "Yes, sir."

He took another sip of his coffee. Meta-space ghosts aside, Captain Disraeli of the heavy cruiser *ISS Kerouac* was having an awful day.

For starters, he'd just found out that because of the recent real estate bubble on *Britannia*, he'd most likely lose half a million credits in some beachfront property he'd invested in last year. He shook his graying head at the thought—there goes any hope of an early retirement.

Next, it came to his attention that he was about to lose his chief engineer and best friend to a reassignment. That was something every Integrated Defense Force officer had to be prepared for, but it still came as a shock since Admiral Yarbrough had promised him there would be no more crew rotations among his senior staff for at least the next year, and dammit all if he was going to go on these deep space patrol missions with some tight-ass newbie lieutenant straight out of IDF academy.

His reply message to Admiral Yarbrough had not been professional, and it would probably earn him some type of bureaucratic reprisal from the old battle-ax.

But worst of all, he'd lost his fifth straight game of Kluger's Squares to his first officer, a bubbly red-headed commander whose shrill laughter anytime she won or found something even remotely humorous not only got on his nerves but also created within him the burning desire to wrap his lips around a .45 blaster and just end it all.

She wasn't that bad. In fact, she was the best first officer he'd ever had. Professional, friendly, and utterly capable.

But, sweet mother of Stalin—that laugh.

Still scowling, he swiveled his chair to face the sensor station, mug still in hand. "Midshipman? Status of sensor sweep?" he said between sips.

The young man, barely out of IDF Academy himself, nodded. "Almost complete, sir. No abnormalities from the meta-space sensors, and all the EM frequencies are quiet. The meta-space discrepancy we read earlier must have been a ghost reading off our own transmitters."

2

It was an exercise this bridge crew had repeated three times a day, every day, for the last six months of their most recent assignment: the dreaded deep space border patrol. The most boring, uneventful, pointless assignment possible for an advanced Pulsar class heavy cruiser like the *ISS Kerouac*. Border patrol was for the old scout cruisers, or even the Legacy Fleet. It was not an assignment suitable for a state-of-the-art military vessel complete with smart-steel armor and petawatt class laser systems.

And the border in question was a border in name only. Hell, on the other side there was probably nothing. Just more stars, nebulae, interstellar gas and dust. But mostly, nothing.

But *they* were still out there. Somewhere. At least, that was still the current military doctrine.

They were the Swarm. No one knew what they called themselves, and so naturally humanity had come up with all manner of names for them, some insulting, some descriptive. The Swarm, Pixies, the Greeners (a play on "little green men", he supposed), Ghosts, along with several other more colorful designations, such as Sodders, Cumrats, Pusbots, and a few that even he blushed to repeat.

They'd earned their monikers—an Earth nearly devastated seventy-five years ago served as a testament to their unpleasantness.

But they'd disappeared. As suddenly as they'd come. And since then, Earth's Integrated Defense Force had patrolled, ever vigilant, guarding humanity against their return. And in all the decades of reconstruction and prosperity that followed, the fear of the Swarm had waned—people had started to question whether the Swarm even still existed at all. Hell, we'd *beaten* them last time, right? Maybe we'd beaten them for good. Permanent extermination.

"Thank you, Midshipman." He turned to the navigation stations that occupied a third of the bridge. "When sensor sweeps of sector 521 conclude, prepare for q-jump to sector 522."

"Aye, sir," said the chief navigator, an older woman, near retirement herself. Captain Disraeli inclined his head in approval at her—he liked the woman. Reminded him of his grandmother, years ago, before she died. Stiff. Proper. But swore like a sailor whenever her assistant navigator's calculations were slightly off.

He raised his head, which the "all the bells and whistles" computer immediately recognized as a sign to prepare to address someone in another section of the ship. "Disraeli to Commander Gooding, report to the bridge."

A few minutes later his XO appeared, saluting the marine guard as she crossed the threshold to the bridge, which sensibly resided deep within the armored core of the ship rather than being perched precariously on the top of the vessel like an old-style soda can on the fence, ready to be picked off as alien target practice.

"You called, sir?" Commander Gooding took her position at the center of the operations center.

"We're about to q-jump to the next sector."

"Well, it's about time. I think we've had far too much fun in sector 521. Shall I recall the crew from shore leave early?" She winked at him. He forced a strained smile back. She was always making her jokey small talk—in reality it annoyed the hell out of him, but he couldn't let his crew know that. And she meant well.

"Indeed, Commander. Let's try to keep the frivolity to a minimum in sector 522—we've got an important mission to accomp—"

"Sir! I...." A voice called out, but trailed off.

Disraeli snapped his head over to the sensor station where the voice had originated. "Well?"

The midshipman cocked his head in confusion, scrutinizing his readout. "Sorry, sir. It looked like there was a massive quantum fluctuation in the background vacuum energy, but it's gone. Running diagnostics now—could've been another grounding problem with the sensor array."

Disraeli turned back to his XO. "Well! That was the most excitement we've had around here in weeks." He heard scattered chuckling around the bridge. Still, after the ghost meta-space reading earlier, it was suspicious. But nothing Gooding couldn't handle—he had to get to sickbay. "As I was saying, Commander, please take the next shift. I've got a doctor's appointment this afternoon that I don't want to miss."

"Yes, sir. Is Doctor Evans giving you a sucker this time?"

"No, but he told me that my fifth visit is free, and I'm cashing in." He winked at her. She didn't need to know about his decade-old case of Rigellian warts. Especially since the only place one tended to contract it was in the red light district of New Mumbai on Rigel Three.

He stood up, grabbed his coffee mug, and walked to the door, saluting the marines with a half-hearted wave.

But stopped mid-stride.

He held still, putting his hand out to feel the bulkhead nearby. A faint vibration.

That shouldn't be there.

"Sir?" The XO stepped towards him, a questioning look on her face.

"Midshipman," he said, momentarily ignoring his XO, "what's the status of that diagnostic?"

The young man fingered his console. "Completed, sir. All systems functioning normally."

The tremble intensified. Now his XO and the rest of the bridge crew could feel it—he could see it in their faces.

He bolted back to his station. "Full sensor sweep! I want to know what in the blazes that is." He raised his head. "Engineering, Disraeli. What the hell is going on? Is there an engine test I wasn't told about?"

The faint vibration grew to a shudder.

"No, sir," replied the chief engineer.

"Then what the devil is this shaking?"

A pause at the other end, and before the engineer could reply the captain heard an odd noise from one of the sensor stations. The midshipman's face had gone white, and a choking noise escaped his lips. He pointed a shaking hand at his console.

"Midshipman?"

The young man fiddled with his console and sent the image on his screen to the large holo-viewer on the starboard wall.

Captain Disraeli turned to look at the screen.

And dropped his coffee mug, which shattered in a steamy puddle at his feet.

"Holy Mother of God…."

CHAPTER TWO

Veracruz Sector
Operations Center, Starbase Heroic

Admiral Ryten glared at the report before tossing aside the datapad. It was highly unusual, but from everything he knew about Captain Disraeli, it was not entirely surprising. The man often showed little regard for authority and much less for regulations and procedure. Probably why Admiral Zingano had practically banished him from the core to the periphery, resigning the old officer to patrol duty.

"Ensign Taylor, please check the data logs for the past 48 hours. It could be that their regular reports just got lost in the bog of bureaucratic manure we're drowning in."

The young woman nodded. "Yes, sir, but I personally review every report that comes back from the patrols in the periphery sectors. I'm telling you they haven't reported in for two days."

"Anything unusual in their last report?"

She shook her head. "Nothing. They'd completed their scans of sector 520 and had just q-jumped out to 521. That was the last we heard from them."

Admiral Ryten drummed his fingers on his desk. Damn. Captain Disraeli may have held standard fleet regulations in low regard, but to Ryten's knowledge the man had never missed a daily report. Besides, it wasn't his job anyway. It was his XO's. And Ryten had served with her. She *never* missed a report. The woman practically breathed paperwork.

"Very well. If they don't file it in the next five hours, send a scout ship out there."

"Aye, sir."

CHAPTER THREE

Sol System, Earth orbit
Valhalla Space Station

Captain Tim Granger shook his head. He couldn't believe it. After all this time, after all his years of dedicated service. All the awards, medallions—every worthless pin, bar, and insignia that adorned his left breast meant nothing.

They were taking *her* away from him. Dammit, they were actually doing it.

"Admiral Yarbrough, I don't understand. The *Constitution* wasn't scheduled to be decommissioned for at least another five years."

The thin, gray-haired woman gestured for him to sit.

He remained on his feet in quiet defiance, eliciting a drawn-out sigh from the admiral. She sounded like a worn-out school teacher, and it irked him.

"Tim, you know how ancient the Old Bird is. I'm sorry, but the High Command has decided to—"

"Nonsense," he interrupted. "She's in as good a shape as any ship in the fleet. Why *Constitution*? Why now? Dammit, Vicky, I—"

"Tim, the decision is made." She winced when he swore under his breath. "Look, I did what I could. I tried to extend the decision out another year, but they wouldn't have it."

Granger stared at the pictures on the wall, Admiral Yarbrough posed in handshakes with various government dignitaries—including President Avery—a smattering of favorite vacation destinations, and, of course beautiful shots of all her previous commands, the *ISS Legacy* and the *ISS Baltimore* included. Magnificent ships. Just like his beloved *Constitution*. His home.

"It's the Eagleton Commission, isn't it? They're forcing the military cuts, and Command decided the easiest way to comply with reductions is to scrap her, didn't they?"

"I won't pretend I can read their minds…." She trailed off when he shot a skeptical look at her. "But, you're probably right."

He finally sat down, slumping heavily into the seat across from the Admiral. He remembered sitting in the same chair in the same office fifteen years earlier, when he accepted command of the Old Bird. The *Constitution* was old even then. Hell, she was old during the Swarm War seventy-five years ago.

But they built them right back then. They built them to last.

He sighed, and searched for words. But there was nothing he could say, so he resorted to nostalgia. "When we were at the academy, things were different. You still remember old Commodore Vickers?"

She grinned. "How could I forget? Ninety-five years old and still teaching Orbital Tactical Theory."

Granger stroked his chin, rough from neglecting his morning shave. "I was a year ahead of you, so you might not have been there, but one day he burst through the door of the classroom, waving his cane—bashing the chalkboard and the screen and his desk with it—screaming about a new Swarm invasion—" He broke off as he saw her chuckle, and descended into laughter himself as he tried to finish.

She finished his story. "And then he pulled the fire alarm, and caused the evacuation of half of the academy before they sorted out what happened ... yeah, I remember that. Who could forget?"

Granger wiped his eye. "Who could forget indeed? All it turned out to be was him overhearing some old archived press reports that they were playing in the history class as he walked down the hall. Thought he was listening to a live news feed."

Admiral Yarbrough stood up and pulled a small bottle out of the cabinet behind her, along with two glasses. She offered, and Granger nodded. "Poor old man—probably scared the living daylights out of him. Didn't he die just a few years after?"

"He did." Granger swallowed some of the liquid she'd offered him and grimaced. Jack Daniels. Damn, she broke out the good stuff for him. He coughed, and winced more—he'd been coughing more lately, sometimes with pain. It was probably time to schedule that checkup with Doc Wyatt. "But you know the thing about Commodore Vickers? He was there. He was *there*. He was old enough to have actually served during the Swarm war. He knew what it was like. The action. The danger. The casualties. He was a goddamned war hero. Blew up half a dozen Swarm capital ships with his own light cruiser before they finally got him, and he drifted in high-earth orbit in just his space suit for almost three days before IDF found him —mind you, that's when space suits were rated for only one day at vacuum."

"Hardy old bastard, wasn't he?" She threw back her own glass and winced.

He stared at her knowingly, wondering if she was on the High Command's side or not, if she had actually tried to dissuade them from decommissioning the *Constitution*. "And you know what he would say to the Eagleton Commission?"

"As I recall, he was not fond of politicians," she replied, pouring another two fingers of the amber liquid.

"He'd hobble his way into that capitol chamber, smack a few of the senators upside their heads with his cane, and lecture them about constant vigilance and preparedness. He'd be spinning in his grave if he knew how deep the military cuts were."

"Well, we *are* over seventy years out from the end of the war, and not even a glimpse of the Swarm in all that time. Not even the barest hint. It's natural that people are letting down their guard. Hell, it was natural to do that forty years ago."

"Natural, and stupid." He finished off his drink and slid the cup back over to the Admiral. "They're out there, Vicky, and we're pulling our pants down and pleasuring ourselves, thinking no one is watching."

"Well, let's just hope the Cumrats aren't voyeurs," she said with a wink.

He snorted, and slammed back the second glass she'd

poured for him. "We didn't win the war because we were stronger than them, Vicky. We didn't win because we were better or smarter. We won because of luck. We won because they up and left for no reason at all. If they hadn't, Earth would be a graveyard and all our colonies destroyed. If they come back, do you really think we'll be so lucky? If we're not prepared...."

Admiral Yarbrough interrupted. "I agree, Tim. But those are decisions above our pay grade. For now, there's nothing to do but move on." She regarded him, and scowled. "Look, it's not like you're being forced to retire. You're only sixty-four, for god's sake. Why are you treating this like your funeral? There are other commands out there—"

"But not like the *Constitution*," he said, rising to his feet. "Not like the Old Bird. Nothing compares. She's in a class of her own."

"She's an outdated hulk of mismatched parts and misfit crew members, Tim! She's the last of the Legacy Fleet—all the rest of them are mothballed or destroyed. She's way past her prime. It's time. No young officer in their right mind ever asks for assignment to the Old Bird."

He poured himself a third glass and held it up to the light, watching as the blue-tinted overhead lights refracted through the amber liquid. "I did. It was my second assignment back as an ensign forty years ago, and when Adams retired fifteen years ago, I jumped at the chance to go back."

She glanced at him skeptically. "You were assigned there because after what you pulled that was the only command they would give you."

"How dare you ..." he sneered. Dammit, the alcohol was

affecting his verbal filter. He needed to go.

"How *dare* I?" She stood up. "Tim, I've been *far* more than accommodating all these years. I've looked the other way. I've covered for you. I gave you a chance when no one else would. And that's what you say to my face? How *dare* I?"

He only scowled at her.

"Get off my station," she said with more force than she meant, for after a moment her face softened. "Report with the *Constitution* at Lunar Base in two weeks for decommissioning. There'll be a nice ceremony. Dignitaries, historians, celebrities … all that shit. You'll love it. Make a two-minute speech. Eat some expensive hors d'vours. Shake a few hands. Get a little drunk. Then, when it's over, we can discuss your next assignment."

"I hate speeches."

"I'll write it for you, then. Dismissed."

"Sir." He nodded a casual salute, and stepped toward the door.

"Tim?" She called out to him as he passed the threshold, and he glanced back. "It won't be so bad. You'll like one of the newer frigates the shipyards are putting out. They're faster than any old clunker from last century."

He nodded with a thin-lipped smile. It was all he could do.

If he spoke again he knew he'd regret it.

CHAPTER FOUR

Veracruz Sector
Starbase Heroic

Starbase *Heroic* was built with one thing in mind: rock solid defense. In the aftermath of the Swarm War, the newly united Earth governments vowed to never be caught unawares again and undertook a massive building program, in parallel with Earth's reconstruction. At the forefront were a series of defensive outposts at the edge of United Earth space, scattered in the direction of space the Swarm had come from, and among these was Starbase *Heroic*.

Admiral Ryten stalked the labyrinthine web of corridors long after the nighttime shift had started, running his hands along the hard steel walls, feeling every pulse, tremor, and vibration from the various ships docking and undocking, the shudder of the power plants deep in the core, the pounding of the marines' feet as they played basketball on the court two decks above.

It was like a small city, but one armed with several dozen multi-megaton tactical nuclear torpedoes and hundreds of mag-rail guns and laser turrets. No Swarm fleet would ever make it past the Veracruz Sector. At least, not without paying a heavy penalty.

He paced the halls because he was worried. The scout ship had left over twenty-four hours earlier, and had not returned. No sign of any report, either. It was damn peculiar—the ship was small and fast enough that if there was any trouble on the other end it shouldn't have had any problems immediately q-jumping right back to *Heroic* to raise the alarm.

Something was wrong. But what could he do, send another scout ship? Lose another dozen crew members?

The Swarm was gone—he'd been one of the few flag officers entrusted with the top-secret report from IDF intel five years ago. That report formed the basis of the decision by the Eagleton Commission to heavily cut back on military spending. The evidence was incontrovertible—all the Swarm's former haunts deep within their space were completely and utterly deserted. Entire underground cities left uninhabited. Desolate.

The top brass at IDF intel assumed they'd all been killed off in some kind of plague or infestation, though the lack of bodies made that hard to prove. But the fact remained that they were gone.

Ryten continued down the hall, feeling the rising vibration of the power plant as he neared the core of the station, and turned the corner into the Operations Center, saluting the two marines stationed at the entrance.

"Anything yet, Ensign Taylor?" he asked the woman at

communications.

"No, sir. Nothing from the scout ship, and nothing from the *Kerouac*."

Ryten drummed his fingers on his desk before coming to a decision. "Very well. Prepare a report for IDF CENTCOM. Tell them the details of the situation and ask for guidance."

"You think it's the Swarm?"

He shook his head. "No. We have reason to believe they no longer pose a threat. But the Russian Confederation?"

"You don't really think…." Ensign Taylor trailed off, but Ryten finished her thought.

"That the Russians would dare start anything? They've been blocking our expansion plans for decades now. Every time we bring up the idea of new settlements in the United Earth Council, they veto. I'm starting to wonder if maybe the bastards have got plans of their own out in the border sectors —there's plenty of habitable planets out there. Plenty of resource-rich territory to exploit and settle. Something tells me that the *Kerouac* may have stumbled onto one of their secret projects."

Taylor bit her lip. "After all this time? I can't believe they'd risk starting a war over something so petty as resources and territory."

"They've been doing it for years—undermining the United Earth government, throwing up extra red-tape and bureaucratic nonsense while they go out, establish new colonies and build up their own fleet, separate from IDF. Really, it's the same pattern over centuries. They never change."

Ryten paused, reaching over to check the status of the power plant. As if reading his mind, Ensign Taylor asked, "Are they doing maintenance in engineering tonight?"

"Not that I know of. So I'm not crazy then? You feel it too?" The throbbing had intensified. It felt just like the customary faint hum of the engines, only magnified slightly, almost imperceptibly.

He raised his head to speak through the comm. "Engineering, something wrong with the plant?"

A voice rang out of the speaker. "No, sir. There seems to be an imbalance in the phase of the generator. That might be why we're feeling the shudder. I'll see if we can't lock down the source of the problem."

"Thank you, Lieutenant. Ryten out." He turned to Ensign Taylor. "Wake up the chief engineer. Have him report to engineering."

"Aye, sir." She busied herself with the command. "You think this is related to the missing ships?"

The rumbling in the deckplate was now intense enough to hear. "I don't know. But if it is I want to be ready."

CHAPTER FIVE

L-2 Lagrange point, Earth
Conference room, ISS Constitution

Captain Granger looked up and down the conference table and around the room, trying hard to hide his anger from the equally angry faces of his senior staff.

"Sir, it's outrageous. Why now? Why not just wait until our scheduled decommission date?" His XO, Commander Haws, a grizzled old man from whom drifted the distinct odor of the previous night's self-medicating, pounded a fist half-heartedly on the table. His frayed uniform was slightly disheveled, but at least he hadn't brought a bottle to the meeting.

"I know, Abe. It stinks to high heaven. But orders are orders."

"Are they just scrapping her? They can't scrap my baby," said his Chief Engineer, Commander Rayna Scott, a short middle-aged woman whose uniform was a perpetually greasy set of blue coveralls. She ran a greasy hand through her dull blonde hair. It was hard to tell if the gray speckling fringes came from her age or her work.

"Ironically enough, that would be too expensive. But the muckety-mucks managed to procure funding from the Smithsonian to turn her into a museum."

Silence reigned around the table. Several jaws hung open. Commander Scott covered her face with a hand.

Commander Haws broke the silence with a vulgar snort. "What a load of lukewarm rat piss. A museum? They're turning the Old Bird into a goddamned *museum*?!"

Granger nodded humorlessly. "It's my understanding that she'll be in permanent high-earth orbit just a few klicks from *Valhalla Station*. Given all the shops they're building in the new annex … well, makes it easy for tourists—"

Another snort from Haws at the word "tourists" silenced Captain Granger, and he grit his teeth as he frowned back at them all. "Look, people, I hate this just as much as you do." He looked up at the ceiling, which had water damage in several places. "The Old Bird is my home. I started my service to the fleet on the *Constitution*, and I intended to end it that way. But not like this."

Commander Scott cleared her throat. "Cap'n, would you be very disappointed if we suddenly had engine trouble?"

"What?" Granger cocked his head. She hadn't mentioned anything in the engineering briefing early in the day.

"Oh, you know, I mean if we weren't able to maneuver out to Lunar Base in time due to persistent unexplained engine failure? They'd have to reschedule, and we all know how much time it takes to shuffle the schedules of so many dignitaries and senators…."

A smile tugged at Captain Granger's lips. Haws snorted again, but this time with a grunt of approval.

"Rayna, I ..." he began, but stalled as he saw her dead-serious expression. "You're a gem. No, I'm afraid this is it. This is goodbye. You'll all be reassigned"—he turned to Commander Haws—"except for you, Abe. I expect you'll probably take the plum retirement package they'll offer you—"

"Like hell ..." began Haws with a grumble, before Granger cut him off.

"And I can assure you that you'll all have the highest recommendation from me." He looked them all in the eye, one by one. The XO, his diminutive and greasy chief engineer, and the CAG—Tyler Pierce, who'd remained silent and scowling. Standing near the wall were the operations chief, Colonel Hanrahan—who commanded the marine contingent—and the chief medical officer, Doctor Wyatt. Half a dozen other men and women stared back at him from around the table. "It's been an honor serving with you all, misfits and misanthropes included," he added with a wink.

He stood. The rest mirrored him. "One more thing. We'll be taking on a new officer, Commander Shelby Proctor. She'll oversee the conversion of the ship to its new, ahem, status. She's been given operational authority aboard the ship for our remaining time here—hold on, Abe," he held a hand out to touch his XO's elbow. Haws had tensed when he mentioned operational authority. "You will all please defer to her. We've got to get the ship ready for tourists, you see," he added, unable to keep the derision out of his voice.

"Over my dead body. I'm the XO, Tim," growled Haws.

The captain sighed. "I wish it were different, Abe. I really do. Just—give her a chance. Let's make our last few weeks here something we can be proud of."

He was tired. More tired than he'd ever been—even during that short bout with cancer five years previous. In a sense, he was relieved to be moving on.

The officers filed out, followed by Granger and Haws, who grumbled, "Oh, I intend to."

CHAPTER SIX

Sol System, Earth orbit
Valhalla Space Station

Admiral Yarbrough glanced out her window at the dance of ships flickering in and out of view, with the blue marble of the Earth in the background. Mostly cargo freighters and crew transfer vehicles, but several large tourist cruise ships sailed among them, bound for one of the outer moons in the solar system or possibly on their way to one of the handful of planets Earth had settled within a few hundred light years or so. Probably Mercia—one of the worlds run by the British government—or Jefferson—an American colony.

Ha. Colony. Most of the *colonies* were now larger than their governing nations on Earth. Hell, Jefferson was up to three billion already. And Merida, in the Veracruz Sector? Closer to four billion. They'd even gone so far as to declare formal independence from Mexico—not that the old country could do anything about it, seeing how they had never really fully recovered from the Swarm War.

A fluttering tone from her desk indicated the arrival of an IDF communique. She waved her screen open and read.

From: Fleet Admiral Zingano, Commander, CENTCOM
October 21st, 2650
Attn: Admiral Yarbrough.

Vicky, we're getting strange reports out of the Veracruz Sector. A few colonist transport ships never showed up to Merida and have not reported in. Veracruz Sector is close to Russian Confederation space, and CENTCOM is worried that Confederation President Malakhov has approved the use of covert force to expand Russian interests in the region.

Dispatch a few intel ships to the Veracruz Sector and figure out what's going on. Do not engage if the Russians are hostile. The diplomats are all telling me we have nothing to be worried about, including Ambassador Volodin, but all the same, see what you can find out.
-Bill

Dammit. Russians. By some stroke of luck, their region of space was mostly spared the worst of the destruction of the Swarm War. Continental Russia fared nearly as bad as North America, but the Russian colonies somehow generally escaped the attention of the Swarm. Perhaps they were too small to notice. Or perhaps the wafting odor of vodka-soaked day laborers bubbled up through the atmosphere and assaulted whatever the aliens used for olfactory sensation.

Either way, sounded like the people in the Veracruz Sector

needed IDF assistance. Why hadn't Zingano sent the request to Starbase *Heroic*? Surely Admiral Ryten was closer to the situation and could dispatch ships faster than she could.

Maybe he didn't have any intel ships at his disposal. The military cuts from the Eagleton Commission were leaving nothing untouched—even IDF intel services were feeling the pinch. But he was sure to have a few scout ships at least. A Corvette or a Skiff. Just a quick meta-space message to Ryten would get there far faster than q-jumping a couple of intel ships out there, even as quick as the newer ones were—a light-year per hour.

She looked up and spoke to the comm. "Lieutenant Aelian, prepare an intel ship and meet me in my office in twenty."

"Yes, sir," came the curt reply through the speakers. "Problem?"

"I hope not. We've lost contact with a few colonist transport ships in Veracruz Sector."

"Why not send them out from Starbase *Heroic*?"

Good, she wasn't crazy. It didn't make any sense to him either. "Those are my orders from CENTCOM, Lieutenant. See you in a few."

CHAPTER SEVEN

L-2 Lagrange point, Earth
Captain's Ready Room, ISS Constitution

"Commander Shelby Proctor, reporting for duty, sir."

Captain Granger forced out a thin smile and tried not to groan as he rose out of his seat. Dammit, he needed exercise. His belly bulged against his uniform, straining the buttons. The desk job was going to kill him one of these days. And for some reason, his chest felt like someone was wringing his lungs with their fists.

"Commander. Welcome aboard." He looked her up and down. Young. Fit. Approaching middle age. Black hair but pale skin. Was she Asian? No. Well, maybe an ancestor or two in the distant past. "Has Haws shown you to your quarters yet?"

Her brow furrowed. "No, sir. Was he supposed to?"

He muttered a profanity under his breath. *Dammit, Haws, it's not like she's after your job or something.* "He's been busy." Holding out a hand to indicate the doorway he continued, "If you'll follow me...."

Granger walked to the door of his ready room, but she didn't move. "Actually, sir, I wanted to get started right away. We've only got two weeks and I want to hit the ground running. You still have a full contingent of V-wing X-25 fighters on board, no? I want to gut about half a dozen of them, strip out all their weaponry, and use them as hands-on display pieces down in the hangar. You know, so kids can get up inside of them and pretend they're fighter jocks for a few minutes. That should take the longest, so I want to get started early.

"Next, I want to convert most of the command consoles on the bridge into interactive displays and configure them to run in simulation mode. That way we can run guests through in groups and give them the chance to command a warship in battle for a few maneuvers. We can wire them together with the environmental controls to simulate the inertia changes with the artificial gravity deckplates. Then, I want to—"

Granger had held up a hand, but she steamrolled right over his gesture. Finally he had to raise his voice. "Commander?"

"—the galley into a full service restau—" She looked up from her datapad in surprise. "Yes, Captain Granger?"

"No."

She lowered her datapad and pursed her lips, looking as if she were about to stab him with her beady eyes. "Excuse me? Sir?"

"No." He desperately wanted to stop the conversation there, to let the single word of defiance hang in the air as he sent her packing, but reluctantly he went on. "Not today. We'll start tomorrow. We're almost at the end of the day shift, and tonight we've got a standard maintenance of the main engines —"

"But you're not going to need those engines in two weeks, Captain Granger," she interrupted. "I suggest that—"

"Regardless, my orders stand. I'm still in command of this ship, and if you want to protest that inconvenient fact you can take it up with Admiral Yarbrough." He glanced at the old leather-strap watch on his wrist. "And by my reckoning she's dead asleep by now, so you may as well go kick back, have a few drinks at our bar—"

"You have a *bar*?"

"They call the place *Afterburners*. Well, technically it's just a satellite service counter from the galley down in the observation deck by engineering, but some of the boys put together a little distillery. It's actually quite good if you can believe it. Just don't drink too much of it or you'll spend an evening in the detox unit in sickbay. " He turned back to the door and nodded to the marines as he passed, Commander Proctor hot on his heels. "Dismissed, Commander. See you in the morning."

"I—" she began. But the conversation was over. He'd left.

She pounded the air beneath her hanging fists at her side and muttered, "Dammit. This is going to be a long two weeks."

"Ma'am?" One of the marines looked at her questioningly.

"As you were, Corporal."

He snapped back to attention and she strode down the hallway to the elevator shaft. Maybe if she found the astrometrics lab she could get a head start on converting it into a planetarium.

The captain's blunt declaration repeated in her mind and grated her nerves. *No*, he'd said. How dare he? Admiral Yarbrough had recruited her herself for this job. She'd promised her that if she could successfully handle a smooth transition of the *Constitution* into one of the *Smithsonian's* centerpiece museums then she'd be up for a command position.

Ha—command. Something she'd always dreamed of in her previous life as a scientist. It wasn't until she gave that career up and joined IDF that the prospect suddenly became more real, especially with her well-placed friends higher up in IDF's Science and Research Division. And with Yarbrough as her new patron, Proctor would rise quickly. She might not be the youngest captain on record, but definitely the captain with the fewest years of service.

But Yarbrough had warned her about Granger. A washed-up, cantankerous old soldier who'd had more than his share of discipline problems. The admiralty was doing its damnedest to ease him out of command, and it seemed decommissioning the Old Bird a few years ahead of schedule was the easiest way to do that.

The doors to the astrometrics lab slid open, revealing banks of computer access stations and walls of monitors, which, at the flip of a switch could project three dimensional holographic images of whichever starfield or planetary system the user wanted. Perfect for the future museum's new planetarium.

"Excuse me, Commander?"

An older lieutenant peered up at her from his station. His eyes squinted, and the frown indicated she wasn't going to like what he had to say.

"Yes, Lieutenant?"

"I'm sorry, but the captain called down a few moments ago. He informed me that the astrometrics lab is closed for the rest of the duty shift today, and will not reopen until the morning."

Granger, you old bastard.

"Excellent—with the lab closed that will help me be able to get a head start on the modifications to—"

The Lieutenant held up a hand, breaching decorum by interrupting her. "I'm sorry, sir, but he was quite clear. No modifications are to happen before tomorrow morning."

She bristled. How dare he? She had half a mind to get on the comm and ask Yarbrough to beat the old fart into submission for her.

But no. That was not the way to impress the admiralty. If she had Yarbrough fight her battles for her, how could they ever trust her with command?

No, she'd have to be patient. Persistent. Granger may try to oppose her at every turn—in fact, she was sure by that point that he'd throw up every roadblock he could. But she'd push forward anyway.

That captain's chair would be hers, dammit. But not on this piece of junk, thank God, Proctor indulged, allowing herself to feel superior. Her ship would be new—top of the IDF line. All she had to do was get there.

She looked down at the waiting man. "Thank you, Lieutenant. I'll see you in the morning, then."

And with one last glance around the astrometrics lab, she swept out the door, leaving a slightly disappointed-looking lieutenant. Granger had probably instructed him to prod a reaction out of her. Well, she wasn't going to play along.

In fact, she'd just have to prod harder.

CHAPTER EIGHT

Veracruz Sector, Leon System
IDF Intelligence Ship ISS Tirian

"Navigation, time to the Merida system?"

The officer at navigation tapped a few spots on his command console. "We're on the outskirts of the Leon system, sir. Thirty-nine q-jumps left until we reach Merida."

Commander LaPlace fiddled with his uniform—there was a loose strand at his sleeve and no matter how much he picked at it, more seemed to unravel. "What do you say, about an hour?" he said, calculating in his head how much time it would take to make that many q-jumps. Each only took about a minute to complete, but only advanced them about a tenth of a lightyear closer to their destination.

"That's about right, sir. Fifty-five minutes, to be precise."

The IDF Intel ships were small, but blazingly fast. Most larger capital ships like the Lancer class heavy cruisers the IDF built a decade ago were lumbering sloths in comparison, only able to q-jump every two minutes or so—it took that long to build up a sufficient charge in the solid state capacitor banks. And the old blocky ships like the Galaxy class carriers, well, those were more like slugs. Not too many of those left, and once the *Washington* was decommissioned, that would leave only the *Thatcher,* and the *Norfolk.* And that didn't even include the Legacy Fleet—the ancient heavy cruisers from the last century. Thankfully, only the *Constitution* was left from that bunch, and IDF only kept her around as a piece of living history.

"Still no meta-space signals?" If there were any problems at Merida, or Starbase *Heroic,* they would have heard something by now. Meta-space signals were extremely low bandwidth, but they effectively travelled at a hundred times the fastest q-jump drives. Only twenty-four bits per second, but that was better than nothing.

"Still nothing, sir. Not even from *Heroic.*"

That was damn peculiar. Not that the starbase was constantly sending out meta-space transmissions—it was relatively expensive to do so since each signal consumed upwards of a terawatt—but for there to be no response to CENTCOM's repeated messages requesting their current status, well, *that* was unusual.

And it was also classified. CENTCOM hadn't told Admiral Yarbrough the reason they were sending Intel ships out from Earth's *Valhalla* Space Station rather than the much closer Starbase *Heroic.* The truth was that they'd lost contact with *Heroic* over three days ago. But that was classified top-secret. She'd find out in a few days, but CENTCOM played its hand close to its chest, even with its own admirals.

"Ready for q-jump," said the navigator.

"Proceed." Commander LaPlace's fingers tightened slightly around his armrest. The q-jumps were benign enough, but they still always made him momentarily queasy. Not unreasonably so, given that he was effectively going into nonexistence for the barest fraction of a second as the quantum fields worked themselves out. Less than a Planck-second, and therefore imperceptible, but still.

The bridge was small, and a little cramped, and as such LaPlace knew something was up the moment his sensor officer's brow furrowed.

"What's up, Andy?"

"I'm getting a strange reading from one of the planets in the Leon System."

LaPlace craned his neck to glimpse the sensor station. "Such as?"

The officer shook his head. "I don't understand it. It's a meta-space signal, but it's gibberish. It's like a pulsating oscillation. Pretty regular—maybe three hertz, with some overtones."

"How many overtones can there be at only 24 bits per second?"

"Not many. And I'm not sure it's even regular. But ... I've never seen anything like this."

LaPlace bit his lip. Continue on to Merida and Starbase *Heroic*? Or investigate this new mystery? His gut told him all the events were related. "Hold q-jumps. Andy, can you triangulate a source?"

"Maybe. Can we increase lateral speed? That'll help."

LaPlace nodded. "Navigation, aft and starboard thrusters

at fifty percent."

A few moments later the sensor officer nodded. "Got a lock. The source is the fourth planet from the star in the Leon System."

The tactical officer to LaPlace's left tapped his screen, indicating to the Commander a local star map. "Sir, the fourth planet is where the new Mexican settlement is. Nueva Leon. They're governed out of Merida."

"How close?"

The nav officer checked his board. "Just two q-jumps away. We can be there in four minutes."

LaPlace nodded slowly. "Anyone else think we might have found a lead?" LaPlace asked his bridge crew. Nods all around. "Thought so. Comm, send a meta-space signal to CENTCOM. Text as follows: Meta-space disturbance detected near Nueva Leon. Will investigate before proceeding to Veracruz."

CHAPTER NINE

L-2 Lagrange point, Earth
Afterburners Bar, ISS Constitution

Captain Granger knew it was probably a mistake to antagonize the newest officer on the *Constitution*, but dammit all if it didn't feel wonderful. But that preening paper-pusher of a commander, Shelby Proctor, would probably complain to Admiral Yarbrough that he was interfering with her mission, and he knew his official record could do without *another* corrective administrative action. He'd been on good behavior for the past decade or so, but Yarbrough made it clear to him years ago that she wouldn't tolerate another *incident*, no matter how many good-old-boy buddies he had up the chain of command.

"So you're just going to let her do it? Strip out our starboard fighter bay and turn it into a friggin petting zoo?"

Granger glowered at his XO, and tipped his glass back. "What the hell am I supposed to do, Abe? Lock her in her quarters until the decommissioning ceremony and hope for the best?"

"Yes." Haws pulled his flask from his boot and uncapped the lip, grinning at the thought.

"You and I both know that we're on a tight leash here."

"Even after all this time? Hell, Tim, it's been nearly fifteen years since your little stunt." The old officer swigged the remainder of the contents of the flask, which he'd probably been working on since waking up that morning.

"Regardless. I don't want to risk your retirement. Or my next command—assuming I get one. Or the futures of the rest of the senior staff."

"You know we'd have your back."

"That's what I'm afraid of. No, Abe, it's time. It's time we let her go. She's had her run." He glanced up at the ceiling of *Afterburners*, then lowered his eyes to the officers scattered around the room at the tables and benches. The walls were adorned with various mementos and pictures the proprietor had picked up from around the colonies. A fossilized tree ring from the blue forest on Deneb 3, nearly three feet in diameter and glazed in lacquer. A pair of old, dusty leather boots hanging down from a nail driven into the bulkhead—the footwear of the very first captain of the *Constitution,* who commanded the Old Bird over a hundred and twenty-five years ago. He smirked as his eyes passed over a picture of President Avery of the United Earth League, her stern, lined, grandmotherly face taped atop the barely-clothed busty figure of a supermodel in a pose so suggestive that it would give a regular person hip-dysplacia.

Dammit, he was going to miss the Old Bird.

Granger swallowed another mouthful of the *Afterburner's* distilled rotgut. "You know, it's not all that bad. The original *USS Constitution*—the old sailing vessel George Washington commissioned, the one that saw service for nearly a hundred years—it's still in Boston harbor, taking on tourists every day. Are we better than her?"

"Did you hear what Proctor wants to do with the engines?" Haws motioned over to the bartender and pointed at his empty flask.

"What's that?"

"Oh, only strip out the lead ballast from the main drive. Says she wants to bolster the shielding of the main reactor."

Granger did a double-take. "She what?"

"You heard me. Thinks that the level of radiation coming off the reactor poses a threat to visitors."

Granger shook his head. "It's well within norms."

"Within military norms, sure. But it's slightly above accepted civilian dosage rates. So she wants all the ballast stripped out and the quantum reactor core shielded with at least five centimeters of friggin lead."

The captain rolled his eyes. "If we do that, we're as good as dead in the water. As it is, we have to wait over two hours between q-jumps. Without that ballast it'll be a day or more."

Haws burped after slamming back the latest round the bartender had brought to the table. "That's kinda the idea, Tim. That's what decommissioning means. No sense in keeping the engines in shape if your ship is a goddamn museum."

Granger studied his empty glass, then shoved his chair away from the table and let the glass fall with a crash to the floor. Every head in the bar turned and a hush fell over the place.

"Over my dead body."

CHAPTER TEN

Marseille, France, Earth
L'hotel Sur Mer, Presidential Suite

"Yuri, I want the bitch dead."

United Earth League Vice President Eamon Isaacson kicked his loafers up on the chrome countertop of the bar in his presidential suite and puffed smoke from his cigar. Cuban. His last one. He made a mental note to tell his assistant to pick up a new case on the next campaign swing through the Caribbean.

"I thought the plan was to publicly discredit and humiliate her. Force her resignation. Clear the way for your presidency." Yuri Volodin, the Russian Confederation ambassador to the United Earth League, held the glass of sherry up to his eyes, his sallow cheeks glinting with the sparkled light from the crystal chandelier above refracting through his drink.

"It'd be so much simpler if she was dead. Avery is popular. Her approval ratings are only going up with the implementation of the Eagleton Commission. The economy is booming. Consumer confidence is at an all-time high. Shit, even the Cubs won the world series last year. And somehow the bitch seems to get all the credit for everything."

Volodin set his drink down on the bar and rested his hands on his lap. "Should I call President Malakhov? We can suspend the operation and prepare a hit squad instead. It would be a simple matter to frame the Caliphate."

Isaacson waved him off. "No. We're already too far down our path. We've been preparing this operation for years. Once the attack happens, and we're caught with our ass hanging out of our pants, I'll present the no-confidence motion. I've got two dozen senators who've told me they'll second. Coming from her own party, that'll be plenty devastating—between that, and a ravaged Europa Station, people will be calling for her head for letting our guard down."

"Of course," said the ambassador, picking his drink back up.

"And in a few weeks, you can call me President Isaacson."

"I admit, it has a nice ring to it," Volodin nodded. "And President Malakhov will be most pleased. He feels you're someone he can work with."

Isaacson snuffed out the end of the cigar. Best to save the rest of it for later. Could be weeks before he got another. "You're sure they're under your control? They won't go berserk and attack everything in sight? Just a targeted incursion through the fringe sectors, a quick stab at the Jupiter lunar system, and then they're gone?"

"I assure you, Vice President Isaacson, the Swarm have been under our control for the past decade. They are as benign now as small puppies. Ever since we discovered the meta-space link to their homeworld and learned how to simulate it, we can basically tell them to do whatever we want. And with the intelligence you provided us last week, I'm sure the plan will go down flawlessly."

"Just don't blow it. Those smart-steel modulating algorithm codes can be easily changed. They only get one shot at this before IDF resets the codes, and then the smart-steel armor will be impenetrable again."

"I assure you, Eamon, by this time next week, you'll be sitting at home in the White House, toasting my good health."

Isaacson poured himself another drink, raised it to Volodin's, and smiled. "Good. A toast to our new world. More secure and prosperous than ever."

CHAPTER ELEVEN

Veracruz Sector, Leon System
IDF Intelligence Ship ISS Tirian

"Arrived at Nueva Leon, sir. We're in high orbit forty-one thousand kilometers above the surface," said the nav officer.

Commander LaPlace nodded. "Sensor sweep. What have we got, tactical?"

The tactical officer frowned at his screen. "Lots of debris in orbit, sir. I'm picking up metallic and radioactive signatures, and organic too." The man looked up. "Bodies. Pieces of ships. There was a battle here recently, sir."

LaPlace leaped to his feet. "Full spectrum scan of the surrounding space, and the surface. I want to know if the aggressors are still here. Any sign of them?"

"Negative, sir. No active ships in orbit."

"Swarm?" LaPlace glanced at the tactical officer.

"No sign of them, sir. At least, nothing like their ships from the war."

The Commander stroked his chin and considered his choices. They needed information. At this point it could still be the Russians. A surprise attack, most likely, and then a raid on the surface to destroy key industry targets. Set the colony back a few years. Give them the chance to get a leg up in the sector before more colonists showed up.

"Insert into a lower orbit. We need to see what's going on down there. Three-thousand kilometer orbit."

"Aye, sir," said the nav officer, and LaPlace felt the changing inertia as the ship accelerated towards the surface and increased its speed to attain the lower altitude.

"Still no sign of the aggressors?"

"None, sir. But from the looks of these readings the battle couldn't have happened more than a day ago—the reactor cores are still pretty hot. At least the ones that are still intact."

Very odd.

"Give me an ID on the destroyed ships."

The tactical officer studied his data readout. "Mostly a handful of merchant freighters and colonist ships. Several Mexican Fleet Zafano class cruisers...." The officer looked up, his face whiter than it was. "And one IDF Nebula class cruiser, sir. The *Nimitz*. Completely destroyed."

Dammit.

"Captain Smith ..." said Commander LaPlace. That was her first command. They'd entered the academy together, fifteen years ago. "Do you have a visual?" His stomach churned a little as the inertia cancellation struggled to keep up with their acceleration. The hull vibrated slightly with the strain.

"Aye, sir. Coming up on your console now."

The data stream on the screen in front of him disappeared, replaced by a graveyard of ships.

"Good Lord."

There she was. The *ISS Nimitz*. Broken completely in two, electrical arcing still glittering at the exposed seams. Wicked looking carbon-scored holes peppered the hull, indicating heavy weapons fire, and several sections of the ship were completely blown away. Most of the section containing the reactor core and q-jump drive was merely a skeleton of steel-titanium girders and warped, blackened deckplates.

"No life signs?" he said, hopefully.

"None, sir. Life support is gone. The whole ship is at vacuum."

"There could be survivors. In space suits…."

The tactical officer shook his head. "No thermal signs either. It's all cold."

The *Nimitz* rotated slowly, and soon the blackened nameplate passed into view, a gaping hole appearing where the 'z' should have been.

LaPlace took a deep breath. "Fine. Move us closer to the surface and get some visual scans."

A few minutes later, they were close enough for visuals. The tactical officer passed the scans directly to Commander LaPlace's screen for him to see.

Utter devastation. Several blackened, smoking pits where he supposed cities might have stood.

"How many people were down there?"

The first officer, who'd been studying the sensor images, finally spoke up. "Fifty million. Five cities and about a hundred smaller towns around them. All gone."

With a start, LaPlace remembered his first officer, Lieutenant Lopez, had family out in the Veracruz Sector. It hadn't dawned on him until then which planet they actually lived on.

"Lopez? You ok?"

The first officer sat stock still, gazing at the images passing on his screen. As the camera zoomed in they could make out the details. The city on the screen looked as if several high-yield thermonuclear bombs had hit it. A few scattered buildings still stood around the edges of the city, but it was mostly a barren, ash-stricken wasteland.

"My grandparents are down there. And cousins. And my … my sister."

LaPlace snapped his attention back to the tactical officer. "Confirm—are those nuclear blasts?"

"Unknown. Maybe, but they're … off, somehow. I'm reading some isotopic signatures similar to those of a thermonuclear explosion, but the blast characteristics are wrong. It's like…." He looked up at LaPlace. "It's like the blasts came from *under* the surface, and exploded upward."

CHAPTER TWELVE

L-2 Lagrange point, Earth
Long-range Comm Center, ISS Constitution

Lieutenant Jessica Miller had only been aboard the *Constitution* for less than two months, but somehow it felt like an eternity. Especially on days she called home.

"Are you being good for Grandma and Grandpa?"

Her son, whose small face filled up the entire left half of the split screen and whose eyes continually darted offscreen, only said, "You fly today?"

"Yes, baby, I fly every day. Momma's a pilot! Momma flies spaceships!"

"You go fast?"

She smiled and nodded. "Super fast!" Winking at the right hand side of the screen, she added, "But Dad flies faster! He flies a *big* spaceship." She held her hands out in front of her and apart by a meter.

The big blue eyes grew as round as cookies, and her

husband's voice cut in—he was orbiting the Earth, though usually the *ISS Clyburne* was on patrol duty out in the Paredes Sector. When he came in from deep space on occasions like this, they always tried to set up a three-way call between them and Jessica's parents in Sacramento.

"Zack, Momma asked you a question. Are you good for Grandma and Grandpa?"

"Yes," came the small reply, and Zack's big eyes darted momentarily offscreen.

"Do you do what they say?"

"Yes."

"Do you—" Her husband cut off as Zack ran offscreen, and they could hear his voice hollering at the dog. Jessica's mother's face appeared on the screen.

"Oh, sorry, I'll go get him."

Jessica waved a hand dismissively. "Oh, don't worry, Mom. Let him play."

"Well, all the same, you two talk while I go sort things out —" The older woman glanced offscreen, and winced. "Oh, he's into the dog food again. ZACK! No, *no!*"

She disappeared, leaving Jessica to talk to her husband, who she'd not seen in over a month. "So, how long is the *Clyburne* here for?"

"A few days. Then we're off to Lunar Base as escort for some diplomatic shindig—"

Jessica could hardly believe her ears. "You're going to Lunar Base? But that's for us! I was going to tell you in a few minutes—"

He furrowed his brow. "Tell me what...."

"They're decommissioning the *Constitution*! There. At

Lunar Base. I'm sure we can get shore leave at the same time. At least for an evening."

His furrowed brow had given way to a smile. "Yeah, I'm sure Commander Ashworth will let me coordinate our schedules."

"Did you talk to him? You know, about what we discussed?" she asked, expectantly.

His smile broadened. "I did."

"And?" She both loved and hated it when he played coy with her. He hadn't changed a bit in their four years of marriage. Not that she'd know—they'd both been on nearly constant duty for the last two years, ever since her maternity leave ended.

"He said ... probably."

She squealed. She hadn't squealed since she was a little girl, but even with the looks the other officers and pilots threw her way in the Comm Center, she let the giggles fly. "Perfect! Tom, don't you realize? With the *Constitution* being decommissioned and all, they'll have to rotate me into another ship. And if Commander Ashworth is for it, then now is the perfect time. Just think of it: finally serving on the same ship...."

"Yeah. That'll at least cut down on my Comm Center use. I had to barter away my weight room time for today's session, right on top of yesterday's session."

"Oh, Tom, the sacrifices you make for your family." She feigned a tear. "It really touches me. Right here." She touched her chest.

His eyes flicked lower. "Wait, do that again, but move in closer to the cam," he murmured. "And pull your uniform down a little...."

"Tom!" She held a finger to her lips. "My mom's right there. She can probably still hear us!"

"No, I can't," came the disembodied voice of her mother from offscreen.

She put her face into her hands as her husband started to laugh. *Men.*

"Hey, Miller! You done yet? My girlfriend's waiting!" She glanced up at the man waiting near the door. Lieutenant Volz —one of the fighter jocks. Young, cocky, and eminently impatient.

"Yeah, hold on, Volz. Don't get your panties in a bunch," she said, waving him off.

"You're ten minutes over your time." He pointed to the clock on the wall.

She rolled her eyes. "Look, honey, gotta go...."

Yet somehow, with the good news about the *Constitution's* decommissioning, her husband's imminent arrival at Lunar Base, and the distinct possibility they would soon be on the same ship, the rest of the day became more bearable.

With the Old Bird's current assignment at L2 Station, she had the duty to pilot one of the crew transfer vehicles to shuttle officers and enlisted back and forth between the ship and the station. Normally, it was just a routine part of the job that made her want to gouge her eyes out from boredom, but today she punched the engine and pushed the g-forces.

"Whoa, easy there, cowgirl," said Commander Pierce from behind her. As CAG, he ran a weekly training exercise with the fighter wing based on L2 Station, and he was just returning to the ship with his pilots.

"Sir, you're from Britannia—"

"York, actually," he interrupted. His patrician accent was oddly soothing to her ears. "But close enough—they're both in the Britannia Sector."

"Sir, you're from York," she corrected herself, "and I'm pretty sure no one from York is allowed to call me *cowgirl*. Have you ever even seen a horse? A cowboy? Corral? Tumbleweed? A six-shooter?" She glanced back at him, seated in the midst of a few dozen of his fighter jocks returning from their training exercise.

"I'll have you know, I own two horses. And my father has an original Ruger 22."

She gave him a skeptical look.

"Well, the gun is in an airtight display case. And the horses —well, I'm told they're quite well cared for...."

"Exactly," she replied with a smirk, and pulled the controls to angle the ship around one of L2 Station's nacelles.

"Why are you so happy, anyway? Haven't you heard we're being decommissioned?"

Exactly, she repeated in her head, but didn't want to give the impression she was eager to leave. "Yeah. But I just heard I might get to be reassigned to my husband's ship."

"So you're taking it out on us? Seriously, slow down a bit." He clutched onto his armrest as she put the transport ship into the final tight curve that would take them back into the Old Bird's fighter bay.

Glancing at her speed indicator, she saw that he was right —she hadn't been paying attention and they were coming in way too fast. Seeing that she only had a few seconds to correct their speed and approach vector, she shoved the thrusters into reverse, which had the added effect of throwing them all forward into their restraint harnesses.

But she'd overcompensated, and now, just as the landing gear extended, the back of the shuttle spun to the right, and with a flick of the thrusters she halted the spin and fishtailed left.

"Miller!" shouted Commander Pierce.

In the struggle to keep the craft flying straight, she still hadn't reduced the speed to something normal for landing, and as a result the landing gear hit the ground with a screech and showered the deck with sparks as the shuttle scraped across the landing zone, still fishtailing slightly as it finally came to rest.

"Oops," she said, after a momentary silence. Some of the fighter jocks in the back heckled her and Commander Pierce gave her a stern warning eye.

Lieutenant Volz, who she recognized as the fighter jock from earlier, laughed. "Well, she's no fighter pilot, but I think she deserves her own callsign. What do you say, Fishtail?" The pilots stood up to disembark, still laughing and joking at her expense.

She glanced down at the gouge she'd torn out of the deck and winced. "Sorry, sir."

Pierce eyed the damage, and shook his head. "Well, good thing she's being decommissioned next week or Commander Haws would have your ass mopping floors for a month. But what with that new Commander setting this place up as a museum, he'll probably give you a commendation for making her job difficult."

The other pilots were exiting the craft, and she ran the shuttle through its post-landing procedures. "Are you going to write me up, sir?"

"I suppose not. Just get your head out of the clouds, all right?"

"Yes, sir."

He ducked out, leaving her to park the shuttle back in its alcove off to the side of the landing runway.

Dammit, she thought. *Way to leave the Constitution on a bad note, Miller.*

CHAPTER THIRTEEN

L-2 Lagrange point, Earth
Captain's Ready Room, ISS Constitution

The Old Bird floated in nearly empty space, accompanied only by a few surveillance arrays, data-com satellites, astrometric telescopes and dishes, as well as L2 Station, a squat-looking, rotating starbase crewed by a few dozen officers who, like most of the crew aboard the *Constitution* herself, found themselves on the blunt end of a long, punitive assignment.

L2 Station may have had some strategic importance in the distant past, during and before the Swarm War, but these days it was a dead end post for dead end careers. Keeping watch over one of Earth's Lagrange points—where its gravity exactly cancelled that of the Sun, creating a stable point ideal for space stations and ships to float without any fuel consumption—was the worst assignment an IDF officer or enlisted could draw.

Out of his ready room window, Captain Granger watched

the station rotate slowly against the steady backdrop of stars and data-com arrays, wondering if his next assignment would be there. Or worse: chained to a desk deep within the IDF Command Center outside Omaha, destined to push papers every day for the rest of his career.

The door opened behind him. "Captain, you wanted to see me?" Shelby Proctor's voice grated on his nerves. He already hated it, and it had only been less than a week.

"I hear you want to strip apart my engines."

He turned around and stared her in the eyes, not inviting her to sit or even to stand at ease. It appeared she sensed he meant business, and so maintained a stiff composure, staring at a point just above his shoulder, and yet he could just barely detect the slightest tug at her lips, indicating she was relishing the occasion.

"Strip? No, sir. We need that shielding around the reactor core to—"

"I know your reasoning, Commander!" He spoke more loudly than he meant to, and he could see the corner of her mouth tug higher.

"Sir, need I remind you that this ship is due to stand down in less than a week? Your engines are useless. They simply won't be needed during her next mission."

"That may be." He swiveled his chair around and sat, still staring at her. "But we still need to make the trip to Lunar Base, and for that we need our engines."

"Correction, sir. We need one of our engines. Not all six. The thrust of one of them will be more than sufficient to get us to—"

"You're betraying your ignorance of the capabilities of my

ship, Commander. On paper, one of those engines can produce just enough thrust to get us to Lunar Base within the week. But she's old, Proctor. She hasn't operated above sixty percent thrust for well over twenty years." He glanced down and picked up a datapad, handing it to her. "I've temporarily denied your request for the lead shielding. It'll have to wait."

"But sir! I'm under a tight schedule here! I can't have you interfering—"

"I'LL INTERFERE WITH WHATEVER I DAMN WELL PLEASE ON MY SHIP, COMMANDER!"

His fist was clenched, and he felt his face grow hot. He knew he shouldn't have lost control. And that was confirmed as Proctor's face broadened into a full smile. From her pocket she produced her own datapad and tossed it on the desk towards him.

"There. Have a look. You'll find Admiral Yarbrough has given me the authority to do just about whatever I want, up to and including going over your wishes, *Captain*." She said that last word with a wink.

He scanned the orders, and sure enough, Yarbrough had indicated that Proctor was to have all command authority necessary for her to complete her work.

Dammit.

He studied the wording of the orders as she droned on about the importance of her mission, how securing the legacy of the *Constitution* was vital for the education of future generations, and for the Old Bird to serve as an ambassador from the fleet to civilians, creating good will and yada yada yada….

"Commander Proctor," he interrupted, his eyes glazing

over a phrase within the orders, "my orders stand."

"Excuse me, sir?"

"Yarbrough was clear that your authority over my ship only extends to your mission. She explicitly left line management to me. And part of line management includes ensuring the safety of my crew."

"I assure you, Captain, I'm being completely safe—"

"I'm sure you are. However, I disagree about the safety of removing the ballast from the engines. You see, should the remaining engine fail en route to Lunar Base, we'd sail right by it, or worse—get pulled into the moon's gravity well." It was his turn to smile at her. And he did.

"The chances of that happening are about a billion to—" she began to protest, but he interrupted her again.

"Regardless, I am responsible for safety, and in my judgement, that is far too high a risk. My order stands. You're dismissed, Commander," he added, before she could protest again.

She furrowed her brow and stormed out the door. "We'll see about that, Captain."

Still smiling, he followed her out a few minutes later and made his way down to the bridge, saluting the two marines posted outside the doors.

The regular day shift was just settling in, relieving the night crew and transferring console access and control to the new operators. He noticed they were more sluggish and informal than usual—he should really run a readiness drill to keep them on their toes. He shook his head. What was the point? They were due at Lunar Base in less than a week.

Granger glanced around the bridge for his XO,

Commander Haws. But he knew exactly where he was. Probably hungover, staring at himself in his bathroom mirror, unkempt and unshaven.

To his surprise, the old man strode through the doors to the bridge, grumbling greetings to a few of the departing crew members. He may have been unkempt and unshaven, but at least he was awake and alert. Granger called that a win for the day.

"Commander, time to get under way to our final destination, wouldn't you say?" Granger leaned onto the main command console, looking up at his old friend.

Haws grumbled something under his breath. "If you say so, Tim."

"I do. Take us out."

Haws barked orders to the navigation and engineering crew, working them through the process of spinning up the remaining engines, checking safety interlocks, securing decks for inertial transport, and marking off the checklists for departure from the Lagrange point. Granger nodded approvingly whenever a department chief called out for his final authorization, but otherwise stood back and let Haws handle the affair. It would be his final command, after all. His old friend deserved to go out with dignity.

Within the hour, Haws barked from across the bridge, "She's all ready, Captain."

Granger nodded slowly, and walked to the center of the bridge, glancing around at all of the crew. A hush fell over everyone as they realized he was about to speak.

"I'm not one for speeches." He glanced up at the ceiling with a frown, and turned to look at all the various departments scattered around the command center. "She's a good ship. The best. It's been the highest honor serving with you all." He turned to navigation. "Time to Lunar Base at fifty percent drive?"

The answer came without a pause—they'd already made the calculations. "Three days with a two-hour acceleration burn and a four-hour decel burn on final approach."

"Very well." He glanced back at Haws, who kept his face stiff and frowning. "Let's take her home."

CHAPTER FOURTEEN

Veracruz Sector, Leon System
IDF Intelligence Ship ISS Tirian

"Sir, we're approaching the other southern continent. ETA is three minutes."

LaPlace glanced at his readout. "Major cities down there?"

"Just one, with several outlying towns and settlements. All orbital traffic is silent on this side of the planet as well."

Minutes ticked by, and the ocean passed underneath them, peaceful, unaware and uncaring of the devastation on the land nearby. Soon their orbit brought them over another brown and green landmass, and before the sensor officer announced anything, LaPlace saw it.

Distant flashes of light, like lightning from a massive thundercloud, and a clutter of objects in the lower atmosphere, just at the edge of sight.

LaPlace jumped to his feet, still staring at the scene. "Report."

The sensor officer shook his head. "Lots of ships out there. Unknown identification. Unknown design and configuration. They're…." The officer swore and pounded the console. "Looks like the surface is under attack. There are a few orbital defense ships nearby, but they're mostly destroyed. The city is a sitting duck, sir, and they're getting pounded."

"Any indication we've been detected?"

"No, sir. All ships have maintained their attitude and orbit."

And then it came time for a decision. Get away while they could, or linger for a few more minutes to record more data? If this was the beginning of a full-scale Swarm invasion then they would need all the intel they could get. It was also imperative that they determine the attacker's identity. For all they knew, this could be a Russian Confederation force.

"Keep sensors on passive scan only. Zoom in with the cameras, all wavelengths. Let's get a closer look."

CHAPTER FIFTEEN

Halfway between L2 and Lunar Base
Sickbay, ISS Constitution

"How long do I have, Doc?"

Granger braced for the reply. He knew what was coming. He'd put off the appointment far too long. He'd managed to avoid his chief medical officer, Doctor Wyatt, for months now —ever since the lumps and pain returned.

"It's hard to say, Tim. Two months. Three. Four, if you're lucky."

"*Months?*" That took him by surprise. He'd assumed a few years. "What about Hitraxin? Won't that knock the tumors out for another few years?"

The doctor scowled at him. "Well sure, it *would* have done that, had you come to see me at your regularly scheduled appointment *six months ago*. Hell, Tim, what did you think would happen? Did you really think ignoring it would make it go away?"

"I've been busy," Granger demurred.

"Bullshit. You've been irresponsible. Now it's metastasized and soon your lymph nodes will be fatter than your damn head."

Shit. He didn't need this right now. First they take away the Old Bird from him, and now he gets his life taken away too? He shifted uncomfortably on the examination table, studying the scans Doc Wyatt had given him. The tumors were unmistakable: white, black, and dark red blobs interspersed all throughout his midsection, some larger, some smaller, but each deadly.

"Look, I can give you Metastacin—that should stabilize them for a month or so. And Flaginox will keep the pain and tissue inflammation at bay...."

Doctor Wyatt was fiddling with his handheld medical scanner, avoiding eye contact. They'd served nearly a decade together, and he counted him as one of his best friends on board—and Captain Granger didn't make friends easily. Why make friends when they'll inevitably disappoint you?

"It's ok, Doc. It's my time." He said the words, but they rang hollow in his own ears. "Look, I've got to do a walkdown of the ship one last time before we arrive at Lunar Base. Make sure our new guest hasn't mothballed the whole place before she's supposed to." He stood up to leave.

"Are you going to tell the crew?"

Granger walked to the door. "Now why the hell would I do that, Doc?"

"Are you at least going to tell your—" began Doctor Wyatt, but the doors sliding shut cut him off.

Granger stalked the halls, aiming vaguely towards

engineering, nodding at crew members as they passed. When he reached the only elevator that would take him down to engineering, the door didn't even open—the mechanism merely groaned in protest as the gears ground unfruitfully against each other.

Damn, she's as sick as I am.

Digging his fingertips into the joint between the sliding door sections, he grunted as he struggled to pull them apart. When a two-inch space appeared, the mechanism finally caught and the doors sprung open.

"Engineering," he grumbled to the empty air inside the lift.

A soft beep indicated the computer's acknowledgement, and the lift moved. Momentarily, the speaker announced, with a fair amount of distortion, "Engineering." Hell, even the speakers were going out. Maybe it really was time to just pull the plug on the whole ship.

"Sir, glad you're here," began a frazzled Commander Scott before he could even get a word in, "I tried contacting you before about this but couldn't find you. She's gone too far this time, Cap'n."

Somehow, he knew exactly which *she* his chief engineer was referring to.

"What is it this time, Rayna?"

She led him to one of the vast engine bays that housed one of the six main drive units, and pointed. "Look. I go to bed last night with engine four *not* disassembled, and when I wake up this morning, it *is* disassembled. Anything wrong with that picture, Cap'n?"

Granger ground his teeth together. The entire unit was taken apart, and the lead ballast was clearly gone. "Where's the ballast?"

"Where do you think, sir?"

Granger spun around and strode back toward the lift. "Prepare a launch tube, Commander."

"Sir?"

"A launch tube. We're going to need it to aid the disembarking of our guest."

He didn't stop to look, but he could almost feel the broad smile cross Rayna's face. Hell, he'd love to press the launch button himself if it meant he could be rid of Shelby Proctor a few days early.

CHAPTER SIXTEEN

Veracruz Sector, Leon System
IDF Intelligence Ship ISS Tirian

Commander LaPlace peered at the screen, trying to see the ships firing down at the surface. The sensors were recording every last detail, but he wanted to visually verify the identity of the attackers. He knew, from years of military and intel training, what the Swarm ships should look like. At least the ones that attacked Earth seventy-five years ago. They were quite literally a swarm. A few central carriers acting as bases for thousands, tens of thousands of fighters. Earth's defenders were simply overwhelmed by the sheer numbers, not to mention the superior technology and firepower.

"Comm, have a q-jump data pod ready to go. I want to have something ready to send just in case…." He let the words hang in the air—his bridge crew would know exactly what he left unsaid.

"Aye, sir. Data pod loaded and currently downloading all

available telemetry."

LaPlace nodded. "Good. Append the bridge's audio recording as well. They may as well hear what we're talking about." He turned to his nav officer. "Ensign, I want q-jump coordinates laid in and your finger hovering over the initiate button. Understood? We're talking hair-trigger here."

Satisfied that the ensign was ready to hightail them out of there, he redirected his attention back to the sensor log.

"Ops, am I seeing this right? Those are not Swarm fighters. At least, not according to our historical data."

"You're right, sir. These are slightly larger. We're detecting around two hundred of them, all around the size of one of our V-wing fighters. Maybe double the size of an X-25."

A Swarm fleet from seventy years ago would have sported many times that number of fighters. And the central carrier in the middle of the screen was possibly even more massive than the old Swarm carriers. But the design—it looked vaguely ... human? Nothing like the Swarm cruisers from the history books, with their dozens of nacelle arms and vast jagged pylons that presumably acted as fighter bays.

As LaPlace watched, about three dozen of them broke off from the main engagement over the city and moved sharply towards one of the partially destroyed IDF cruisers.

"Captain, I've got power readings from that Zafano class cruiser. Transponder signal is that of the *ISS Vallarta*. Their main reactor has restarted and several of their mag-rails are energizing." The officer looked up at the screen to watch. "They're firing at the incoming ships, sir."

LaPlace glanced up. Sure enough, the battered cruiser, still steaming air, smoke, and debris, had angled itself such that several starboard turbo-mag-rail cannons had a clear shot at the large fighters. He could almost imagine the pulsating rhythm of the shots—the cannons fired around five rounds per second at speeds approaching ten kilometers per second.

Several of the enemy fighters flared up into fireballs, but the rest accelerated at incredible speeds towards the *Vallarta*, and fired their own streams of high-velocity projectiles at the ship. The rounds exploded with ferocious energy into the side of the IDF cruiser, which spewed debris and fire—quickly extinguished by the vacuum of space. Soon, a gaping hole was exposed. But that was only the beginning. One of the large carriers, a massive behemoth of a ship lit by sickly green running lights, veered towards the *Vallarta* and unleashed a dazzling green energy beam.

The beam blazed toward the hole in the starboard side of the *Vallarta*. LaPlace glanced down at his sensor readout and knew what was about to happen without asking his ops officer, who nevertheless called out, "I'm reading a radioactive signature, sir! That beam's got anti-matter in it, and it's interacting with the—"

But the flash on the screen cut him off. Even though it was only a holographic viewscreen and therefore limited in the amount of energy it could put out, they all automatically shielded their eyes. When the screen desaturated, the *ISS Vallarta* was gone.

A moment's silence permeated the bridge.

"Ensign, have you scanned those fighters for life-readings yet? I want to know who we're dealing with and then get the hell out of here."

"Working on it, sir. There's some kind of odd interference

messing with our sensors. I can't get a good reading on what's inside those things. At this point, could be human. Could be ... well, even back during the Swarm War we were never able to get life-sign readings from the Cumrat ships—"

"Sir! The ships...."

LaPlace snapped his head back to the screen. The surviving belligerent fighters had changed course and were now flying directly towards them.

"Ensign! Now!" He yelled at the nav officer, who hit the q-jump initiation on his console with a jab of his poised finger.

The viewscreen held steady.

"Ensign, I said NOW!" The fighters appeared to speed up.

"Trying, sir. I think whatever is interfering with the sensors...." The ensign drifted off, tapping buttons on his console furiously.

LaPlace pointed at the ops officer. "Launch the data pod. Get that thing out of here." He turned back to navigation. "Ensign, evasive maneuvers. Swing wide and Z minus fifty. Put some distance between us—maybe we can clear their distortion field."

He felt the ship lurch as the inertial canceling system struggled to keep up with the maneuvers the nav officer was keying into the console. Movement on the screen caught his eye.

"Sir, they're firing!"

"Keep swerving, Ensign!" He craned his neck around. "Is that data pod away?"

"Aye, sir!"

"Did it make the q-jump?"

An explosion erupted across the bridge and Laplace

shielded his face from the flames. When the emergency system extinguished the fire, he looked back to ops. The officer was slumped against his console, his head and torso scorched black and blistery red. Glancing down at his own readout, he swore —the data pod had failed to q-jump.

IDF headquarters would not be warned.

"Ensign, maximum acceleration! Get us to the wreckage of the *Vallarta*! Maybe we can put some debris in between us and—"

But the nav officer never got the chance to acknowledge. Another explosion ripped through the bridge, and a giant section of bulkhead blasted away, revealing the blue-tinged atmosphere of the planet far below. As the air spewed out, sucking the nav officer with it, LaPlace glared at the enemy fighter speeding directly towards them. The forward guns of the other ship glowed, and, using his last breath which erupted out into the vacuum, he spat towards the incoming fighter out of spite before blacking out.

CHAPTER SEVENTEEN

Halfway between L2 and Lunar Base
Fighter Bay, ISS Constitution

Captain Granger strode up to the doors of the fighter bay's maintenance hangar, pointing to the two marines stationed there.

"You two, with me. Your orders are to arrest Commander Proctor at my signal. Understood?"

The marines looked at each other nervously. One of them cleared his throat.

"I said, AM I CLEAR?" he barked, and one of the marines stiffened his back.

"Uh, sir, she gave us the order that if you interfere with her work, we are to confine you to your quarters. Said she had authorization from Admiral Yarbrough herself."

The marine flinched as Granger marched up to him. Unbelievable. She'd crossed the line. He stood toe to toe with the marine and yelled in his face. "I am the captain of this ship, soldier! How would you like to spend the next five years rotting in the brig for insubordination and mutiny?"

He hadn't realized he was waving his fists in the air, and he self-consciously lowered them. Dammit. He'd lost his ship. Five days ahead of schedule.

"Tim?" Granger turned to the voice. It was his CAG. Commander Tyler Pierce.

"What the hell do you want?" he replied gruffly, still eyeing the nervous marines, who clearly were quite torn. What was the military coming to? Had the decades of peace and prosperity made them all fat and complacent? What was Yarbrough thinking, undermining him like this?

"Just wanted to show you something, sir." The CAG thumbed in the direction of the Air Group's mission room. He was a younger gentleman, clearly the son of some patrician senator or oligarch on one of the more prosperous worlds, perhaps York, or Versailles, judging by his decidedly upper-class accent and the overly conservative part in his hair.

Still glowering at the two marines, he followed his CAG into the mission room—a mini-amphitheater surrounding a podium in front of a holoscreen. Several technicians were busy installing a few extra rows of seating in the front and another was fiddling with the terminal on the podium.

"What are they doing?" Granger asked, indicating the techs.

Pierce's expression betrayed his annoyance. "Do you really need to ask?"

"Proctor?"

Pierce nodded. "They're turning this into a fighter combat simulation room. Bring fifty tourists in at once, show them a cute battle sequence up there on the screen, brief them on their mission, then off they all go to sit in the cockpits of the fighters out there." He thumbed in the direction of the fighter bay, which Granger now had zero desire to see, even though Proctor was in there and he was itching to blast her out one of the fighter bay airlocks.

"Is it bad? Are they all stripped down?"

The CAG shrugged. "Well, not all of them. Just twenty or so. And all of the fighter's systems are still intact. They've just rigged them with dummy torpedoes Proctor printed out in the fab, and upgraded ... uh, downgraded the computers with some new battle simulation program she brought with her from the Smithsonian. But they're all roped off and repainted some god-awful shade of purple and yellow—she thinks it'll make them look more futuristic for the visitors, you see...."

The captain groaned. "Purple and yellow?"

"Yeah, tell me about it. But Tim, this isn't why I asked you here. Come into my office for a moment."

Granger followed him into the CAG's office and took a seat next to the terminal next to Pierce. He smiled at the pictures of the man's family displayed neatly in dark metal frames on the desk—two little boys sitting on the lap of a gorgeous blonde woman posed in front of some pine trees. "Family's on York?" He nodded towards the picture, the faintly purple tinge to the deep blue sky clueing him in to where it was taken.

"Yes, sir. My family's lived in Londinium for centuries. Fourth great grandfather was one of the first settlers there. Helped build Londinium from the ground up. Well, at least his workers did. Never did enjoy getting his hands dirty, the old sod."

"You talk about him like you knew him."

"I did. He only died twenty years ago. Right before I joined IDF."

Granger looked at him askance. "Your fourth great grandpa died just twenty years ago?"

"Well, when you own half the city of Londinium you can afford all sorts of age extending procedures. Replaced half his body at least four times before he finally came down with a common cold and died of pneumonia. One hundred and eighty-nine. Oldest man on York when he died."

Captain Granger whistled. And to think he was going to die at a paltry sixty-four. Sixty-five, if he was lucky. Unless they came up with a miracle cure for stage four lung cancer, a malignant brain tumor, and pancreatic cancer that didn't involve replacing his entire body and flooding his head with high-energy protons to zap the free-roaming malignant cells. He breathed in as deeply as he could, stifling a wince at the pain. "What did you bring me here to see, Tyler?"

The CAG flipped the computer on and brought up several star maps and fleet movement schedules. "The British and the Russian fleets were supposed to conduct joint training exercises in the Britannia system yesterday. I know because my father commands the *ISS Gallant*, which is the flagship of the third British fleet. We talk every other day for a few minutes, and this morning he mentioned something that struck me as quite odd."

"Yes?"

"The Russian fleets never showed up."

"Strange," said Granger. "The Russian Confederation

space is right there next to British space, out towards Sirius. Practically neighbors. Did he have any idea why they didn't show?"

"No. But that wasn't the only odd thing. He received some special orders from IDF High Command to go patrol the border between British and Russian space. Out near the Veracruz Sector."

"Did he say why?"

"He didn't. The orders were classified priority one top-secret. Hell, he shouldn't have even told me what he did."

Granger stroked his chin. Damn the Russians. Slippery bastards as always—Earth nearly lost the Swarm War because of their antics, refusing to coordinate planetary defense with the allied powers right up to nearly the last moment. It took several Swarm nukes over St. Petersburg to finally convince them that it was in their best interests to cooperate with the rest of the civilized world. What were they up to this time?

"Probably just on guard against whatever President Malakhov has up his sleeve," said Granger.

"Oh, they're calling him President now?"

"He did win the last five elections." He paused and smirked. "Albeit with only ninety-eight percent of the vote."

"Sounds like they love the guy. I wonder what he promised the voters?"

"Probably made them an offer they couldn't refuse. Promised to take the Veracruz Sector and re-annex Mongolia, all while masturbating shirtless on top of a bengalese tiger."

Pierce snorted, and shook his head. "Yeah, it's probably just his regular old chest-thumping. Still, my father sounded genuinely worried. He knew something he wasn't telling me.

Has anything come down from High Command?"

"To me? Hell, they didn't tell me about my own ship's decommissioning until a week ago. I doubt I'm high on their list of officers to keep up to date on hypothetical Russian aggression."

The CAG picked up a picture frame and looked at it, his two boys smiling back at him. Granger wondered how long it had been since he'd seen them. "Well, let's hope nothing out of sorts is going on. I know Malakhov is a crazy bastard, but this isn't like him. The politicians have never been friends, but we've always had good inter-military relations. They've never missed a joint training exercise."

Granger studied the star map. Sure enough, eight IDF carriers, a handful of heavy cruisers, and an assortment of lighter vessels—missile frigates, destroyers, tow barges, and supply ships—were gathered at the outskirts of the Britannia system, the main population center of British space. Nearby, Russian space shimmered red, and opaque, as the Russians no longer shared near-real-time sensor data with the rest of IDF. There could be a Russian fleet just on the other side of the border—in the Liv system, and they'd never know it until they decided to show up.

"You think something's up? I mean not just the Russians? You think the Swarm is back?"

Pierce shrugged. "The Swarm? They've been gone for over seventy years. Not so much as a peep out of their space in all this time—assuming we know where their space is. Hell, we don't even know what they look like. All we ever found in the debris from their ships was gray goo."

After their first engagement with the Swarm, humanity

tried to study the ships they'd managed to cripple or destroy. It wasn't easy work since most of the defeated ships self-destructed—any vessels that survived intact were heavily damaged, and there were never any survivors. No bodies, either. Somehow, they'd managed to program their ships to either be entirely automated, or to automatically vaporize any dead bodies. All that was left behind was a thin sheen of organic liquid coating the floors and walls. The hallways and compartments were so small that IDF supposed that the aliens couldn't be more than a few feet tall, if that.

And yet their technology was stunningly advanced. They used energy weapons—some form of accelerated negative ion beams. Anti-helium particles, if he remembered his academy classes correctly. Granger wondered if the new armor every new ship had been constructed with since then would make a difference—hell, even the *Constitution* only survived the war because of her ten-meter-thick tungsten plating. She was practically built out of an asteroid back in the last century—SG10551 was the rock's designation. By the time she was finished, there was hardly anything left of the asteroid.

But not only were their weapons advanced, they seemed to be able to achieve huge accelerations and tolerate massive changes in inertia—changes that IDF's inertial cancelers could only dream of handling. As such, the Swarm fleets were far more maneuverable and faster compared to IDF. That, and their computer control systems put IDF's to shame—each fleet they encountered was so well coordinated, each fighter so well connected to the whole, that it was like fighting one large organism rather than a few hundred little individual ships. Their own targeting computers and command and control centers were simply no match. They'd had to rely on the grit and gumption of their individual pilots, and in many historians' estimations, that made all the difference.

"Let's hope it's not the Swarm. I'd much rather fight a few chest-thumping Russian thugs than those bastards again."

"You think it'll come to that?"

Granger shrugged. "Honestly? No. There's too much space—such an abundance of resources that there's just no point. That's what the Russians have always wanted: territory and resources. Since there's no shortage of either, it's just senseless to fight. No, things will blow over in a few years, Definitely when Malakhov hits his term limits—"

"Wait, you haven't heard?"

"What?"

Pierce grunted a laugh. "The Duma voted away the presidential term limits a few months ago. Old Malakhov is in for life."

The captain snorted. "You'd think he would just save time and call himself Emperor Malakhov instead of spending all this energy on pretense." Granger stood up to leave. He was glad his CAG had pulled him into the office—he'd calmed down enough and was far less liable to toss Proctor out the airlock. "So how many fighters have we got left in operational status?"

The CAG rose to his feet to follow the captain out. "About a quarter. Maybe twenty? Proctor took around forty, and twenty were down for overhauls before she showed up. Why? Expecting trouble?"

"In the five days we have left? Doubt it. But if we're not ready for anything fate throws at us, it's our own damn fault."

CHAPTER EIGHTEEN

Sol System, Earth orbit
Valhalla Space Station

"Admiral Yarbrough? The Vice President's shuttle has arrived."

She stood up from her desk and nodded her head to the empty room. "Thank you, Commander. Please see that he's escorted to the *ISS Winchester*'s docking tube. I'll meet him there."

Pausing for a moment by the window before heading out to meet the second most powerful person on the Earth, she stared down at the green and blue globe far below. *Valhalla Station*'s orbit was about double geosynchronous, and at 50,000 kilometers from the surface it only orbited once every thirty-seven hours, affording them an uninterrupted view of whatever continent they flew over, which at the moment was North America. Squinting, she could just make out the slightly grayish look of the major cities—New York, Washington,

Miami. Nashville was obscured by clouds, but she could imagine seeing the giant civilian spaceport there, rivaling the size of even the IDF port in Omaha.

So small from up here, she thought. Letting her eyes drift farther north, she could barely make out the huge scars left by the Swarm War—circular pockmarks indicating where several cities in Ohio and Michigan had stood. The multi-megaton warheads the Swarm dropped had completely wiped those cities off the map: Cincinnati, Detroit, Cleveland—all gone. And in the aftermath of the war the government had seen little point in rebuilding them, opting instead to let nature take its course, and now the blast zones were covered in lush green. Dense radioactive forests. She remembered schoolyard rumors that the wildlife there had glowing eyes.

But the Swarm was gone. The surveillance missions to known Swarm worlds following the war had indicated that there was not a trace of them left. All their cities abandoned. Not a single ship, not a single alien left behind. Some fundamentalist religious leaders went so far as to claim that the Swarm was simply a scourge manufactured by God for the punishment of mankind for her many sins. And once the punishment was delivered, the scourge was taken away by God without a trace.

IDF intel thought otherwise, and spent decades searching for them, to no avail. They were entirely, and inexplicably, gone.

But now there was a problem in the Veracruz Sector. The *ISS Kerouac* was missing, Starbase Heroic had gone silent, and the scout ship she'd dispatched to investigate had similarly not reported back in for over thirty hours.

She turned to the door—a lowly IDF admiral should not keep the vice president waiting. As she left, a flashing indicator on her desk monitor caught her eye.

Returning to her desk, she examined the report.

A badly damaged data pod from the intel ship *Tirian*.

Her eyes bulged as she watched the video surveillance play out.

Dammit. They're back.

CHAPTER NINETEEN

Halfway between L2 and Lunar Base
ISS Constitution

"Captain, we're within 150,000 kilometers of Lunar Base," said Ensign Prince.

The bridge, which had been humming along just moments earlier, came to a quiet. Granger stood up. Everyone knew that this would be the final time the *Constitution* would fire her engines as a commissioned IDF vessel. The ship needed to slow down sufficiently to enter orbit around the moon. He hoped they weren't expecting another pep talk. "Thank you, Ensign. How's the power plant?" he said, turning to the engineering section.

"Operating at nearly full capacity, sir. Commander Scott says we're good to go."

"Very well. Full reverse. Fire forward thrusters. Sixty percent power."

"Sir? Since we're down a few engines, that won't slow us

down enough." Ensign Prince hemmed, and returned his gaze to his computer readout. "That is, sir, ever since engine number six was scrapped and——"

"Thank you, Ensign, for the reminder," he said, cutting off the young man and mentally sending choice words down towards Commander Proctor in the fighter bay. "Eighty percent on the remaining engines should do it."

"Aye, sir."

"Notify me when we're an hour out."

He grunted a greeting as Commander Haws staggered onto the bridge. Dammit—he'd been drinking again. The odor was noticeable from a dozen feet away.

"We fired the engines yet?" he slurred.

Granger advanced on his friend and gripped his upper arm, pulling him along beside him towards the door.

"Come with me."

"Ah, Tim, it was nothing. Just a glass."

"A glass? You sure it wasn't ten?"

He saluted to the marines posted at the entrance to the bridge and pulled the XO past some wary-eyed officers paused in conversation outside the operations center next door.

"Look, we're throwing in the towel tomorrow anyway, what's the big—"

Granger shoved Haws up against the wall and stared into his face, just an inch away. "What's the big deal? Dammit, Abe, I've stuck my neck out for you so many times I'm frankly getting a little tired of it. I've warned you about showing up for duty drunk. There's only so many times I can sweep this under the rug. You're hurting morale and you're disrespecting me."

Haws snorted. "Stuck your neck out for me, my fat white

ass. You wouldn't even be here if it wasn't for me, after that stunt you pulled. They were about to dishonorably discharge you, but because of me they promoted you. Imagine that—the rogue commander of the Khorsky incident, getting his own damn ship."

Granger's fists tightened around Haws's uniform. Looking both ways down the hall to make sure they were alone, he leaned in close. "You and I both know that's not true. The fleet's been on the decline for decades. They needed a kick in the ass and I gave it to them. Just like I'm doing with you." He released the XO and shoved him down the hall. "Go. Sober up then report back."

"Is that an order, *Captain*?" Haws growled.

Granger let his shoulders hunch over. "Does it need to be, Abe?"

An officer rounded the corner and walked past them, nodding a quick salute. Granger let her disappear through a door down the hallway before going on. "Look, Abe, you're my best friend. We've given the Old Bird a good run. Let's not sully it by—"

Haws brushed past him. "Save it, Tim. Save it for someone who cares. You and I both stopped caring years ago, when they sentenced us to the Old Bird."

"Sentenced?" he asked. Haws didn't stop.

"You heard me."

He turned around the corner and disappeared out of sight.

And Haws was right: their assignment was a sentence. A subtle effort to get the two of them out of the way. To silence and discredit them. A court martial would have brought too much publicity, and a discharge, honorable or otherwise, would have given them the ability to speak out. But a dead-end assignment?

Granger rested a hand on the wall. The ship hummed with the distant pulse of the ancient engines. Her engines. *His* engines. Haws called it a sentence, and it may have been, but it was the best damned sentence he would have ever dared to ask for.

CHAPTER TWENTY

Earth's Moon
Main Auditorium, Lunar Base

Vice President Isaacson of the United Earth Government beamed out from the podium, flashing his toothy politician's grin at the auditorium full of reporters, dignitaries, politicians, celebrities, and civilians—there was even a class of students from some well-to-do private elementary school in New England.

Granger glanced at his watch—an ancient gold and silver time-piece with leather straps given to him by his mother several decades ago. Damn, this ceremony was taking forever. Isaacson sure knew how to talk.

"—in fact," the Vice President continued, "some might say that we've gone too far in our efforts to modernize the military. They think we should remain constant. Fixed. Unchanging. Well, ladies and gentleman, times change, and with those changes we rise to meet them. The challenges we'll face in the twenty-seventh century will be unlike those we faced in the twenty-sixth. The Swarm is long gone, as our intelligence and science expeditions have claimed. There is no sign of any other alien civilizations for all the many thousands of cubic lightyears we've explored. Again, as we've seen throughout the millennia, our most difficult challenges will come from within, and so we must be prepared for that threat —"

Granger suppressed a wry grin. He knew the Russian president was probably seething if he was watching, which he almost undoubtedly was—who wasn't watching the decommissioning ceremony of the oldest ship in the history of Earth's spacefaring fleets?

"—and so we say to you future generations"—Vice President Isaacson inclined his head down to his left, towards the rows of seated students—"the future lies with you, if you will rise to meet it. We deliver into your hands a safer galaxy, a safer humanity, a safer world. Study hard, learn as much as you can, follow in the footsteps of your heroes, and for god's sake, come up for air from your video games every now and then, ok?" he added, to a roomful of delighted, polite laughter.

And before he knew it, it was his turn. Isaacson sat down, and all eyes turned to Captain Tim Granger as he lifted slowly to his feet, trying hard not to wince from the sharp pain in his lungs.

He approached the podium, and set his hand-written speech down next to a glass of water set out for him. They told him he had fifteen minutes, but damn it all if he wasn't able to write down more than five minutes of material. Guess he'd have to wing it. Stalling for as much time as possible, he picked up the glass of water and downed it.

Granger cleared his throat and stared down at his notes, squinting before realizing that his reading glasses were still tucked snugly into his pocket. Placing them on his face, he mumbled, "They say your eyes are the second thing to go in old age, followed quickly by your ears." He waited a moment for comedic timing. "But I'll be damned if I can remember the first thing."

More polite, measured laughter. God, he hated speeches.

"One hundred and thirty years ago, our forefathers had a vision," he began, reading his speech from the beginning. "A vision of safety, and progress. We had started spreading among the stars, and with that spread came unknown dangers. It seemed we were alone in the universe, but those early leaders of a United Earth had the foresight to realize that might not always be the case. And fortunately, almost serendipitously, we built warships. Fleets. Far more overpowered than what we thought we needed."

He coughed, and it turned into a full-blown fit. An admiral seated behind him reached under the podium and handed him another glass of water, which he accepted gratefully, and continued, "The *Constitution*. The *Chesapeake*. The *Congress*. The *Warrior*. The *Independence*, and the *Victory*. What we today call the Legacy Fleet. We built some ships before, and some after, but those were the finest. Our golden age."

He paused, glancing up at the waiting audience. "And then the Swarm came. Without the handful of carriers, cruisers, and frigates that we had at the time, humanity as we know it would have disappeared."

Another pause. "But we won. We survived. We lived to

fight another day. But that day never came...." He trailed off. He just wasn't feeling it. The words seemed hollow. Like he was repeating politicized platitudes designed to soothe the ears of everyone present. To not offend. To keep everyone comfortable.

The hell with it. He picked up his speech and flipped it over, and clearing his throat, he stared up at the audience again.

"But the truth is, we were lucky. Damned lucky. It wasn't skill, or grit or gumption or bravery or brilliance that got us through that war. It was dumb luck. They handed our asses to us, and we almost paid the ultimate price. Now we say the Swarm has disappeared. We say they've abandoned their worlds and that they'll never come back. We develop tests and analytic techniques to confirm this conclusion and we pat ourselves on the back for our ingenuity, for surely it must have been us. Surely it's because of our brilliance, our excellence, that we've driven off the Swarm. And so we sit back. We relax. We pretend we're perfectly safe."

He glanced over at the collection of seated dignitaries on the rostrum, and saw that several of the officials were nervously checking their watches, some staring at him, some shooting daggers out of their eyes at him, Vice President Isaacson included. Admiral Yarbrough slowly moved her head back and forth at him.

"Just because something is old, doesn't mean we need to throw it away. What kind of society have we become, what happens to our values when we say that just because something or someone has been around a hell of a long time that they've outlived their usefulness? We become a society of vacant, immature materialists. Moving from one new thing on to the next. Devaluing age and experience." He was talking about the *Constitution*, but he couldn't help but feel like he was talking about himself as well.

"And what does this old guy say? He says: be careful. Be watchful. Be vigilant." He grit his teeth. He knew he needed to make this speech politically palatable to the muckety-mucks up on the rostrum behind him. "And it is for that reason that IDF CENTCOM has decided to not simply retire the *Constitution,* but to turn her into a museum. A place of learning. A place to remember. Where future generations will see her legacy directly, and be inspired to continue the watchful peace that she oversaw."

The words felt hollow and distasteful in his mouth, but it was the best moral compromise he could come up with. "And so we commit the Old Bird into your hands. A gift from the past and present crew of the *ISS Constitution* and IDF to the people of Earth." He glanced down at the rows of wide-eyed elementary school students. "Take care of her. Be true to her, and she'll fly you safely home. Thank you."

Applause, and a few waves and handshakes later, it was finally over. Thank god. Where the hell was the adult beverage table? Wherever Haws was, probably. He glanced the auditorium over, and, sure enough, his XO was camped out next to a long table holding hundreds of glasses half full of champagne. He made a b-line towards him, ignoring half a dozen hands reaching out to pat his shoulder or grasp his hand.

"What the hell…." He nearly tripped over a small obstacle in his path.

"Watch where you're going, Captain!" said a small voice

almost directly under him.

It was one of the schoolchildren. A boy. Maybe ten years old, but obviously very small for his age. But his attitude was ten times the size of his body.

"Excuse me?" said Granger.

"You heard me, Captain. Say, nice speech. I fall asleep during half the speeches our teacher takes us to, but yours was great! I like short speeches. Especially when you swear." The small boy stuck his hand out, which Granger tentatively grabbed. He didn't quite know what to make of this boy, but he liked him.

"Glad to hear it. Are you thinking of joining IDF someday? Be a starship captain?"

The boy rolled his eyes. "Oh, god no. Are you kidding? How boring!"

Granger chuckled. "Well then, what *do* you want to be?"

"A motorcycle racer, of course!"

"Isn't that a little dangerous?"

"Not as dangerous as piloting a starship."

Granger grunted—the kid had a point. "What's your name?"

"Cornelius Dexter Ahazarius."

He repeated the name slowly, as the boy had blurted it out quickly. "Cornelius Dexter—"

"Ahazarius. The third. And sorry, Captain, gotta go. My teacher is giving me *the eye*. Probably thinks I'm annoying you or something."

The teacher bustled through a nearby group of children and confronted the boy. "Dexter! I told you not to bother anyone important!" He turned to Granger. "I'm terribly sorry,

Captain Granger. Mr. Ahazarius here is a little incorrigible."

Granger raised an eyebrow. "Indeed."

"Come along along, Dexter. Leave the man alone—he's earned his retirement."

The teacher ushered the boy away, leaving that word grating on his ears. *Retirement.*

Granger found the drinks and looked around for his XO. Looked like Haws had already made his retreat out of the auditorium. Damn. Granger downed a whole glass of champagne and then quickly reached for another.

He was just settled into light conversation with a senator when Vice President Isaacson sidled up to him through the crowd. "Captain Granger! Excellent speech, sir. You're a natural."

Granger painted a stiff half-smile on his face. If he was a natural at giving speeches, then poo-flinging monkeys were naturals at etiquette and manners. "Thank you, sir. Very kind."

"You know, when President Avery asked me to stand in for her here, I was like a little kid—so excited. To think that I would get to be the one to welcome the Old Girl home, I was just—"

"Old Bird."

Isaacson stopped mid-sentence. "Sorry?"

"She's the Old Bird. Not the Old Girl." Granger noticed the vague show of false embarrassment the Vice President put on. "Common mistake, sir. And we appreciate your presence here." He grabbed the man's hand and intended to move on to the next dignitary, but Isaacson held his hand firm.

"I just wanted you to know," he said, leaning in close to Granger, "that we are of similar minds. We've grown soft.

Complacent. As far as I'm concerned, you're a prophet, Captain Granger."

Ugh. Flattery. If there was one language common to every politician everywhere, it was flattery. Granger's smile thinned. "You're too kind."

"I mean it, Captain. There are those of us in the government that don't agree with the findings of the Eagleton Commission. We should be building up our military. Not stripping it down like President Avery wants."

How odd. The man was President Avery's second in command. He was her biggest cheerleader, her most tireless campaigner and surrogate. What the hell was he doing cutting her down in private?

"Well, I don't know that we need a military buildup, Mr. Vice President. But a little vigilance and preparedness go a long way."

"Indeed," Isaacson said, flashing his politician's toothy grin. "In fact, after this whole affair is over and you're reassigned, would you mind stopping by my office in Washington?"

An invitation to the Vice President's office? Granger felt like he was stepping into an alternate reality. "I'd be honored, Mr. Vice President. And what shall we be talking about?"

"Your future, of course."

Granger's smile vanished. "I have no future, Mr. Vice President. I'm just a sailor at the end of his tour. The Old Bird is retired, and soon, so will I." He thought of the plague of tumors invading his chest, his abdomen, his brain. The drugs Doc Wyatt had given him seemed to help with the pain, but this level of metastasis was terminal.

Isaacson came in close again. "Please reconsider, Tim. I think you'll find that in a few weeks, the political climate may have changed somewhat. There are rumblings in the Senate— key people are nervous about the Eagleton Commission. And if the chips fall where I think they might, I'll need someone in the military I can trust. Someone of like mind."

His eyes were oddly insistent. But what in the world was he talking about? He almost asked when he heard his personal comm device go off, pulsing with the arrival of an urgent message.

Simultaneously he heard dozens of other comm devices go off all around the vast hall. The crowd, which had up to that point been chatting and laughing amiably, fell into an uncomfortable silence as dozens of eyes looked down to read their messages.

Granger pulled his out of his pocket.

It was from CENTCOM, Priority One.

UNIDENTIFIED VESSELS SIGHTED ON TRAJECTORY TOWARDS EARTH. ETA 1 HOUR. ALERT CONDITION RED.

CHAPTER TWENTY-ONE

Earth's Moon
Observation Compartment 2, Lunar Base

Lieutenant Miller leaned over the railing and rested her head against the window, looking out at the gray, barren moonscape. The glare from the sun was harsh in her eyes, though the protective coatings on the composite glass at least made it bearable to look out the window and take in the magnificent view. Just above the white glare of the regolith, the half-illuminated blue, green, and white globe of the Earth hovered.

"Seems so small from up here, doesn't it?" she murmured.

"You'd never even know ten billion people lived down there just by looking at it from space," replied her husband, who was leaning his head against the window next to her.

"Ten billion people. And little Zack-Zack." She squinted against the glare, trying to make out the coast of California under the cloud cover. "Do you think we're doing the right thing?"

"Hmm?"

"You know"—she tapped a finger against the window, pointing towards the Earth—"both of us being out here on duty. I should just take an early discharge. It's not fair to him. It's not fair to my parents."

He shrugged. "Oh, they love it, and you know it. And Zack-Zack will be fine. It'll only be like this for two more years and then you can at least draw early retirement and go reserve. I'll join you in just a few years after that, and we'll have it made."

He was right, but it didn't mean she had to like it. The guilt wracked her at times, knowing that someone *else* was taking care of her son. Raising him. Teaching him. Cuddling him at night before bed. Sure, that was her own mother, but it still killed her inside. And though her husband hid it well, she knew it killed him too. "Yeah, I guess. But we could manage, you know, if I left now. It'd be tighter, but we'd figure it out."

A silence. Was he mad? Why wasn't he looking at her, or saying anything?

"Commander Ashworth said yes."

At first she didn't realize what he'd said, but then it hit her. "He said *yes*? Really?"

"Really." He turned to grin at her.

"So I'm cleared to transfer to the *Clyburne*?"

"You're clear. He said he'll handle it—already put the request in yesterday."

Her chest swelled and she felt flushed. *Finally.* After four years, they'd finally get to serve together. See each other every day. Have sex.

And before she knew it he had grabbed her and pulled her in close, kissing her with the full force of three months of pent-up sexual tension. She kissed back, eagerly, drinking him in.

Finally.

The sound of a klaxon immediately overhead made them both jump, and they pulled apart.

"What the hell is that?" she said, noticing the red flashing lights down the empty hallway—everyone was at the decommissioning ceremony, but soon, several doors down the hall burst open and several officers dashed down towards another set of doors.

"That's a red alert," said Tom, turning to her. "Get back to the *Constitution*."

"Red alert? In space dock? Here?" It was almost incomprehensible.

He nodded. "Probably just a drill. Some jackass pencil-pusher over in the admin building decided to make life difficult for Granger, just as a parting shot."

"They really don't like him, do they?" she remarked, as they turned down the hall and made for the space dock where their ships hovered.

"No one in fleet admin likes him, and half the captains and admirals despise him. That's why he's been shuffled off to the *Constitution* all these years—they wanted him out of their hair."

They reached a junction where the hallway split, each branch leading to the airlocks of a different starship—one branch ending in the *Constitution* and the other in the *Clyburne*. Dozens of other officers and crew members were streaming around them, jogging towards the ships.

"Wait," he said, and reached in one more time for a kiss. And then he was gone, pulling away and joining the throng of men and women rushing towards the *Clyburne*. "See you in a few days," he called back.

She waved, but her stomach clenched as she turned to jog towards the *Constitution*. "What's up, Ballsy?" she asked the man running past her. Lieutenant Volz.

"Haven't you heard?"

"No." She ran to keep up with him, and they passed through the airlock.

"The Swarm. Little Cumrats are back."

Oh, god. Her thoughts immediately went to California. To her son. Her parents.

And her husband, on another warship, possibly heading off into battle.

Her stomach clenched even more.

CHAPTER TWENTY-TWO

Earth's Moon
Main Auditorium, Lunar Base

Within seconds of reading his message the klaxons rang out, followed by flashing red lights. The civilians in the room panicked; several schoolchildren screamed. Granger tucked the comm device back in his pocket and stood up straight, scanning the room for Yarbrough or any of the senior admiralty. He spotted them leaving the room in a rush, and he hurried to catch up with them. He noticed Commander Proctor jogging after him out of the corner of his eye.

"What's the situation, Admiral?" he said as he fell into step behind her, next to one of her aides.

"Several ships q-jumped into orbit around Jupiter. Complete communications blackout on all the moons and orbital platforms. And ten minutes ago a cargo freighter imaged the ships en route to Earth at incredible speeds."

"How incredible?"

Yarbrough turned her head to flash him a pained glance. "They'll be here within the hour."

Granger's mouth hung open. "But that puts their speed at around—"

"Nearly point five c, yes, I know," Yarbrough replied. They were nearly to the Lunar Base Command Center, and officers were streaming through the halls, reporting to their duty stations.

"But isn't that impossible?" said one of her aides, a young lieutenant.

"Kid, nothing's impossible when it comes to the Swarm —"

"We don't know it's the Swarm, Captain Granger," interrupted Yarbrough.

"Care to take any guesses as to who else it might be, Admiral?" he said icily. He knew it was politically correct to think the Swarm threat was finished, but he couldn't believe her intransigence on the issue when an entire fleet was bearing down on Earth.

"CENTCOM isn't sure. We knew there was a threat out in the Veracruz Sector and sent scouts to investigate."

"And?" he said, as they rounded the corner into the Command Center.

Yarbrough demurred. "And, well, we lost contact with them." She saluted the commanding officer of Lunar Base, Rear Admiral Tully. "What's the latest, Sheldon?"

"ETA fifty-five minutes. The cargo freighter managed to image most of their fleet in decent detail. We're looking at six to eight large carriers or cruisers."

"Origin?"

Admiral Tully shrugged. "Not any design I've ever seen. Certainly not Swarm."

Yarbrough cast a glance back at Granger. "See?"

"We know next to nothing about the latest Swarm technology, Admiral. It's reckless to assume it's not them just because it doesn't look like their ships from seventy-five years ago."

"Are they aggressive?" said Yarbrough, turning back to Admiral Tully.

"Still no long range comm signals out of Jupiter. Ganymede Station is silent, as is Callisto Depot. Hell, the only way we knew they showed up was from an old scientific satellite in high-Jupiter geosynchronous orbit that was out of range of whatever jamming signal they've got going on."

"What do our defenses look like here?" asked Granger.

"Lunar Base is no sitting duck, Captain. Plus we've got a dozen ships sitting out there in honor of the *Constitution*'s decommissioning. The *Qantas*, the *Clyburne*, the *Petain*. If this is Swarm, and if they're anything like the ships from last time, they don't stand a chance against us." Admiral Tully smiled smugly.

Commander Proctor stepped forward. "We already know these are not the ships from last time. They've evolved. Or improved. Or whatever it is they do."

Yarbrough took a deep breath. "Mobilize the ships that are here. Get me on the horn to all the captains—I'm taking temporary command of the portion of the fleet that is here and will run battle operations from this Command Center, with your consent, Admiral." She nodded to Sheldon Tully—not that she needed his permission, since she outranked him by a star, but they were old friends. "Get all the civilians off the base and loaded back on to the transports immediately," she said to her aide. "Captain Granger, I want the *Constitution* to escort them back to Earth—"

"What?"

"You heard me. The Vice President is here, not to mention the dozens of senators, congresspeople, and governors. And don't forget about the kids. We can't have them in a combat situation."

"If that fleet makes it past Lunar Base, there might not be an Earth to go back to. Keep the *Constitution* with the fleet."

"No. We can't afford to lose such a significant portion of the civilian government if we fail here. No, get to Earth, and report in to Admiral Zingano at CENTCOM. That's a direct order. Move."

She shoved him out of the way and made for the command console where Admiral Tully was directing operations.

Commander Proctor fell into step next to him as he stormed out of the Command Center. "Well sir, looks like you're stuck with me for awhile longer."

Dammit.

CHAPTER TWENTY-THREE

Earth's Moon
Bridge, ISS Constitution

"Tim, what the hell is going on?" Commander Haws was still buttoning his old frayed uniform when he met Granger and Proctor in the hall on the way to the bridge. It seemed he had managed to escape from the decommissioning ceremony early.

"An unidentified fleet is en route to Earth."

"Swarm?"

"Unknown."

"Bullshit," grumbled Haws as they approached the two marines standing guard outside the bridge.

"Exactly." Granger paused before entering the bridge, glancing for a moment at the two officers. Proctor technically had operational control over the *Constitution* given the Old Bird's decommissioning ceremony not an hour earlier, but given the emergency at hand....

"Commander Proctor, I'm re-assuming command of the *Constitution*. If you wish to lodge an objection with CENTCOM—"

"No need, sir. I understand," she replied, with a curt nod. Good. She wasn't going to pull anything stupid—when called upon, she seemed to be someone who understood the need for action. He'd prefer to just tell her to go to her quarters, but that would be going too far.

"Good. I'm assigning you as assistant XO. Commander Haws will delegate any duties to you that he sees fit—" He held up a hand of silence to Haws, who'd started to protest. "Not now, Abe. This is an emergency, and we both know that being on a war footing is different than being on watch duty for our entire careers. We'll need all the help we can get, and I want her with you."

He hoped his friend didn't read between the lines: he really wanted Proctor shadowing Haws to make sure the old man, probably still hungover from over-indulging at the reception, wouldn't make any sloppy, fatigue-induced mistakes.

"Fine," Haws grumbled. Satisfied his friend would not give him anymore guff, Granger strode onto the bridge.

"Battle stations. Sound general alert status orange."

The bridge, which had been half-deserted due to the decommissioning ceremony, fell to a shocked silence. The lieutenant sitting in the command chair opened his eyes wide.

"Sir?"

"You heard me, Diaz. Get back to ops and sound the alert. Get the bridge crew back here. Tell Commander Rayna Scott to report to the bridge—I want an update from her on engine status. And assemble the weapons crew chiefs—we need to know what the status is of the mag-rail cannons and the point-defense RPOs—"

"Sir," interrupted Commander Proctor, "I'm afraid I had the point-defense rapid pulse ordnance turrets all decommissioned yesterday. I thought it wise to ensure civilians couldn't accidentally activate them somehow during the simulations...."

Granger paused. "*All* of them?"

"Yes, sir," she said, with the slightest of winces.

"Very well. Get the crew chiefs up here," he turned to Haws and Proctor. "Get those RPOs back in service. As many as you can. You have thirty minutes."

Haws grumbled an affirmative, and barked some orders to a few ops midshipmen to assist them. Granger strode over to the fighter command terminal. "Is Commander Pierce back from Lunar Base yet?" he asked the Lieutenant CAG sitting in for him.

"Aye, sir."

"How many fighters are still in service?"

"Twenty-three, sir."

Damn. Twenty-three out of eighty-two. They were effectively going to be a sitting duck, unless they could manage to convert some of the fighters that had been turned into simulators back into fighting craft.

He spun around to Proctor who was huddled over a terminal with Commander Haws, discussing the RPOs. "Proctor, tell me about the fighters. The simulators. How much were they altered?" He wanted to say, *how much did you screw them over*, but thought better of it.

"All live ordnance removed, and their power plants are all

decommissioned. But other than that just some software upgrades."

Granger squinted at her. "Define *decommissioned*."

"The fuel cores have all been removed and the initiator matrices are all cold."

Dammit.

"Fine. Let Haws handle the RPOs. You get down to the fighter bay and assist Commander Pierce in getting all those birds back into operational status. You have one hour."

"All of them up and running in an hour? But that's—"

"Crazy? Unrealistic? I'm sorry, Commander, but I didn't set that particular deadline. The Swarm did."

Proctor closed her mouth, frowned, and nodded. "Understood." She rushed out the door, sweeping past another woman entering the bridge.

"Cap'n, what's going on?" said Commander Rayna Scott. She didn't have her characteristic smudged coveralls on but rather the dress uniform, having come straight from the decommissioning ceremony.

"Swarm." He paused, watching her blue eyes enlarge. She opened her mouth, and closed it. "I need my engines, Rayna. What's our status?"

"How soon?"

"One hour."

She didn't move, but her eyes flashed back and forth, as if reading some imaginary computer terminal in front of her face. After a moment she snapped back to attention. "You got it, Cap'n."

"Good girl," he murmured as she too rushed out the doors without another word.

What next? They had one hour to get a decommissioned battle cruiser, which hadn't seen a day of real action in over seventy years, ready for the fight of its life. He breathed deep and closed his eyes, ignoring the sharp pain stabbing into his lungs. *Dammit, not now,* he thought, noting the pain had increased since the morning.

But no time to worry about himself. He had a crew to lead. A ship to protect.

A world to save.

CHAPTER TWENTY-FOUR

Earth's Moon
Captain's Quarters, ISS Winchester

"I thought you told me their fleet would stop at Jupiter, shoot the place up, and leave? What the hell are they doing? Straight towards Earth! They're heading straight towards the damn Earth!" Vice President Isaacson's hands were sweating, which didn't help as he wiped the sweat from his forehead.

Ambassador Volodin was seated at the computer terminal in the captain's quarters, which Captain Day of the *Winchester* had given up to his VIP guest. He frantically punched keys and commands, trying to backdoor his way into the *Winchester*'s meta-space communications transmitter.

"I don't know. They should have stopped. They should have turned around." Volodin motioned for Isaacson. "Here. Enter your credentials. If you do it, IDF will never know we accessed the system."

Isaacson snapped his head towards Volodin. "How do you

know that?"

"We know a lot of things, Mr. Vice President. Hurry."

Isaacson keyed in his credentials, and the access to the meta-space system popped up on the screen. "Is it too late to make them turn around? Do they commit to a target once they engage?"

"I don't know." Volodin took out a personal datapad and scrolled through it. Finding what he was looking for, he began tapping a message into the meta-space transmitter. "But I know the pattern that subverts their link to the homeworld. If we can disrupt their current mandate and replace it with something else, like a basic command that says *return home*, then we may be in the clear."

Isaacson paced the room, looking up at Volodin every few minutes. He perused the captain's bookcase and framed pictures, recognizing Fleet Admiral Zingano in one, shaking Captain Day's hand in front of the IDF flag. "Well?"

"The message went out a few minutes ago. No reply yet."

"They reply?"

"Yes," said Volodin. "When we first disrupted their meta-space link a decade ago, we were as surprised as you. The Swarm had never replied to any of our attempts to communicate during the war. Not once. But when we first subverted the link, they not only replied, but acknowledged receipt of instructions. They *obeyed*. That was unthinkable, but when we directed them to hollow out a particularly large asteroid in the Beta Ceti system as a test, and they complied, finishing within days, well"—he looked up from the terminal—"that was when we believed it, and started to plan for how to use it."

"Why didn't the Russian government inform IDF about this?" Isaacson demanded. "We're talking about a species that nearly wiped out Earth."

Volodin sniffed. "Same reason IDF didn't share smart-steel technology with the Russian Confederation. You don't trust us. Never have. And when we found the aliens were not monsters, that they could be reasoned with, we believed we'd found our ally. Or, at least, a counterbalance to IDF influence out in the colonial sectors."

"Counterbalance? Reasoned with? I thought you controlled them."

"After a fashion, yes. But they still have will, and intelligence. After the initial test, where they hollowed out the asteroid for us, they required an exchange of knowledge. So they sent us schematics for better gravity field emitters, allowing our ships to sustain greater changes in inertia."

Isaacson didn't like the direction this conversation was going. "And what did you give them?"

"The Russian Academy of Science is at the forefront of quantum field technology. We taught them how our fusion cores use artificial nano-singularities. Increases our fusion efficiency by some five hundred percent over IDF's. Seemed like a fair trade for their inertial compensators."

"And how do you know that they're not going to just turn around and use the tech on us? What makes you think they're suddenly tame?"

"I told you, Eamon, we've been controlling them for years. The exchange happened nearly a decade ago, and in all that time they've never been anything other than docile and cooperative."

A binary code flashed up on the screen, and Volodin tapped out an instruction for the computer to decode it into characters.

His face drained white.

"What does it say?" Isaacson yelled, pushing Volodin aside to look at the screen.

Only two words comprised the translated message.

You die.

CHAPTER TWENTY-FIVE

Earth's Moon
Bridge, ISS Constitution

"Lieutenant Diaz, get on the horn to Lunar Base. Find out what the status is of the civilian evacuation, and when we leave to escort the civilian fleet."

"Aye, sir."

Granger strode around the central command console to sidle up to his XO. "Where are we at, Abe?"

The old XO grumbled. "Tim, it's going to take a lot longer than one hour to get all these RPOs operational."

The captain pointed at the readiness summary on the console. "Focus on the lower-hanging fruit. Get as many as you can operational before the hour is up. And that's just the time it'll take the Swarm to arrive at Lunar Base. By then we'll be escorting the civvies back to Earth, so we've got a little more time than that."

"You think the ships we've got assembled here can stop

them?"

Granger paused. "Who knows? CENTCOM is q-jumping a few more ships in from Earth, so Lunar Base is not exactly a sitting duck. And the base itself is not lightly armed either. They'll put up a hell of a fight. If all goes well, we may not even need all these RPOs and fighters."

The XO grunted. "Yeah, but if it doesn't, I can't imagine what one more ship will do to them if they decide to continue on towards Earth. Especially if that one ship is the *Constitution*."

"She'll hold," said Granger, patting the console. "Hell, I'll wager she'll hold together better than most of those new ships IDF has pumped out in the last fifty years. Ten meters of tungsten shielding ain't nothing to sniff at. Those new ships have barely a twentieth of that, and it's all made of that new smart-steel. The stuff is supposed to be stronger than anything, but only if the computers are working."

"What happens when the computers go down?" Haws glanced up at him sideways.

"The electron energy orbitals in the smart-steel are regulated by a central processing unit. Or some physics shit like that. Makes it a thousand times stronger than regular steel, and far more than that for short periods of time in anticipated impact zones. All I remember from my briefing is that if the computers go down, or if the attacker knows the quantum modulation patterns, the smart-steel becomes very, very dumb."

"I can't imagine CENTCOM would have cleared smart-steel to be used in starships if it's not safe."

Granger eyed his XO. "Abe, we're talking about the same

CENTCOM that has agreed with the Eagleton Commission about the need to strip down the fleet. I'm not sure I'd put all my faith in their judgement these days."

His XO's eyes narrowed. "You don't think the fleet is at risk?"

"Of course it's at risk. Whether it's at existential risk remains to be seen."

Lieutenant Diaz raised his head towards the captain. "Sir, Lunar Base reports that most of the civilian transports are loaded and ready for evac."

"How many?"

Diaz glanced at his display. "Most of the political delegation came on the *Winchester*, but we've also got the *Roadrunner*, the asteroid mining ship *Redeye One*, and the *Rainbow*, along with a handful of merchant and industrial freighters that requested our escort back to Earth. The total caravan should be fourteen ships."

Fourteen ships. That's a lot to defend.

"Available armaments on any of them?"

"Negative, sir," said Diaz, with a downward glance.

Granger sucked in a painful breath, careful to let his face remain steadfast. "Very well. We go to escort duty with the caravan we've got." He stood up and called back to Diaz as he passed through the doors to the bridge. "Lieutenant, inform me immediately when all ships report ready. I'll be in the fighter bay."

"Aye, sir."

The corridors were strangely silent, except for the occasional bustle of activity as a crew member ran past with whatever urgent business they had to get the ship on a war footing. Hardly any of them stopped to salute the captain as they sprinted past, but Granger didn't care. In an hour, they could all be dead anyway.

No. He couldn't think that way. *She'd pull them through*, he thought as he traced a hand down the corridor wall. The *Constitution* had performed admirably in the first Swarm War, suffering substantial damage, sure, but she'd always pulled through. After each battle, after each skirmish, the Old Bird carried her crew home—one of the only ships during that war to do so.

But times had changed. The Swarm had changed, if the early sensor readings and intelligence were accurate. It was either a completely new enemy, or the Swarm had radically overhauled its technology and ship design in the past seventy-five years.

Granger strode through the doors to the fighter bay, saluting the two marines stationed at the entrance.

"Captain, we're nearly done restoring about a dozen fighters back to operational condition—alterations had only just begun on those. But we've still got over forty fighters down," Commander Proctor called out to him breathlessly from the command station near the side wall. The entire maintenance section—several hundred meters long and almost a hundred wide, was a bee's nest of frenzied activity. Maintenance crews and whoever else Commander Proctor had managed to deputize were busy on about fifty fighters, frantically working to restore them to operational status. Granger was actually impressed at the scale of the operation that Proctor had managed to put together in such a short period of time.

"Very good, Commander. Excellent work. How many birds will I have in forty-five minutes?"

A hint of a grimace tugged at her brow. "Just shy of fifty, sir."

Granger breathed a curse. "We'll need more than that, Commander." He saw her steel her jaw slightly. "Even so, excellent work," he added with a curt nod.

"Thank you, sir. In another hour and a half we should be up to sixty fighters total. Unfortunately the twenty or so that have been completely stripped and outfitted for simulator service will take quite a bit more time."

"Understood. Carry on." As Commander Proctor turned back to her assistants, Commander Pierce came bounding up.

"Captain, you realize we don't actually have fully trained pilots for all these fighters, don't you?"

Granger half-smiled, and turned to leave. "Define *fully trained*, Commander."

Pierce followed him out the door. "We basically only have a half-complement of full-time pilots. The rest are trainees. Assigned to the *Constitution* fresh out of IDF Flight Academy. They were supposed to finish a six-month tour here before officially earning their wings."

Granger continued down the hallway towards the bridge. "And?"

Pierce huffed. "*And,* sir, these boys simply aren't ready for combat. I've only had them for about a month."

Granger stopped and turned, letting two technicians rush past before staring his CAG in the eye. "You go to war with the army you have, Commander. They either die out there in their birds defending the *Constitution* and the rest of the caravan, or they die in here with their fat asses in their bunks. Ask them which they prefer and get back to me."

He could tell his CAG still hadn't quite understood the gravity of the situation, which mystified him a little. "Commander?" he asked, letting his voice soften a hair.

"Sir, it's just that I still haven't heard from my father. The *Gallant*. Word is that the entire third British fleet is ... missing."

Pierce's voice wavered slightly. Granger reached out to his CAG's elbow. "I know. CENTCOM thinks ... well, let's just say they don't have high hopes that the third fleet survived its encounter with the Swarm." He looked Pierce in the eye. "I'm sorry, Tyler."

"So it's confirmed, then? CENTCOM knows the third fleet engaged the Swarm?"

"No. Nothing's known for sure. But given that we now have a Swarm fleet bearing down on Lunar Base within half an hour, I'd say the chances your father is alive are slim. But now is not the time, Commander. Right now we need to give these bastards a good old-fashioned whoopin'. Let's hand their asses to them. Exterminate them. Then, when Earth is safe, we'll grieve. Agreed?"

His CAG steeled his jaw and nodded. "Yes, sir."

"Good man." Granger turned once again to return to the bridge. "I want every available fighter ready to launch in forty-five minutes, Commander. And if you have to deputize the shuttle pilots, do it."

"Yes, sir," came the reply from down the hallway.

But Granger hardly heard it over the red alert klaxons that sounded shrilly through the corridor.

CHAPTER TWENTY-SIX

Earth's Moon
Fighter Pilot Briefing Room, ISS Constitution

Commander Pierce stormed into the fighter bay's briefing room where the pilots were still assembling. Running through the numbers, he knew there were simply not enough pilots for the ships that Proctor would have ready for him, even counting the trainee pilots fresh out of the academy. In addition to his regular crew of twenty, and his twenty new trainees, he still had up to forty more spots to fill.

And that meant anyone on board who had any flying experience whatsoever was fair game, and the captain had given him a blank check to draft who he needed.

Most of them had arrived—a handful of former freighter pilots who'd joined IDF as mechanics or gunnery sergeants, and of course the entire ship's complement of shuttle pilots. He nodded a quick greeting to Lieutenant Miller, who'd seated herself alongside the rest of the fighter jocks.

The room fell into a hushed silence as he reached the podium. None of them had joined IDF expecting war. Becoming an IDF pilot usually meant one was preparing for an eventual career flying the giant tourist spaceliners, or colonial transport ships, or merchant freighters.

But war was upon them, whether they were ready or not.

"I'm sure by now you all know this is not a drill. The Swarm is back and they're out for blood."

One of the fighter jocks interrupted, Lieutenant Volz. "Same ships as last time? Like what we've trained against?"

"I don't know, Ballsy. All we've been told is that the entire Veracruz Sector has been laid to waste, and they're on their way here."

As the gravity of his words sunk in, he turned to the group of newcomers. "As you can see, the situation is grim, and we need every available fighter. That means some of you who are joining us now are being called up as pilots—"

"Sir," began one of the enlisted crew, a mechanic, who was still greasy from working on a bird. "I haven't flown a freighter in five years. What good will I do out there?"

"You'll do better out there than you will in here. All that matters now is firepower. Plus, not every fighter is ready to go —there are thirty-odd birds still being brought back into service. That means we'll start with the most experienced of you lot, and get the rest of you into simulators in the meantime. Each newbie will be paired with an experienced pilot, and two pairs will form a squad for a total of twelve squads now, twenty squads when all fighters are brought into service. Your assignments have been made and are now on your consoles."

The pilots all looked down at the tiny computer screens on their armrests.

Lieutenant Volz nudged Lieutenant Miller, "Look at that, Fishtail, you're with me. Try to keep up."

She looked stunned, but managed to murmur, "Sure thing, Ballsy."

The CAG continued. "You've got one hour. Newbies, get to the simulators. Experienced pilots, go with your trainees. Teach them the essentials. How to fire, how to cover, basic defensive and offensive patterns. Nothing fancy, just the tried and true."

The red alert lights and klaxons blared behind him. It was showtime.

"Go! Be in your birds in one hour!"

CHAPTER TWENTY-SEVEN

Earth's Moon
Bridge, ISS Winchester

Vice President Isaacson stormed out of the captain's quarters and raced down the hall. The two secret service agents assigned to him jumped out of their chairs and bolted after him. Ambassador Volodin followed close behind, huffing and struggling to keep up. "Where are you going?" he called.

"We've got to get the hell out of here," yelled Isaacson.

Volodin huffed something else but was breathing so hard Isaacson couldn't understand, and before he knew it he was approaching the two marines stationed outside the bridge who held up their hands indicating that they stop.

"I'm sorry, sir, only authorized personnel are allowed on the bridge."

Isaacson bristled. "Then you get the hell in there and tell the captain that Vice President Isaacson wants to come on his bridge!"

"Yes, sir!" One of the marines disappeared through the door, and reappeared within moments. "This way, sir."

Isaacson barreled past the remaining marine and strode onto the bridge, which was humming with activity. The ship was only a smaller Cincinnati class corvette, mainly used by IDF for transporting personnel and dignitaries around the solar system, but they apparently were gearing up for battle.

"Vice President Isaacson, we're a little busy here, sir—"

Isaacson interrupted. "Captain, we need to get to Earth immediately."

The captain shook his head. "I'm sorry, sir, but the *Winchester* does not currently have q-jump abilities."

Unbelievable. "Currently?"

"That's correct. As such, we'll be escorted in by the *Constitution*."

"THE *CONSTITUTION*?" Isaacson yelled. "You're telling me that the oldest ship in the fleet, the same one we decommissioned today and is missing half its engines and is being flown by a bunch of washed-up failures is the ship that will be escorting the second-in-command of the government of Earth?"

Captain Day shifted uncomfortably. "Yes, sir."

"Get Yarbrough on the comm. Now." He pointed to one of the consoles. The captain nodded to the officer at the comm station, and within moments, Admiral Yarbrough's voice boomed over the speakers.

"Yarbrough. What is it, Mr. Isaacson?"

"Admiral, am I to understand that the *Constitution* is the only warship escorting us back to Earth?"

"That's correct, Mr. Isaacson. We simply can't spare any

modern cruisers. If there's any chance we can stop them here at Lunar Base, then that's what we'll do. I need all available ships—"

"Preposterous, Admiral. I demand you send another, more modern warship as our escort. Not just that bucket of bolts out there."

Silence came over the speaker as Admiral Yarbrough weighed her options. Finally, she sighed. "Very well."

"Send the *Qantas*."

"But, Mr. Isaacson, that's the flagship of IDF. We need her defending Lunar Base."

"We need her defending the Earth, and her elected leaders. End of conversation."

Another silence. "Fine. Yarbrough out."

Isaacson nodded in approval. Good—it was time the admirals learned to listen to him—they'd better get used to it.

"Now, Captain Day, tell me why we can't just make the q-jump. Tell me why we don't *currently* have that ability."

Day walked around the tactical station to face the Vice President. "The problem, sir, is that while we do have a q-jump drive, the need for it has not existed for years—at least for this ship. We mainly take on duties involving short-range transports and missions within the solar system. If we want to re-engage the drive, we'll need a functioning quantum field coupler, and you don't just find those lying on a shelf somewhere. It's a delicate, expensive piece of equipment, and it doesn't make sense to maintain them on vessels that—"

"Then *find* one."

"Excuse me?" Captain Day looked confused. Isaacson rolled his eyes—were all fleet officers this dense?

"Find one, Captain. Get on your comm to Lunar Base, the *Constitution*, the other ships—someone must have a spare. Do it now. That's an order."

Captain Day grit his teeth, but nodded.

"Yes, sir."

Good. They were learning to respect his authority already. That would come in handy after his inauguration next week.

CHAPTER TWENTY-EIGHT

Earth's Moon
Bridge, ISS Constitution

"Report," barked Captain Granger, as the bridge doors slid back into their pockets.

The XO grumbled, "CENTCOM sounded the alarm a few minutes ago. Seems our approaching friends made a little pit stop at Mars. Before it blew, Phobos Station recorded images of the alien fleet."

"And the Mars colony?"

Haws snorted. "Bastards took out the whole thing. In a matter of minutes."

The entire Mars colony. Gone.

"Impossible. What did they use? Nukes?"

"No," continued Haws. "See for yourself. Looks like … well, not like anything I've seen before."

Granger bounded towards the command console and tapped the video display showing the priority message received from CENTCOM. A zoomed-in image of Mars appeared, and a handful of grainy-looking ships snapped into orbit, decelerating at incredible speeds. After a brief battle with a handful of defending orbital patrol ships, a harsh white light appeared in the midst of the invading fleet. As the light intensified, the image started to pulse with static. Suddenly, the brilliant light disappeared in a flash.

Moments later, an enormous red plume rising up from the surface was all the evidence Granger needed of the colony's demise.

"Dammit," he whispered.

Haws growled. "Close to a hundred thousand souls down there, Tim. Or, there were, at any rate, god bless 'em."

As they watched the video continue, the alien fleet accelerated to a huge speed, and the pixellated images grew larger on the screen, which pulsed with a regular static. Moments later, several bright green beams lanced out from the lead ship and the video went dark.

"Has CENTCOM analyzed this?" The captain glanced up at Haws.

"They're working on it, they said. But they called a general red alert—the alien fleet will be here in minutes—sooner than they thought."

"Why the static?"

"Tim?" The XO limped over next to him.

"That pulsing during the video. What was that?"

"Power surge?"

Granger stroked his chin. It had seemed like more than that. It was regular. Pulsing. "No, I don't think so." He walked over to the signals intelligence station in the tactical section of the bridge. "Ensign, I want a team analyzing that vid from Phobos Station."

"What are we looking for, sir?" asked the fresh-faced young woman.

"I don't know. Pull it apart. We need everything we can get at this point. Get me the highest resolution images of the alien ships you can, and see if you can determine the source of that pulsing."

"Aye, sir."

Granger turned back to Haws, but before he could say anything the communications officer caught his attention. "Sir, Lunar Base is signaling us. It's Admiral Yarbrough, sir."

"Send it to my station," said Granger. At the terminal, he tapped the button to initiate transmission. Admiral Yarbrough's weary face filled his screen.

"Tim, it's time to get out of here. And you're going to have some company. Vice President Isaacson requested that another capital ship accompany him back to Earth."

"You mean," Granger deadpanned, "he's not comfortable with just the *Constitution* holding off an alien attack on his ship?"

"Something like that. The *Qantas* will join you—it's a newer battlecruiser, and should set the Veep at ease."

Granger thought it was a bad idea—the fleet's flagship should be in the battle for Lunar Base, but nodded nonetheless —there was no time for an argument. "Will that leave you enough firepower?"

"We'll be fine. Lunar Base is no sitting duck—we'll hand their asses to them. Assuming they have asses."

Granger chuckled—it was true, they'd never found so

much as a finger from the Swarm vessels they'd managed to salvage. Even the most intact ships were completely devoid of life. Just a translucent mucus smeared everywhere.

"When you get back to Earth, report to Fleet Admiral Zingano. He's heading up the defense of Earth. We're not stretched so thin back there as out in the Veracruz Sector. These bastards won't know what hit them. Get out of here, Tim."

The tired face disappeared, replaced by the Laurel and Earth seal of IDF. Granger glanced up at the communications officer. "Is the caravan ready?"

"Aye, sir. All ships reporting in. The _Qantas_ has moved into formation with us. Also, sir, the captain of the _Rainbow_ would like to talk to you."

"Fine," he said, glancing at the countdown timer. They had less than fifteen minutes before the alien fleet showed up at Lunar Base. "Put it on my screen."

An older woman appeared on his console's screen. "What can I do for you, Captain?"

"Captain Granger, as you know, we've got a boatload of kids over here."

"I'm aware of that, Captain."

"This is a Cincinnati class corvette, but our q-jump capability was stripped a few years ago when I bought her. Too expensive to maintain. But all she needs is a quantum field coupler—if you have a spare, I can get it installed in under thirty minutes and be on our way. One less target for you boys to protect."

He nodded. "We'll look around for one. In the meantime, be prepared to head out with us. We're your best hope for now.

Granger out." He leaned back to the comm officer. "Have operations look down in storage for a spare quantum field coupler. If they find one, get it down to Proctor and have her send it over to the *Rainbow* on a shuttle."

"Aye, sir."

"Good. Helm," he said, turning to the navigation pit. "Get us out of here. Half-power to main drive. And get me on speaker to the caravan," he called back to the comm.

Pausing for the comm officer to patch him through, he cleared his throat. "This is Captain Granger of the *Constitution*. Set your headings toward Earth, at an acceleration of two g's. We'll maintain that thrust for fifteen minutes and then we'll coast the rest of the way in and make a coordinated deceleration. Stay close to either the *Constitution*, or the *Qantas*. If the alien fleet overtakes us, keep the two warships in between yourselves and the rat-bastards. Granger out."

Haws nodded at him. "Short and pithy. Just how I like it."

Granger motioned to the helm. "Take us out, Lieutenant."

With a distant roar, the main engines surged to life as ultra-high-temperature plasma blasted out the rear thrusters. The internal gravity field took a few moments to adjust to the new acceleration and Granger swayed a bit. He noticed that no one else swayed—was he tired? Was the damn tumor spreading in his brain?

Hell—all he needed was a few weeks. Enough time to save his ship.

And his world.

CHAPTER TWENTY-NINE

Earth's Moon
Bridge, ISS Constitution

The time inched forward slowly, but inexorably. On the main viewscreen was a split-screen image of the Earth, which loomed far off in the distance but grew almost imperceptibly larger with each passing minute, and on the left-hand side was the gray orb of the moon, with the Lunar Base complex still just visible, sprawling across Mare Tranquility.

Granger drummed his fingers on his console, watching the time tick down until the expected arrival of the alien fleet. Ten minutes, twenty-five seconds.

"Captain?" The comm buzzed on his console, and he tapped it in reply.

"Go ahead, Commander Proctor."

"Sir, we now have sixty-two operational fighters. The remaining twenty will require at least another day, sir."

Sixty-two. Better than nothing, he supposed, and better

than he'd expected Proctor to pull off, though it was still woefully short of what he wanted. The *Qantas* brought another ninety-five fighters, all of which were far more technologically advanced than the *Constitution*'s, but in spite of their almost impenetrable smart-steel armor, Granger had deep misgivings about them. They'd never been tested in actual live combat. Not like the *Constitution*'s fighters. Granted, those hadn't been tested in live combat for over seventy-five years, but still.

"Very good, Commander. Wrap things up there, and then head to RPO fire control. We're up to twenty guns, but that's still only half of what we've got." Granger didn't know exactly what she would do to speed things up, but she'd proved herself on the fighter deck—somehow, against all odds, they were going into combat with over three quarters of their fighters operational, up from less than a quarter just a few short hours ago. Despite his earlier frustrations with Proctor, he was beginning to respect her.

"I'm assuming you want them all operational by the time the enemy fleet shows up, sir?" she replied with the slightest sarcasm in her voice. He let it pass. "Also, sir, we've confirmed —we have another quantum field coupler here in storage. Shall I arrange for transport to the *Rainbow*?"

"Of course. You have twenty minutes. Granger out."

He glanced at Haws, who flashed a quick wink, and grumbled, "Putting her through the wringer, aren't you, Tim?"

"She deserves it. As penance for stripping everything down for the past two weeks. But I've got to hand it to her: she's good."

"Let's hope she's good enough."

Granger's console beeped. He glanced: incoming

transmission from Vice President Isaacson. In annoyance, he flipped it on. "Yes, Mr. Isaacson?"

"Captain, am I to understand you have a spare quantum field coupler on board?" The Vice President's narrow face appeared on his screen.

"Mr. Isaacson, have you been monitoring the *Constitution*'s transmissions?" Damn old fool. Didn't he have anything better to do?

"I haven't. But Captain Day reported to me that you're in the process of transferring a quantum coupler to the *Rainbow*."

"That's right. There are thirty kids onboard the *Rainbow*, and a war zone is no place for a child."

"True, but it is also not the place for senators, government ministers, cabinet officials, governors, or the Vice President of the United Earth League. Captain, the *Winchester* is the same design as the *Rainbow*. You will order that shuttle to deliver her cargo to this ship immediately."

Politicians. Several choice words and insults came to mind. He was half tempted to just switch the comm off, but they were out of time. Either send the damn thing over there, or be harangued and pestered until they did.

"I hope your new quantum coupler gets you safely to Earth, sir. I can't imagine what we'd do without a tenth of our government. Granger out."

He hoped the sarcasm didn't come across too strongly. Hell, who was he kidding? He hoped it *had* been strong—strong enough to shame the bastard. This crisis was not improving Granger's already dismal opinion of politicians generally, and the Vice President particularly. "Comm, order the shuttle to the *Winchester*."

Granger turned back to Haws.

"Disgusting old bastard, that one." Haws flipped a middle finger at the dark display on his monitor. "Want to shuttle me over there so I can punch the piece of shit in the nose? I'm retiring anyway...."

Granger chuckled. "Politicians will be politicians. Truth be told, the kids might be safer with us at this point if the aliens are intent on pressing through to Earth. I just don't—"

"Sir!" interrupted Lieutenant Diaz, the officer at the sensor station. "Lunar Base reports engagement with the enemy fleet!"

Granger snapped his eyes to the timer on his console, which said they still had five minutes before the aliens were supposed to show up. "Damn. Their drive tech is not just more advanced than ours—it puts us to shame." He turned to his XO. "Sound red alert, combat stations. All retrofit and recovery operations cease immediately and all crew report to battle stations. Except the RPO gun repair crews—we still need every damn gun we can get operational in the next twenty minutes."

Haws started barking orders to the various department chiefs. The bridge, which had been collectively holding its breath for the last half hour, now burst into a flurry of activity.

He watched the screen, which now showed a small cluster of tiny white dots converging on the moon. They were already far too distant to actually watch any of the operations—the resolution just wasn't high enough—but perhaps one of the satellites....

"Lieutenant," he said, nodding to the comm station, "tap into one of the science satellites in orbit around the moon.

133

The Armstrong satellite I believe will do. Redirect it to the battle zone and give us a live feed."

"Uh, sir, that's a civilian craft run by the Unified Science Federation. We can't just—"

"Actually, we can, Lieutenant. When asked for credentials, pipe it through to my console. Every captain in the fleet has backdoor access to every single spacecraft, satellite, defense platform, and data pod. If it's in space, I can access it. A nice little feature we implemented after the Khorsky incident a decade ago." He glanced around the bridge. "That's classified top-secret, by the way."

"Aye, sir. Sending it to your console now."

The access authorization script appeared on his screen, and he entered in his personal red-level security code. He hoped against hope that IDF hadn't already deactivated it. It was an irrational thought—they weren't relieving him of his rank, just his command. But really, what was the difference?

"There you go, Lieutenant."

Granger watched as the monitor on the side wall of the bridge flipped from a split-screen Earth/Moon image to a nightmare.

Eight alien ships, all larger than IDF's largest carriers, lurked in stationary orbit over Lunar Base as the remnants of the IDF fleet engaged them. Remnant was the best word to describe the defenders, as at least a dozen smaller frigates and most of the heavy cruisers and carriers careened, broken and fragmented, through space.

A flurry of defensive fire blasted up from the surface— Lunar Base's robust orbital defense was giving the alien fleet a run for its money. Granger heard a few abortive, quiet cheers as one of the alien vessels broke apart under the withering fire from below, but they soon fell silent as they watched another huge alien ship bear down on the *ISS Clyburne*—itself a massive carrier—and slice it in two with a devastatingly effective directed energy weapon that arced across space in a lethal, brilliant green light.

Granger heard several officers behind him moan. After entire careers of waiting and training vigilantly for an enemy that never came, they were unprepared for the emotional impact of real threats and losses. He knew several of them probably had friends on that ship. He knew Captain Arenson personally, and a giant pit formed in his stomach as he watched one of the halves of the *Clyburne* burst into a massive explosion as it was hit by a second devastating beam.

CHAPTER THIRTY

Earth's Moon
Bridge, ISS Constitution

"Captain, something's happening," called out Lieutenant Diaz. Granger peered at the screen and saw that he was right—something very odd was happening, just as in the surveillance vid from Phobos Station. A piercingly bright light had appeared in the midst of the alien fleet.

And as before, the video feed began to pulse.

But this time he noticed something else. A faint humming in the deckplate. Like a distant vibration, low and rumbling and barely perceptible.

He turned to Haws. "You feel that?"

"Feel what?"

Dammit—was his head playing tricks on him again? If they survived the day he'd have to go down to Doc Wyatt and get his brain scanned. The headache, combined with the faint vertigo from the deep pulsing in the ship were evidence enough that the cancer had spread.

"That pulsing. It started just when the video began shaking, and that light showed up next to the alien ships." He glared at his XO. "You're telling me you can't feel it?"

Another voice sounded out across the bridge from the doors sliding open. "I feel it."

Granger breathed an inaudible sigh of relief. "Good, so I'm not crazy. Why are you not down in fire control, Commander Proctor?"

"Not much point. They're going to have about eighty percent of the firing systems up in the next fifteen minutes. Not much more I could do, so when I heard the alarms I came down here. Thought you could use some of my expertise on the Swarm. Such as it is," she added with a faint grimace. "No one knows much, but my doctoral dissertation was on Swarm anthropology."

He regarded her with a skeptical eye. "How in the world did you study Swarm anthropology without any living specimens? Or dead specimens for that matter."

But he hardly heard her answer, as his attention had swiveled back to the screen to watch as the brilliant light increased in intensity, even as the bombardment from the defenses on the surface intensified. One of the alien ships erupted in a massive explosion as one of the high-yield quantum thermonuclear warheads found its target, but the other ships held formation around the growing point of light.

Granger knew what was about to happen. They'd seen it less than an hour ago, and the next moment confirmed his fear. The light disappeared—it moved so fast his eyes couldn't track it. He wasn't even sure it moved, possibly because when it disappeared the video feed was overwhelmed with static and distortion. But a second later a massive explosion erupted out of the lunar surface far below, blasting outward, taking the entire Lunar Base with it.

Someone across the bridge in environmental operations vomited.

"Well, Commander? What does your Ph.D. in Swarm Anthropology tell you about that?"

Proctor was silent as the entire bridge watched the aftermath. A giant plume of rock, dust, and debris wafted up from the surface, the low gravity of the moon permitting the cloud to extend hundreds of kilometers upwards. Soon, it was nearly where the alien ships had been, though they had quickly moved off after their doomsday weapon launched. They were now finishing off the remaining IDF vessels that survived the initial onslaught.

"Well, for one, they're an evolutionarily cyclical species. This is just the latest of a series of regular leaps forward for them. Each cycle they expand outward from their core systems or homeworld, clearing out the space around them, before retreating back."

Granger stared at her. "How the hell do you know all that? I thought we knew nothing about them. All of IDF's expeditionary forces came back empty handed. The Swarm disappeared seventy-five years ago, inexplicably, without a trace, and now you're telling me you somehow know more than IDF intel about our deadliest enemy—"

"Oh, they know all this. Or rather, they've been told. None of this is corroborated. You're right, all the expeditionary forces sent out in the early years after the Swarm War came back empty handed, so I had to rely on ... more indirect methods. I studied the worlds they left behind, reconstructed maps of their expansion, networked with technological anthropologists to glean what we could from their ship design. In the end I couldn't come to many firm conclusions beyond what IDF scientists have come to, but I have my hypotheses. Or rather, I used to. I left my science career fifteen years ago for the military."

Granger considered her for a moment, wondering if they could glean anything from her previous studies that might help them, but out of the corner of his eye, movement on the still-playing video feed caught his attention. An IDF ship breaking off from the melee, which had become more of a mop-up operation for the aliens.

"It's the *Thrush*, sir," said one of the tactical crew. "My brother is on—" but he broke off as he watched a brilliant green beam flash out from the nearest alien ship and lance right into the heart of the *Thrush*, a smaller light cruiser. The beam emerged from the far side, and within a few seconds the entire ship burst into a muted flame, quickly extinguished by space.

And then it was over. Every IDF ship had succumbed, and without hesitating, the alien fleet started moving as one.

Straight toward Earth.

Straight toward them.

CHAPTER THIRTY-ONE

Near Earth's Moon
Flightdeck, ISS Constitution

The simulator training was intense, but over far too quickly. In a sense, flying the simulated fighter was like flying her usual shuttle, only with guns. And now she was encouraged to fly at breakneck speeds and take the curves as fast as she could.

"Did pretty good for a newbie," said Lieutenant Volz as she pulled herself out of the simulator, using his offered hand as leverage.

"Thanks, Ballsy."

"Just don't fishtail your landing, Fishtail, or that callsign's gonna stick."

The hour was up, and the two of them jogged through the fighter bay, which swarmed with activity as the work crews frantically pushed to get as many birds into service as humanly possible. The interactive museum displays, models, and soft ropes and poles for queue formation were shoved unceremoniously into a corner—all trappings of retirement had been tossed aside.

"Ok, you're in that one there. Stay close to me. Our squad will fly in three-man attack wedge formation with single backup while we're out there, just like you practiced in the sim. You, Dogtown, and Hotbox will fly point and I'll back you all up."

She climbed up into her bird, and before she knew it she was initiating the engines and lifting off the deck. The pulsing screen of the energy airlock shimmered around her as she passed out into the vacuum at the end of the runway where she awaited with her squadron the inevitable order to deploy.

Voices of the other pilots chattered excitedly over the comm, and she felt a thrill of adrenaline. But after a minute of waiting, she reached into her back pocket and pulled out a picture of Zack as a baby, held in her husband's arms. It was when they were on a hike up in Yosemite right before her redeployment.

She reached and jammed it into a small space between the dashboard and one of the indicators so that it popped up vertically on its own. Her two favorite people in the world right in her view as she readied the rest of her fighter's systems for combat.

Ballsy's voice rang over her headset. "All right, bitches, we've got confirmation! Get ready!"

Glancing one more time at her baby son and Tom, she gunned her engine.

She swore she'd see them again.

CHAPTER THIRTY-TWO

Near Earth's Moon
Bridge, ISS Constitution

"Sir, they're accelerating rapidly!" said Lieutenant Diaz. "I don't know how, but they're at thirty g's. At this rate they'll be on top of us in five minutes!"

Haws sidled up to him and whispered in his ear. "Tim. This is crazy. We're no match for them—not even with the *Qantas* backing us up. We'll be dead in five minutes."

"What are you suggesting?" murmured Granger.

"Q-jump with whatever civilian ships that are capable of docking with us, and get back to Earth now. Meet up with the fleet. It's our only hope. Maybe fighting alongside the rest of the fleet we might actually make a difference. But this? This is suicide."

Haws had kept his voice low, to avoid any listening bridge crew from hearing their commanders discuss a possible retreat. Worse—a retreat leaving behind defenseless civilians to their certain doom.

"None of those ships have q-jump capability, and we don't have time to let them dock. I'm not going to leave these people to their deaths," he replied in a murmur.

"Tim, if we stay, they'll still die, just a minute or so later," pleaded Haws.

"And if we leave, we'll die just a few hours later. So what's your point?" He said this out loud and several officers glanced at the two of them. He raised his voice to the whole bridge and pointed at the comm officer. "Pipe me through to the ship."

"You're on, sir."

"This is Captain Granger. As you may know, we're about to engage with the enemy fleet. Probably Swarm. I'll be honest with you: the odds don't look good. These bastards just took out Lunar Base and half a dozen IDF vessels in under ten minutes. This is the real deal, folks. This is the moment we've trained our whole lives for."

He paused to glance around the bridge. Except for the hum of systems and the sound of the ventilation, all was silent, all paying rapt attention to the captain. He needed this to be good.

God, he hated speeches.

"We've already lost friends. We've lost family. Ships newer and larger than ours have already met their end. But I'll tell you something." He glanced at Haws, who glared back. "This ship has never met her match. Seventy-five years ago, when she was already fifty years old, she held her own against the Swarm. She and the rest of the Legacy fleet. The *Congress,* the *Warrior,* the *Independence,* and the *Chesapeake,* all lived to tell the tale. So I say to you: do your duty. Stand firm. Keep your wits about you. Remember your training. Be true to her and she'll be true to us. And if we fall, then by God we will fall in defense of humanity, and those after us will tell stories that will pass through the ages. Granger out."

Haws grumbled. "Let's hope there's still someone around to tell stories about us."

Granger ignored him. "Launch fighters. RPO crews stand ready. As soon as the fleet is in range I want firing solutions. Scan their vessels for their power plants and focus on them. I want their power systems crippled as soon as possible. Contact the *Qantas*, tell them to back us up—our armor is ten times as thick as theirs. And if Captain Argus gives you any guff about his precious smart-steel armor, just remind him I have operational authority over this mission." His string of orders came out so fast that those around him at first weren't sure which was directed to whom. But within a few seconds they snapped into action, Haws barking orders to the weapons crew, Commander Proctor relaying orders to the fighter bay, and the comm station chattering into their headsets.

"Time?"

Lieutenant Diaz glanced at his console readout. "One minute, twenty seconds until maximum firing range, sir."

"Begin firing in twenty seconds. I know targeting is less accurate, but I want a barrage to greet them on their way in. Full spread, rate of fifty kilograms per second for the mag-rails. Wait on the lasers until they're in range."

"Aye, sir," said the tactical officer. "Targeting computers engaged, ready to fire. In ten. Nine. Eight. Seven...."

This was it. Granger gripped the edge of his command

station and glared at the viewscreen on the wall, as if daring the enemy fleet to come any closer.

"Two. One," continued the tactical officer. "All guns, fire."

On the screen he could barely make out the flashes of the mag-rail slugs as they shot away at speeds faster than his eyes could track. With any luck, a few would find their targets and soften up the fleet before it arrived. He watched as two by two the fighters sailed out of the fighter bays and glided into formation, flanking the giant ship. Soon, sixty-three were out, and above the hum of general operational activity on the bridge all he could hear was the distant pounding of the mag-rail guns firing their slugs.

"Anything?" he said to the sensor officer. "Any impacts?"

"Not yet, sir. Targeting is difficult at this range, and they have time to move out of—" The officer peered closer at his display, "Hot damn! We hit one, sir. Got 'em good."

"On screen. Maximum magnification."

The view of the distant approaching points of light was replaced by a grainy close-up of one of the alien ships, which was belching fire and debris. "Good work, people," he said, with a nod to the tactical station.

"Twenty seconds until laser firing range. The fleet is beginning its deceleration. Holy mother of god … Sir, they're decelerating at over five hundred kps per second. That's—"

"Impossible?" Commander Proctor finished his sentence for him. "I think not, Lieutenant. I think we'll find the Swarm will be full of surprises today. It's how they've evolved—every cycle they swarm outward, with a whole new slate of technology to throw at their perceived enemies—"

"Cut the chatter, Commander. When I want a dissertation

I'll ask for it." He watched the countdown timer tick to zero, indicating the fleet was in range of the rest of their armaments. "Fire lasers. Target the lead ships—maybe the debris blowback will impact the other ships."

The telltale pulse and thrum of the laser systems sounded in the background. Usually, in practice simulations, the lasers were only fired at half power, tops. And only one or two. Not all of them. Between the lasers and the mag-rails, the ship shivered with the combined rumblings.

"Any effect?" he said, but from the screen he had his answer. None of the alien ships showed any signs of distress, and as the image became less grainy, signifying their rapid approach, the lead ship flashed with green light.

The sensor officer yelled out across the bridge. "They're firing, sir!"

CHAPTER THIRTY-THREE

Near Earth's Moon
Bridge, ISS Constitution

"Who are they targ—" But Granger knew the answer before the question left his mouth as the ship was slammed violently back. The pulsing, shimmering green beam rammed right into the forward section of the ship and began cutting into the hull. He watched as, on the screen, debris and wreckage blasted out into space as the ship reeled.

The deckplate shuddered and the bridge crew cringed at the sound of distant explosions.

Granger lurched over to the operations station, his legs buckling a few times as the rocking continued. "Damage report. How deep is it cutting?"

The terrified young officer shook his head. "Looks like the tungsten plating is doing its job, sir. But that beam is pretty powerful. Two—no, three—sorry, four meters of shielding gone in the section they struck. And it's still firing, sir."

The captain wheeled around to yell at the tactical station. "Redirect all fire to their energy beam emitter. Blast that piece of shit to hell."

"Aye, sir," said the tactical officer, as he motioned to his subordinates to focus their fire on the lead ship. Targeting this far out was still iffy, but Granger was hoping for a miracle.

"Position the ship so the energy beam hits starboard. Let's distribute some of this damage."

"Firing thrusters, sir," called out Ensign Prince, the navigation officer, as the sound of new explosions rang out through the deck plating.

"Twenty seconds until arrival, sir. Sensors show our lasers had zero impact—they have some kind of electromagnetic shielding that deflects the lasers, even with our random modulations."

Suddenly, the rumbling stopped. Granger glanced up at the screen, hoping for good news. And he saw it: the lead alien ship, now more resolved than just a few pixels, began to erupt with minor explosions all over its hull as the *Constitution*'s magrail slugs pounded on its surface. The other ship apparently wasn't immune to ballistic chunks of metal sailing through space at fifty kps, plus the alien's residual speed.

"Good. Signal the *Qantas*. Let's coordinate all fire on that lead vessel. Take them out one by one." He turned to Haws, "Get on the horn to Commander Pierce. I want the squadrons flying interference against the other ships while we take them out one by one with the *Constitution* and the *Qantas*."

He heard Haws bellow into his comm, and the rest of the bridge crew complying with his orders, and he finally sat down in the chair next to the command station. They were hurt, but it was already going much better than he'd thought. They were not only alive, but they'd also heavily damaged one of the alien vessels already.

It couldn't last.

"Captain," began Commander Proctor, sidling up next to him, "when they show up, chances are they're going to deploy that weapon—the one that destroyed Lunar Base."

"Agreed. What do you propose we do about it, Commander?" He was unnecessarily testy, but he couldn't help responding so to such an obvious statement.

She apparently didn't notice, or didn't let it get to her. He liked that—she kept her emotions in check and didn't let it become personal. "Let me work with the science station crew to analyze all the data we picked up on that weapon. We'll come up with some options for you."

He nodded his approval, and she retreated to the rear of the bridge and gathered the small science crew around her. Haws turned to him. "Pierce is ready, Tim. And good timing—look," he added, pointing to the viewscreen.

Granger looked up.

They'd arrived. An alien fleet, now six ships total, and judging from the smaller green beams lancing out from their hulls, they didn't look happy.

CHAPTER THIRTY-FOUR

Near Earth's Moon
Bridge, ISS Winchester

Vice President Isaacson drummed his fingers nervously on the edge of his chair. The feeling of helplessness was utterly maddening.

"Are those damn techs done yet?" said Isaacson, staring nervously at the viewscreen, which displayed an image of the alien ships drawing ever closer. "How long does it take to install a quantum field coupler?"

Captain Day scowled. "Just another few minutes, Mr. Isaacson."

"They'll be *here* in another few minutes!"

As if to punctuate his point, a green flash filled the screen. Isaacson jumped in his chair. "What the hell was that?"

The image on the screen was answer enough. One of the distant dots on the screen unleashed another barrage of fire at the *Constitution,* which cut deep into the hull.

"Looks like some sort of directed energy weapon. Clearly not laser," said the sensor officer. When he looked up again the color was draining from his face. "I'm reading an anti-matter signature, sir! It's very high energy—highly focused gamma ray and x-ray, with a high flux of anti-boron ions!"

Isaacson didn't understand what that meant, but it didn't sound good at all. What in the world was taking those techs so long? "Captain, we need to—"

Captain Day interrupted. "Q-jump drive coming online now, Mr. Vice President. Just hold tight."

Another few minutes passed, and the alien ships grew from tiny dots to gargantuan behemoths, which all began unleashing unholy hell upon the *Constitution* and the *Qantas*. Good god. What in the world was in the Russians' minds when they decided to attempt contact?

The fighter bays of the two IDF cruisers disgorged dozens of fighters which swarmed out to engage the similarly-sized craft being pumped out of the alien ships by the hundreds. Isaacson looked at the captain.

"And"—Captain Day pointed at the navigation officer, still looking at his console—"engage the q-drive."

The viewscreen, which showed the unfolding battle, briefly flashed, and within another moment the familiar, safe image of a blue and green Earth filled the display.

Isaacson breathed a sigh. *That was too close.*

He turned to Ambassador Volodin, who'd stood close by him since they arrived on the bridge. "Looks like we've got some work to do, Yuri."

Work indeed. If the situation could be salvaged, an alien incursion straight to Earth would help him bounce Avery out of office all the sooner.

But if IDF failed to stop the invasion ... well, then it would be time to make a backup plan.

CHAPTER THIRTY-FIVE

Near Earth's Moon
X-25 Fighter Cockpit

Lieutenant Miller pulled up hard on the navigation controls, grunting as the sudden g-forces slammed her down into the seat. The stars wheeled overhead, and she had to use the trick that Ballsy had taught her during her brief, one-hour training session: keep your eyes fixed on a point on the dashboard and keep the spinning starfield in the peripheral vision.

"Fishtail! Level out!" came Ballsy's voice over her headset. She pushed down on the controls and saw the reason for his warning. Three Swarm fighters were barreling towards her, guns blazing. With a frantic squeeze of the trigger on her navigational stick, she shot off a flurry of gunfire of her own.

"Hard left, then loop up and reform the wedge!" Ballsy's confident voice was reassuring, if a bit loud, but she did as he said, firing off another burst for good measure at the lead

Swarm fighter. Out of the corner of her eye she saw Volz swoop in and pick off two of the fighters, while the other newbie in the squadron, Hotbox, blasted the third to fiery pieces.

"Nice shot, Ballsy," came Dogtown's voice over the comm.

Miller risked a glance at the alien ships that loomed large in the viewport, and cringed in dismay at the dozens of fighters disgorging from the massive bays. The lighting within the alcoves of the giant capital ships was a sickly pale green, otherworldly and downright terrifying. A nearby explosion lit up the nearest ship and, horrified, she realized the light was coming from the *Constitution*. A deadly-looking shimmering green beam had lanced out from the alien ship and slammed into the hull of the Old Bird, carving deep into her, releasing an explosion of sparks and fire.

"Head in the game, Fishtail!" came Volz's voice.

She swerved to maintain the wedge formation, and saw their next target: a lone alien fighter that was homing in on one of the *Constitution*'s laser turrets.

"Take it, Hotbox," came Dogtown's voice. She watched Hotbox veer left and blast the alien fighter to oblivion before it could unleash a single shot at the Old Bird.

It was going well. Far too easy, in fact, against an alien fleet that had just devastated Lunar Base and the ships defending her.

Tom's ship.

She grit her teeth. She couldn't allow herself to think about that yet. Her eyes burned and her shoulders began to quiver.

No. No, not yet. Focus on the battle. Stay alive. For Zack.

Stay alive.

Her headset beeped, indicating an incoming message from the CAG. "This is Pierce. All fighters direct your fire at the trailing alien capital ships. Your orders are to engage the capital ships. Keep them busy and focused on you. We need to give the *Constitution* and the *Qantas* a reprieve so they can pound the bastards one by one. CAG out."

Ballsy's voice followed Pierce. "You heard him. Let's bugger over to that second ship and have a field day."

Pulling up on her navigation control again, she held the wedge formation as they veered up and above the first alien ship and towards the second.

"Watch those fighters!" said Ballsy.

"Do we engage?" shouted Hotbox.

"Negative. Maintain course towards the target. We'll engage the fighters once we're there, and in the lulls between bogey engagements we'll pop off a few rounds into that fat mother's ass."

Deadly alien fire lit up her viewport, and she instinctively ducked her head. Luckily, she also pulled down on the control, dropping her ship underneath the line of fire, and to her relief the alien bogey exploded as it caught a few slugs from Volz.

"Thanks, Ballsy," she said, catching her breath.

The second alien capital ship now filled her viewport, and, miraculously, there were no bogeys trailing them yet. "Ok crew, blast the shit out of her. See how much blood we can draw before they swat the mosquitos," said Volz.

Maintaining the wedge formation, they unleashed a full barrage of gunfire at the enemy hull. They had no idea where their sensitive systems were, or for that matter, where their weapons installations were. But they peppered the surface with as much ordnance as they could before the next wave of bogeys showed up.

And show up they did.

"Shit. Dogtown, back me up on this one. Newbies, lay down some suppressing fire for Dogtown. I'm going in."

Ballsy breathed hard into his comm, and with good reason. A swarm of at least a dozen fighters was racing towards them, guns blazing. Ballsy veered and swooped like lightning, blasting craft after craft, and those he didn't get, Dogtown picked up. Jessica and Hotbox picked off the ones who'd veered wildly to escape Ballsy's suicide run.

Intense green light lit up her viewport, nearly blinding her before she squeezed her eyes shut, and she gave a little yelp. Tentatively opening her eyes, she saw the viewport had compensated for the overwhelming brightness of the alien energy weapon. Following the track of the beam with her gaze, she saw that it terminated in a massive fireball erupting on the hull of the *Constitution*, cutting deep into the ship.

The Old Bird belched fire and debris from a gaping hole in her starboard flank, and the fear welled up inside her.

They weren't going to make it.

Zack would be left alone.

If Earth even survived.

Bullshit, she thought, and, kissing her fingers, brushing them up against the photo sticking up out of her dash, she keyed in a set of instructions to the nav computer. She may have been new to the nimbleness of the little X-25 craft, and the fighter's guns, but she'd been programming complicated flight vectors for years.

"FISHTAIL, WHAT THE HELL ARE YOU DOING?"

"Just saving the ship, Ballsy. Don't get your panties in a bunch."

She smirked as she remembered that was her reply to him a few days before when he was pestering her to use the long-range comm station.

But she quickly ran out of time to think at all. Now, all that mattered was her reflexes.

And faith.

With a pull on the navigational controls, she swooped towards the massive green beam still cutting into the *Constitution,* wrapping around it in a tight orbit, and corkscrewing down towards the point on the alien ship's hull where the beam originated.

And released a torrent of gunfire that streaked away and hit hard at the beam's source.

"Fishtail!"

She grinned, but kept firing. Fragments from the blast whizzed past the cockpit and pelted her viewport, but she held her thumb firmly against the trigger as she looped again and again around the shimmering green beam, corkscrewing ever closer to the hull.

Her stomach clenched, and she prepared to pull away. Just another three seconds....

And with a blinding flash, the source of the beam erupted in a terrific explosion. The navigational controls protested as she pushed them to the limit, and the intense g-force threw her back up into the harness and blood filled her head, nearly making her pass out.

But she leveled the craft out, and swooped back into

wedge formation, glancing back to look at her handiwork.

The green energy beam had disappeared, and the hull where it had originated flared with electrical arcing, fire, and a stream of oozing goo, as if the ship itself was bleeding.

"Fishtail …" began Ballsy, apparently searching for words, "that was incredibly stupid."

"Thank you, sir," she replied, hearing the awe in his voice.

Another swarm of bogeys was descending on them, and with another stream of gunfire, they were back in the thick of it, dodging and weaving through the onslaught.

In spite of the rush of adrenaline that still pulsed through her veins after the incredibly ill-advised maneuver that took out the energy weapon, she felt her stomach clench once again as she saw three IDF fighters get picked off by enemy fire and explode in a blaze of quenched smoke and debris.

"We gonna make it through this?" she mumbled, half to herself, half to her squadmates.

"It'll take a bloody miracle," replied Ballsy.

CHAPTER THIRTY-SIX

Near Earth's Moon
Bridge, ISS Constitution

Whereas before the alien energy beam made the ship shudder and quake from the impact, this barrage knocked nearly everyone off their feet. Granger held on to his armrests as Haws flew headlong into the console in front of him, bloodying his nose and face.

Screams and blasts and debris filled the air.

Granger yelled over to the tactical station, pointing at the only officer who hadn't tumbled out of his seat. "Full spread of mag-rail fire! Initiate the point-defense screen. All RPOs fire! Get me some defensive screening!"

Somehow, even with the tactical station only staffed by one officer, the orders were initiated, for when Granger looked up at the viewscreen he saw a dance of white and red streaks that indicated the activation of the rapid-pulse ordnance point defense, and like a storm of sparks it seemed to lessen the impact of the pounding alien energy beams.

The short reprieve allowed most of the bridge crew to get back into their seats. "Tactical status!" yelled Granger.

"Fighters are engaged with the alien fleet—they've dispatched their own fighters," said a tactical officer.

"Sir, incoming transmission from Captain Argus of the *Qantas*." The comm officer punched the command to transfer the audio to Granger's console.

Captain Granger tapped his acceptance of the transmission and Argus's voice boomed over the speakers. "Tim, our fighters are taking heavy fire. Recommend we engage the rest of the fleet to take some of the pressure off them."

"No. Focus your efforts on that lead ship. We'll take them out one by one—"

"But our boys are dying out there, you bastard! They need our cover!"

Granger sneered at the console even though he knew the other man couldn't see him. "Remember who's in charge of this mission, Argus. My order stands. Focus your efforts on the lead ship. When it blows, we move on to the next."

Only silence came over the speakers, though the ship continued to rumble and quake in protest of the pounding it was taking from the enemy's directed energy beams. Thankfully, they didn't seem as intense with the RPOs acting as a shield.

"Captain! The lead ship!"

Granger snapped his head back to the viewscreen, and smiled.

Under a vicious barrage of mag-rail slugs, the alien vessel

was erupting with dozens, even hundreds, of small explosions, until finally the starboard half of the ship exploded in a massive blast. The port half careened off and slammed into its nearest neighbor, a smaller alien ship that was busy firing at the swarm of IDF fighters pelting it.

The second ship's guns fell silent.

"See? They bleed," said Granger. "Argus? Target the next ship. Move the *Qantas* to point five mark two and commence firing. Granger out."

He coughed violently, and held his chest. Haws squinted at him and offered a hand, but Granger waved him off.

"Sir, the *Qantas* has lost half her compliment of fighters. There's only sixty or so left," said the wing commander's liaison.

"They're getting ripped apart out there, Tim," said Haws, with a characteristic grumble.

"I know. But so will we if we directly engage."

The tactical officer nearly jumped out of his seat. "Sir! The *Qantas* is changing course. They're moving to provide cover for the fighters!"

"Damn fool," said Granger.

"The *Qantas* is taking a pounding, sir."

"Status of their armor?"

The officer shook his head. "They're cutting right through it. She's not going to last long at—"

But a bright explosion on the viewscreen cut him off.

The *Qantas* was gone.

CHAPTER THIRTY-SEVEN

Near Earth's Moon
Bridge, ISS Constitution

The bridge was silent for a few moments as the crew watched the *Qantas* break up. The dazzling green beam that was still tearing through it emerged from the far side, burning up a fighter that strayed into its path.

But there was no time to mourn. Granger jumped up. "One down, a second crippled. Four left. Maintain fire on the third ship. I want all fighters from both the Old Bird and the *Qantas* to concentrate on the remaining three ships and keep them occupied. Are those nukes ready yet?" he called back to Proctor, who was still huddled at the science station with the science crew.

"The nuclear chief has not reported in yet, sir," said Proctor.

"I want an update."

"Yes, sir." She rushed back to the XO's station and almost

shoved Haws out of the way, who muttered his displeasure.

Green light filled the screen. A fresh explosion several decks above caught them all off guard and half the bridge crew flew from their seats, Granger included. He landed hard on his side. Pain wracked his chest, and he coughed violently into a hand.

The hand came back soaked in blood.

Swearing, in terrible pain, he pushed himself to his feet and surveyed the damage. One of the operations crew was clearly dead, his head crushed by a girder that had burst through the ceiling. The others, in various states of injury, began crawling back to their seats.

But a body at his feet didn't move.

"Abe?"

He bent over and shook his friend. "Abe?" he repeated. Granger pushed the man onto his back, and noticed the blood streaming from a giant gash on his head as well as several other spots on his torso and abdomen. He must have caught that girder in the head before it landed, along with other debris that had blasted outward during the explosion.

Granger felt for a pulse. It was there, but faint.

Blood pooled up beneath him.

He wasn't going to make it.

Steeling his jaw, he stood up and yelled out for Proctor. "Where are my nukes, Commander?"

"The chief says you have two! And only two. So we'd better make them count. Loaded and ready to fire!"

"Fire both at that third ship!"

The nuclear officer at the tactical station initiated the launch, confirmed, and all eyes darted up to the screen.

Two streaks of exhaust shot away from the *Constitution* towards the alien ship nearest them. Another green beam lanced out from the ship, catching one of them in its sights, frying its detonators, and the torpedo exploded in a tiny muted fireball.

The second, however, found its mark, and plunged into an already gaping hole in the side of the alien vessel. A moment later, the viewscreen went completely white as the explosion momentarily overloaded the imaging sensors. When the image was restored, the alien ship was flying apart in five or six different chunks.

"I want more nukes, Commander!" he yelled.

"Sorry, sir. I've got one that will be ready within the hour, but the rest are thoroughly decommissioned. It'll take a few days to cobble any more from the existing warheads."

He paused, and considered his options. Three alien ships down. But they'd lost the *Qantas*, and at least half their fighters. No more nukes. The point defense RPO screen seemed to take the edge off the devastating directed energy tech the aliens had, and their own lasers were completely useless, but mag-rail slugs managed to punch through whatever shielding they had.

Nothing for it but to keep pounding with the slugs, then.

"Sir, mag-rail crews are reporting they're almost out of ordnance," said a tactical officer.

"Out?"

"There's more in storage, sir, but it'll take several hours to reload."

Damn. So they had nothing left.

A deep, low rumble had begun, pulsing through the ship, as an added layer to the cacophony of destruction that rocked them. He knew what it was without asking.

"And sir, a point source of energy has appeared in the middle of the remaining four ships. It's getting bigger."

CHAPTER THIRTY_EIGHT

Near Earth's Moon
Bridge, ISS Constitution

"Proctor! I want some answers! What have you come up with?" Granger twisted around to face the science station near the rear of the bridge. The low rumbling throb had increased in intensity, and he knew what was coming in the next minute or two.

"It's a forced artificial quantum singularity, sir. No other explanation fits the data we've got."

He glared at her. "Is that even possible?"

"Possible or not, it's there, and it's getting bigger. It's a miniature black hole—its event horizon is just microns in diameter, and somehow when it reaches a certain mass, they're able to entangle the matter trapped inside with another point some distance away, essentially teleporting it. That's what we saw when Lunar Base erupted outward—it was the black hole suddenly appearing a kilometer beneath the lunar surface. And when the surrounding billions of tons of matter collapsed into it simultaneously, it rebounded off the center of the singularity, collapsed the black hole, and blasted all the material upward in a sort of miniature supernova that—"

"BUT HOW DO WE STOP IT?" Granger was yelling now, and he didn't care what his crew might think—they had seconds to figure a way out.

"We can't, sir."

Granger bit his lip and swore. Pounding his console and looking down at his dying friend, he said quietly, "Prepare for q-jump to *Valhalla Station*. Signal the civilian ships—everyone should scatter, each a different direction."

Proctor eyed him, emotionlessly. She wasn't challenging his order, but she apparently wanted to make him actually say the unspoken truth.

He said it. "We're leaving them here." He eyed the bridge crew, and caught several fearful, scornful glances. His thoughts strayed to the boy he'd met after the decommissioning ceremony. Cornelius Dexter Ahazarius. The third. What would he and all his classmates think when their teacher told them the *Constitution* had left? He could almost hear their screams as he imagined the Swarm ships closing in on them, unprotected. Dammit, he couldn't think about that. Not now. "We either die here protecting a few civilians, or die above Earth, protecting humanity."

Ensign Prince cocked his head to the side. "Sir, calculations complete."

"Recall the fighters. Get our birds aboard, and the ones remaining from the *Qantas*."

"Sir," began the comm officer, "the *Rainbow* is signaling us.

One of the civilian ships—the one with the school kids. They're requesting to dock—"

"No," he said, quickly.

"But, sir, they—"

"I SAID NO, LIEUTENANT," he barked. He glanced at Proctor. "Estimated time until that thing hits us?"

She shook her head. "Based on the last one we saw, thirty seconds. At most."

Granger gripped his armrests and swore again. "How many fighters left out there?"

The wing commander liaison checked her console. "Fifteen, sir."

"Initiate q-jump on my mark." He glanced at the clock, counting down in his head to ten seconds from Proctor's time estimate.

Just a few more seconds....

"Sir, look!" Diaz's voice came from tactical, and he snapped his head toward the viewscreen.

The singularity pulsed, then flashed bright, oversaturating the screen.

CHAPTER THIRTY_NINE

Near Earth's Moon
X-25 Fighter Cockpit

"Fishtail, you're too far left. Pull back into wedge—don't worry, you won't hit Dogtown. Trust your squad," said Ballsy.

"Right," she mumbled. Dogtown had in fact nearly collided with her just a minute earlier, but she nudged the craft slightly to the left anyway.

The battle was going poorly. After a few initial successes, they were on defense far more than they could target the alien capital ship, and she watched dozens of her fellow fighters erupt in fiery debris-filled explosions.

And then there was the mysterious shimmering white light that had appeared out of nowhere in the midst of the battle. At the same time, her fighter began to pulse all around her, and the comm kept time with buzzing static.

"Orders are to stay clear of that anomaly," said Ballsy. "It's probably a weapon. The gun crews on the Old Bird are going to attempt to knock it out."

"Contacts, three o'clock." Dogtown interrupted, and Miller snapped her head to see close to a dozen more alien craft bearing down on them, releasing a firestorm of weapons fire.

"Split. Fishtail on me, left. Hotbox on Dogtown, right and negative z. Converge and flip on the other side."

Ballsy shot ahead of her and she followed, laying down covering fire as he blazed a path through the oncoming horde. A stray round blasted into her right wing, and her engine sputtered momentarily, but the ship's attitude and course held steady.

"There's too many—" began Hotbox.

"Just shadow Dogtown and lay down the cover fire," Ballsy barked into the headset.

"I—I can't maintain—"

A loud crackle and static boomed over her headset, and an indicator on her dashboard flashed red. She craned her head momentarily to look.

Hotbox was hit, barrel-rolling end over end, out of control. Smoke and flame streamed from the ship.

"Oh, god," she said, as she saw where the damaged fighter was heading.

Straight towards the mysterious shimmering white globe.

"Dogtown, on me," said Ballsy. "Fishtail, get closer. Shadow my movements."

But she could hardly hear. Transfixed by the tumbling fighter barreling towards the white light, she flew as if on autopilot, matching Ballsy's flight pattern even as she watched....

Hotbox's fighter entered the white maelstrom, and the entire shimmering sphere erupted in a blinding flash.

When she looked again, Hotbox, and the white light, were gone.

A moment's silence reigned over her headset, before she realized that voices were yelling on the other end, she'd just been too shocked to recognize them as language.

"All craft, hot landing on the Old Bird, NOW!"

Hot landing. Hot landing? Right. She was a shuttle pilot, but she knew that term. Hightail it to the fighter bay, and don't slow down for the landing. *Constitution* must be preparing for a q-jump as soon as all fighters were aboard.

"You heard him, Fishtail. Get the hell out of here!"

Ballsy looped around a pair of enemy bogeys, blasted one to fiery bits, and darted towards the Old Bird at maximum acceleration. She followed.

But glanced back towards where the white light, and Hotbox, had disappeared.

Oh, god. Please be alive, Hotbox, she thought, before pushing forward to maximum acceleration, and struggled to breathe against the massive g-force.

Please be alive.

Her cockpit lit up with Swarm weapons fire and she inhaled sharply. The remaining bogey that Volz had looped around was following them in. "Ballsy—" she began.

"I see it. Hold tight, Fishtail!" Ballsy, ahead of her and about to land on the flight deck of the fighter bay himself, veered up in a tight loop and wrapped around behind her and the enemy bogey on her tail. With a few surgically targeted rounds he sent the Swarm craft spinning out of control.

It slammed right into the tungsten armor overhanging the fighter bay doors, ricocheted down and crashed onto the lip of the deck, just inside the energy field that held the air in the massive bay. Fishtail veered right at the last moment as it fell, braking furiously as she came in for a hard landing. Finally, with a screech of metal on metal, her fighter came to a stop.

She was alive. Against all odds, she was alive.

Her comm speaker burst to life with an angry klaxon.

"Marines to the fighter bay! Security alert! Possible Swarm presence on the flight deck!"

CHAPTER FORTY

Near Earth's Moon
Bridge, ISS Constitution

"What the hell was that?" To Granger's eyes it looked as if the singularity had flared, and then disappeared.

But the *Constitution* was still there.

"Sir, the singularity is gone," said Lieutenant Diaz.

"How?"

"Looks like one of our damaged fighters collided with it. It was tumbling out of control and flew straight in."

Commander Proctor called out from the science station. "The mass of the fighter must have disrupted the formation of the singularity. It could be that we can take them out with normal mag-rail slugs."

The bridge had fallen quiet. With the walls and deckplate no longer pulsing with the whatever energy the artificial singularity had emitted, and the alien energy beams no longer pounding against the hull, they'd finally been given a brief reprieve.

It couldn't last.

They needed to get out of there, as soon as possible.

"Are the fighters aboard?"

"Aye, sir. All remaining fighters aboard and accounted for."

"Then get us the hell out of here," said Granger, pointing to Ensign Prince.

"Initiating—" began Ensign Prince, but he was interrupted.

"Sir, incoming signal from the *Rainbow*. They're asking to land in our fighter bay," said the comm officer. He glanced up at the captain. "In fact, all the remaining civilian ships are requesting entry."

Granger grit his teeth. He couldn't leave those kids here. He just couldn't.

"Fine. Get the *Rainbow* aboard. Then the other ships as we have room. Ensign," he turned back to the navigation station, "I want a hair-trigger on the q-jump initiator. When I give the signal, we're gone. Got it?"

"Aye, sir."

Granger turned and watched the viewscreen. Three smaller freighters queued up behind the *Rainbow*, waiting for their chance to board the *Constitution* and escape. But in the distance, near the alien ships, which had still not opened fire on any of them, the same bright, piercing light reappeared.

"Sir, they're regenerating the singularity!" yelled Commander Proctor.

"I see it. Fire a few mag-rail slugs at it. See if we can't disrupt it like before."

The tactical officer gave the signal to one of his gunnery

technicians, and several white streaks lanced out from the *Constitution* towards the singularity. It flared, and if anything, grew in brightness, but it remained quite stable.

"Again. Unload the current magazine into it."

The tactical crew chief gave the signal again and more streaks shot out from the bow, and again the singularity flared, and this time obviously grew into a more intense light.

"We're feeding it," said Proctor, her eyes staring at the screen.

Granger swore. "We've got even less time now, then." He glanced at the screen and saw two freighters still hugging close to the *Constitution*. "Is the *Rainbow* aboard?"

"Aye, sir."

"Signal the rest of the caravan. Tell them to scatter. Full speed. Preferably away from Earth—the aliens will be less likely to chase them down."

"Aye, sir," said the comm officer.

He waited until the comm station had finished warning the rest of the caravan, then pointed to Ensign Prince. "Go. Get us out of here."

Ensign Prince punched the initiator control, and the telltale distortion shimmered in the air all around them as the quantum field established itself around the ship. Within a moment, the view on the monitor shifted, and the alien ships disappeared.

Replaced only by empty space.

"Where the hell is *Valhalla Station*?" murmured Granger.

CHAPTER FORTY-ONE

Near Earth
Flightdeck, ISS Constitution

Jessica Miller jumped out of her cockpit the moment the hatch opened, nearly tumbling down the stepladder the tech had pushed up to the fighter.

As she descended, a platoon of armored marines rushed past her, assault rifles at the ready. "EVERYBODY OUT!" shouted the man in the lead, whom Miller recognized as Colonel Hanrahan. They rushed towards the smoking remains of the Swarm fighter that had followed them in.

It looked relatively unthreatening, given that half of it was a mangled wreck of smashed metal and the other half sported a dozen holes where Ballsy had punched through with his fighter's rounds, but the harrowing idea of aliens on the flight deck made her rush for the exit, towards the debriefing room. Commander Pierce, who was surrounded by a shell-shocked crowd of pilots from the *Qantas*, motioned all the *Constitution*'s pilots back to the locker room.

Her head was light, her feet heavy, and she didn't know whether to shout and celebrate that she was alive, or mourn her fallen comrades. Celebrating felt premature, and it struck her that they had little to feel good about. Glancing around the packed fighter deck, she saw that they'd taken on all the remaining fighters from the *Qantas*, swelling their numbers, but realized that nearly half of the *Constitution*'s pilots hadn't come back.

Including Hotbox. He was young. Just out of the academy. Full of life and enthusiasm and charisma. It just wasn't right. It wasn't fair.

And the thought of fairness drew her mind back to the thing she was suppressing. The thing she couldn't think about, or risk facing a breakdown right there on the fighter deck. Plus, there were probably search crews going through the wreckage of the *Clyburne*, looking for survivors, right?

Of course not. But she couldn't think about it. Not yet. Still too many battles to fight. She had to come home to Zack-Zack whole.

"Fishtail!" Ballsy bounded up to her.

"Hey."

Dogtown joined up with them, and they retreated back to their lockers to sit and recover before they were inevitably called up again. She eyed Dogtown. He was an older pilot, maybe in his mid forties—in stark contrast to Jessica and Ballsy, who were both in their early twenties.

The locker room was subdued. It was only half as full as before, and several of the pilots sat on the benches, their heads in their hands.

Dogtown punched his locker and swore. He punched it several more times, bloodying his knuckles.

"Stop," said Ballsy. "Breaking your hand won't bring him back."

The older pilot collapsed on his bench. "He was twenty. Shit, my son is almost as old as he was. He was just a kid."

Ballsy nodded. He was barely older than Hotbox had been. He reached into his locker and extracted a tiny bottle, and sat down in between Dogtown and Miller.

"To Hotbox," he said, twisting the cap off and raising the bottle up. He took a small swig and passed it to the other two. Miller winced as the burning liquid went down.

A moment of silence passed between the three of them, and they watched the other pilots stream through the doors, some dazed, some amped up on adrenaline. All with a haunted, shadowy look behind their eyes—the look of people who'd seen death.

"Why was he Hotbox?" she asked, turning to Volz. "How did he get his callsign?"

Ballsy smiled. "Funny story." He looked around at the pilots surrounding him, apparently gauging whether it was an appropriate time for said funny story. "There's the official version he wanted everyone to know, and then there's the real story. Officially, it goes like this. He'd been on board for a month, and late one night the master chief walks in on him in the showers, smoking a joint. The whole shower was filled with the smoke. Master Chief says he got high just by walking in. Hotbox." Ballsy shrugged, to conclude the story.

"*That's* the story he wanted people to know? He could get discharged for drug use." Jessica shook her head in disbelief.

"Well, that's because the real story is a little more, ahem, embarrassing. In reality, he was in that shower all right, but he brought a portable long-range comm device with him. You know, those little boxes that let you video call people up to a few hundred thousand klicks away, without passing through the ship's comm array?" He held up his hands to indicate the size of the box, just a few inches square.

"Oh no...." Jessica began.

"Oh, yes," replied Ballsy with a smile. "His girlfriend's in San Diego, see, and well, let's just say things got pretty hot and heavy in the shower that night. When Master Chief stumbled in there ... well ... yeah. Hotbox."

Ballsy chuckled. Jessica rolled her eyes. "And Master Chief? What did he do?"

Ballsy laughed even harder. "Old bastard just went right on showering. Didn't phase him a bit. Hotbox keeps right on going—didn't hear the chief come in. Then, after he's done, when he realizes he'd not been alone the whole time, he blubbers to the chief to keep it quiet, and made up the whole story about the reefer just so Chief could have a juicy story to tell in its place. And ... well, obviously both stories got out, which makes it even better."

Miller snorted.

Ballsy laughed, and wiped his eyes with the back of a hand. "All right, get cleaned up, Fishtail. We could get called up again soon and there's nothing worse than flying in a cockpit with your own rank BO."

"How did you get yours, Ballsy? Your callsign, that is."

Ballsy smirked. "By being Ballsy, of course."

Dogtown pointed at the younger man. "You're looking at

the only pilot in the history of the *Constitution* who's managed to break into her q-jump field as she was jumping away."

"But, that's impossible, isn't it?"

Dogtown shook his head. "Not impossible. Just incredibly dangerous, and stupid, since the quantum field can materialize at any second, and if it does when you're only halfway in, well, it takes that half of the ship with it and leaves the rest behind. Ballsy here," he continued, pointing his thumb at Volz, "was busy *meeting up* with his girlfriend on *Valhalla Station* a few years ago and things went a little long—"

"So to speak," interrupted Volz with a mischievous grin.

"—didn't realize the *Constitution* was about to jump away. So he pulls his pants up, jumps into his fighter, and races off towards the Old Bird, just barely clearing the quantum field in the nick of time. When we appear at Europa station a moment later, there's this little X-25 fighter that's jumped in with us, barreling towards the closed fighter bay doors." Dogtown was chuckling by this point. "Got quite a dressing down by Commander Haws, the old drunk."

"Ballsy," said Jessica, raising her eyebrows at Volz.

"Yeah, sure was." He pointed at her, his head cocked towards Dogtown. "But not half as ballsy as our little Fishtail here. That little stunt you pulled against that weapons installation? Corkscrewing in like that? Crazy. Absolutely chop-off-my-own-left-nut crazy batshit bonkers."

Fishtail shrugged. "Yeah, well. They had it coming."

Ballsy smirked and wiggled out of his sweat-stained undershirt before he stalked off to the shower. "Keep that up and we'll have to exchange callsigns, Fishtail."

A hush fell over the room as Commander Pierce stepped

through the door. "CAG on deck!" shouted one of the pilots nearest him.

"Thank you. You performed like rockstars out there today, people. Absolutely brilliant. You should all be proud." He paused, biting his lower lip. "A moment of silence for our fallen."

The locker room fell absolutely silent as everyone bowed their heads, or averted their gaze from each other to avoid tears.

A moment later, the CAG went on. "I'm sorry, that's all we have time for. We'll have a proper celebration of their lives later. Right now, we've got a war to fight. The aliens are continuing on towards Earth. We should engage them again within the hour. All the *Qantas*'s pilots are now aboard, and we'll be rotating them into our own squads. Team leaders, see me in fifteen. The rest of you newbies, get yourselves to the simulators with your trainers. I want you in those things nonstop until our next engagement."

Pierce stepped to the door to leave, but glanced back one more time. "We're going to beat these Cumrats. From what I saw today out of you boys, they don't stand a chance."

He left. Miller wrapped a towel around her to walk to the shower. Was he just pep-talking them to help them feel better, reassuring them before their impending deaths, or was it sincere? Did they really stand a chance?

Her mind strayed to the picture on her dashboard, and she resolved: they did stand a chance. They would survive.

Somehow.

CHAPTER FORTY-TWO

Near Earth
Bridge, ISS Constitution

"We've overshot Earth, sir," came the reply from navigation, after the officer had conferred with his crew.

"How? I thought you'd made the calculations." This was unacceptable, and Granger was steamed.

"The gravitational distortion from the singularity must have thrown off the numbers. It warped the space metric around us ever so slightly, enough for the quantum field to have decoupled from the vacuum wave function several hundred thousand kilometers farther than we planned."

Granger breathed, ignoring the pain in his chest. They were safe. For now at least.

But Earth was not.

If their experience with the *Qantas* was any indication, the alien fleet would make short work of whatever defenses IDF had mustered in the hours since the invasion.

And the aliens would be there fast.

Granger tapped his comm. "Commander Scott, what's our capacitor status? How soon can we do another q-jump?"

The comm speakers boomed with Rayna Scott's voice. "They're drained, Cap'n. It'll take at least a few hours to get them charged back up enough for a jump."

"Even a short-range one?"

"Right, Cap'n. It'll take at least fifty petajoules, and our power plant took a beating during that scuffle."

He turned to the navigation station. "Fine. Get us to Earth. Full thrust. Do a full burn for the first half, and a full negative burn for the second half."

His comm indicator panel on his command console was going haywire with multiple department heads trying to get through to him. He punched through to Commander Pierce on the flight deck.

"What is it, Pierce?"

"Captain," came the CAG's voice, mixed with dozens of other pilots clamoring nearby, "you should know that I've called Hanrahan and the marines down here. A Swarm fighter crash landed on the flight deck."

Granger jumped to his feet. "Is it contained? What's its status?"

"We're fine, Captain. The thing is shot up pretty good and half the ship is smashed from the landing. Not a chance anything survived. But Hanrahan is here all the same. Best to be safe."

"Good thinking, Commander. I'll be there shortly. No one goes in that thing until I get there. Granger out." He tapped a button and continued, "Doctor Wyatt, Bridge."

"Wyatt here."

"Doctor, meet me on the flight deck in five minutes. We have a Swarm ship that crash landed. I want you to take a look."

"Aye, sir."

Granger tapped another indicator, and braced for bad news from engineering.

"Cap'n," Scott's voice sounded out through the speakers, "engine three is still giving us trouble. I only just got the thing running a few hours ago and it took a beating during the battle."

Granger nodded his understanding, "How much power, Rayna?"

"Forty percent. Maybe fifty."

"Fine. Get to work on restoring full power. I have a feeling we'll be needed at Earth before too long." It was an understatement, and he chided himself for tempting fate with a small joke in the midst of such grave circumstances and devastation. Even with the ten meters of solid tungsten shielding, the alien's directed energy weapon had wreaked havoc on the ship. That last blast was especially devastating, cutting clear through the shielding and piercing straight through into the forward section, taking many lives.

Too many lives, Granger thought, as he glanced at the damage report scrolling past the screen on his command station.

Haws.

His head snapped down to where his friend had lain.

He was gone.

"Where's Commander Haws?" he asked the duty officer,

who was busy dragging the body of a technician from under the fallen girder.

"We took him to sick bay, sir. He was still alive, but barely."

He needed to see his friend. The only one who'd stayed with him all these years. The only officer truly loyal to him, following him to whatever dead end assignment Granger ended up in.

"Commander Proctor, you have the bridge." He turned to leave. "I'll be back in fifteen minutes. When I return I want a status update on the mag-rail reloading. I want the rest of my fighters prepped for duty. And I want my engines at full power, dammit." He looked back at her with a stern, but good-natured nod. "You got all that?"

"Fifteen? We'll do it in ten, sir," she replied, with the barest hint of a grin.

He could still hear her barking orders as he passed down the corridor from the bridge, saluting the two marines standing at attention.

Damn, she's good. Glad I didn't toss her out the airlock.

CHAPTER FORTY-THREE

Near Earth
Fighter Bay, ISS Constitution

Granger burst through the door of the fighter bay, which had been cleared of most personnel. A dozen armored marines stood in a half circle around the wrecked alien craft near the warped, hazy force field holding in the atmosphere from the vacuum outside. Part of the fighter hung outside the field, preventing the giant bay doors from closing.

"Sir, no indication anything is alive in there," said Colonel Hanrahan, a gruff, mustached man who looked like he belonged in one of the old Swarm War holo-vids. His battle armor was sleek, pristine, and shiny, and the assault rifle he gripped looked as if it had been modded by him personally.

"We need to get it out of the path of the doors. Chief?" He turned to the chief technician of the fighter bay who had just come in from the briefing room with Commander Pierce. "I want this moved."

"Aye, sir. I'll get the hydraulics crew working on it." The

chief retreated to the rear of the bay where a handful of technicians were prepping fighters.

Commander Pierce folded his arms. "Captain, I don't want that thing in the fighter bay. How do we really know it's dead? Can't we just shove it out and forget about it?"

Granger shook his head. "No. We need all the information we can get. If we make it through the next engagement and repel the fleet heading towards Earth, IDF intel will want an intact specimen, and this is about as intact as they come."

"But what if the bugger pops out of there in the middle of the next fighter deployment and starts a ground war here in the fighter bay?"

Colonel Hanrahan grunted and stroked his rifle. "We'll be ready for it, Commander."

Granger nodded. "No, you're right. We need to be sure." He inclined his head upward, indicating to the monitoring computer to open a comm channel. "Doctor Wyatt, you here yet?"

He was loathe to bring the doctor there since the man was probably hard at work on Haws, but there was nothing for it— they had to be sure whatever was in the Swarm fighter was in fact dead.

"Be there in a minute, Captain."

Moments later, Wyatt entered the bay through the rear lift. "What's this about, Tim? I've got patients waiting for me."

Granger indicated the Swarm fighter. "We're going to open that up, and you're going to tell me if it's dead."

Wyatt's face paled: he gulped, but then nodded. Granger motioned to the marines to open up the small hatch on the side of the fighter. It was circular, and barely big enough for a human to pass through, which made Granger wonder just how large an individual Swarm was.

The hatch opened and a grayish-green substance immediately started draining out of the opening, causing the marine who'd opened the hatch to spring out of the way. It was viscous—far thicker than oil—and oozed down the side of the craft towards the floor.

"Doctor?" Granger took a step forward and bent down to look at the goo.

Wyatt approached the fighter and held a scanner up to the hatch opening, waving it back and forth. He shook his head, and then held the scanner down to the oozing fluid running down the side of the hatch. "I'm getting no life readings. No heat generation. No electrical impulses. No chemical reactions other than oxidation with our atmosphere. Whatever was in there is dead."

Wyatt crouched down and examined the goo. "I bet they have an automatic system that destroys the body in the event of a catastrophic event. Liquifies it. Maybe as a way to ensure none of them will ever be taken prisoner. Who knows?" He crouched further, bending forward to run a finger through the fluid.

He wobbled and fell backward to a sitting position, shaking his head.

Granger stepped forward. "Doctor? You alright?"

Wyatt nodded. "Yes. I've been on my feet all day. Crouching down like that must have restricted blood flow to my head—I nearly blacked out for a moment, but I'm fine." He shook his head a few more times, and then pushed himself to his feet, rubbing the viscous goo in between his fingers, studying it intently. "Whatever this is, sir, it poses no threat. There's no life in this craft to speak of." He wiped the goo on the surface of the fighter and glanced back up at Granger with a decidedly annoyed look on his face. "Now, can I get back to sickbay and save some more patients?"

Granger nodded. "I'll come with you." He turned to Commander Pierce and the chief as he walked out the door with Wyatt. "Get that thing tucked away somewhere. Don't touch anything—treat it like a biohazard until we know more. Colonel Hanrahan? Keep two men posted by it at all times— see that no one disturbs it. Understood?"

The three men remaining behind replied with a unanimous, "Yes, sir," and Granger strode, with Wyatt in close step, to sickbay.

Time to check on his XO.

Haws, you old bastard, don't leave me now.

CHAPTER FORTY-FOUR

Low Earth Orbit
Bridge, ISS Winchester

Captain Day settled back into his chair, exhaling a sigh of relief. To tell the truth, he'd much rather be back in the thick of things. In the battle. Fighting with his comrades. It was why he'd joined IDF in the first place—to stand among those who defended humanity.

Yet here he was, escorting a bunch of sniveling bureaucrats, diplomats, politicians, and pencil pushers. And the worst of the lot was *him*. Isaacson. The reason they weren't back with the *Qantas* and the *Constitution*, doing their part.

"Mr. Vice President," he began, struggling mightily to keep his voice neutral and respectful, "we're en route to *Valhalla Station* where I presume *Air Force Two* can shuttle you down to the surface?"

Isaacson, who was deep in quiet conversation with the Russian ambassador at the rear of the bridge, didn't so much as look up.

"Mr. Vice President?" said Captain Day, substantially louder this time. Isaacson finally broke off his conversation and shot Day an icy look.

"Yes, yes, Captain, that will be fine," he said, dismissively, then added, "no, wait. *Valhalla* will certainly be a target when they get here. We need to ensure the safety of the senators and cabinet secretaries on board."

And yours, thought Captain Day disdainfully.

"Take us directly to the surface. To Washington, D.C., or New York City." He paused. "No, wait … those would likely be targets too…." The Vice President trailed off.

"To Miami, then. IDF headquarters. It's heavily defended, and our passengers can get connecting shuttles to wherever they need to go—" Captain Day broke off as he saw the Russian ambassador lean over and whisper furiously in Isaacson's ear. How strange.

"No. Not Miami," said Isaacson, with a lingering gaze at the ambassador. "Somewhere else. Omaha, maybe. The spaceport there can handle the *Winchester*, and there's plenty of transport out of the region should the need arise." Isaacson kept looking at Volodin questioningly, and the other man nodded his approval. Very strange indeed.

Captain Day sighed. "To Omaha, Ensign. Full thrust. Deploy reentry aerilons and activate braking thrusters."

Earth rose up to meet them on the viewscreen—the vast green and tan landscape of the North American interior sprawling out in all directions. Off in the distance, hundreds of kilometers below and ahead of them, Day could just make out the distant gray-ish spots of the dozens of ships that dotted the landscape outside the Omaha spaceport—some retired, some in various phases of construction. Day knew that in the weeks and months ahead, ship construction would double. Triple. Perhaps even quadruple, to counter the resurgent Swarm threat.

If they survived the next few days, that is.

The Russian ambassador whispered in the Vice President's ear again. Isaacson nodded, and together they exited through the rear doors, followed closely by the two secret service officers. Day sighed another breath of relief.

"Lieutenant Frum," he said, glancing at the communications station, "send a message to CENTCOM Miami updating them on our status and heading. If they give you any guff, just tell them our orders came directly from our *illustrious* guest."

The Lieutenant snorted derisively. Day smiled—it was good to know he wasn't the only one who felt that way.

"What is it, Yuri?" hissed Isaacson, trying to keep his voice at a level that would only be heard by the ambassador trailing behind him. He aimed for the captain's quarters—the sooner they could get behind closed doors, the better. Volodin seemed far too free with words out in the open.

"Just that, respectfully, Mr. Vice President, you may be safer in Saint Petersburg."

They crossed the threshold of the captain's quarters and the doors slid shut behind them. Isaacson turned to face the ambassador. "But you've lost control of the Swarm! Or don't you remember their message to you? *You die?* Is that Swarm diplomatic-speak for, *we're coming to dinner*? What the hell makes you think we'll be safer in Saint Petersburg?"

Volodin shrugged. "Perhaps my government's relationship with them over the past decade will influence their targeting once they arrive at Earth. Plus, the major Russian cities are heavily defended—far more than even Miami or Washington or New York."

Isaacson peered at him suspiciously. How in the world could the other man know what defenses Miami and the other major North American cities had? How extensive was the Russian espionage operation? "Look, Yuri, we've never even seen a flesh and blood alien. Not once have we ever even seen one of the Swarm face to face. How can you be so confident that now, after all that's happened, they won't hesitate to obliterate every single city on the Earth's surface, Russian or no?"

Volodin sat down at the desk and scratched his arms. "Who says we've never seen a flesh and blood Swarm individual?"

The Vice President sat across from him. "Are you saying you've seen the Swarm? Actual, live bodies? No one in IDF ever saw one. Not once."

"Of course you did. You've seen billions of them."

"What, the ships? Are you saying the ships themselves are sentient? They're bodies?"

Volodin rolled his eyes. "What was inside all those ships from the Swarm War?"

"Nothing! Just whatever goo they left behind when they died or self destructed or escaped, or whatever it is they did to disappear."

"Exactly. That was them. That was our second major discovery after we found we could control them through the meta-space signals." He paused, smiling at Isaacson. "They're a liquid-based life form, Mr. Vice President. Each of those fighters you destroyed seventy-five years ago held hundreds of Swarm. There's hundreds, thousands of billions of Swarm. They are legion."

A shiver went up Isaacson's spine. Legion. The word conjured images of ancient demonic folklore, no less frightful than the actual, deadly aliens out to destroy them. "You visually verified this? Did you encounter any?"

"Of course we did. They are wondrous beings, Mr. Vice President. Intelligent, graceful, and deadly. Those first soldiers who actually physically contacted them were never quite the same."

"Explain."

Volodin folded his arms. He seemed remarkably calm given their dangerous situation. "After the asteroid incident, where we found we could control them, we arranged a meeting. One of their ships was directed to dock with one of our stations deep in the Yalta Sector."

"You have settlements in the Yalta Sector? Since when?"

Volodin ignored the question. "They came. And we docked with them. We sent a few corpsmen into their vessel to investigate and initiate contact. It all went well. We talked with them, though always through meta-space transmissions—even though we were docked with each other. Having the men onboard didn't seem to help or hinder the conversation. But when they came back, they were ... different."

"How?"

The other man paused, thinking. "Wiser. Smarter. Those soldiers that came back rose quickly through the ranks—some are now commanders. One's even a general."

"What do you mean, *those that came back*?"

"The Swarm required several men to stay behind."

Isaacson felt a little ill. "And? What happened to them?"

"They were … consumed. The Swarm demanded it. They didn't give a reason, but we assumed they wanted to familiarize themselves with us. Our anatomy, our brain structure. The Russian High Command judged it a fair trade given what we were accomplishing—given what knowledge they had to share."

"And?" Isaacson leaned forward. "Was it worth it?

Volodin smiled again. "That remains to be seen."

CHAPTER FORTY-FIVE

Near Earth
Sickbay, ISS Constitution

"Doc, is he going to make it?" Granger leaned over his friend. Abraham Haws was a wreck. His forehead was dented —his skull clearly fractured. A part of the support structure of the girder had broken off and impaled him in the chest, barely missing his heart but ripping through his right lung.

"No idea, Tim," said the doctor, adjusting the settings on one of the machines keeping Haws alive. "I've got him in an induced coma right now and pumped his head full of meta-corticals. We've got to repair the damage and reduce the swelling before I can bring him out of it. And he lost a lot of blood, so I ... good god, Tim, are you all right?"

Granger had doubled over in a fit of coughing, wiping a streak of blood from the corner of his mouth. His lungs were screaming at him and he staggered with a wave of dizziness.

"Fine. Don't worry about me."

"Of course I'm worried about you, you stubborn ass! If you're not fit for duty...."

"Don't," interrupted Granger. He stared the doctor in the eye, daring him to continue. "Doc, this is not the time. Earth is just a few hours away from getting blasted apart by an artificial black hole. Don't harangue me about my health when all our lives are on the line!"

"That's my job, Tim, and it's your job to know that if your health is affecting your judgement, then it's my duty to remove you. You understand that, don't you?"

"Screw you," he said, descending into another fit of coughing, steadying himself on the edge of Haw's bed. *Breathe,* he thought. Focusing on the slow, painful rising of his chest, he calmed himself, and added, "Give me a day. My mind is intact. I'm in pain, but that's it."

The doctor shook his head. "Tim...."

"Armand, please." Tim looked into his eyes, pleading. "If you remove me, then it's Proctor that's in charge. And as competent as she is, I don't want her commanding my ship. Not now. Not yet. We've got to save Earth. And if it's to be saved, it's going to be in the next six hours. If I fail, we're all dead anyway."

The doctor considered him for a moment. The man, one of Granger's closer friends on board, seemed oddly distant and formal. Dammit, why was every doctor he ever knew so short-sighted? Always focusing on the symptoms rather than the future? Always on the short term rather than the long. But to his credit, the doctor nodded. "Fine, Captain. If we're still alive tomorrow, I'm placing you on medical leave."

"Understood." He looked down at his severely injured

friend. "Now get me my XO back, and I'll give you a promotion," he added with a sober grin.

"He's not going anywhere for a month if he manages to live a day. I'll keep you updated on his condition. But for now there's nothing you can do." A distant rumble shook the deck and Granger steadied himself on the bed again. Wyatt glanced up at the walls, obviously apprehensive at the prospect of new casualties. The doctor shook his head and rubbed his eyes— was he still light-headed? Granger nearly reached out to him before Wyatt continued, "Get back down there, Tim. The *Constitution* needs her captain."

CHAPTER FORTY-SIX

Near Earth
Bridge, ISS Constitution

The two marines outside the bridge were distracted, pushing aside debris and assisting technicians with securing critical system components on the communications and power routing panel, so no one marked his arrival. Granger came up silently behind Commander Proctor, who, he noticed, was scrolling through the list of casualties. Twenty-six dead. Five missing. Thirty major injuries and at least eighty minor ones.

Not to mention the thousand-odd souls on the *Qantas*, and the hundreds of thousands lost at Lunar Base, on Mars, and the millions, billions, in the Veracruz Sector.

She shook, and brushed her cheek with the back of a hand.

"It gets easier," he said, making her startle.

She turned to look at him. Her eyes were red. She'd served her entire short career pushing paper back at IDF headquarters, and nearly a decade as a scientist before that. She'd never seen death. Not like this.

Nor had anyone in the fleet. There'd been countless drills and fleet exercises, sure, and accidents happen.

But no one had seen death on this scale in over seventy-five years.

"What's that supposed to mean? How could burying our friends get easy?" She let a hint of disdain drop into her voice, but he ignored it.

"I didn't say easy. But burying your friends ... well, you learn how to do it and then move on. And I've buried more than my share."

She said nothing, but turned back to her screen and swiped the casualty list away, replacing it with repair projections. "You've lost a lot of friends?"

"I have. And not just from diseases and sky surfing accidents. No, I'm just about the only one in the fleet who's buried his comrades in the line of duty."

She froze, and turned back to face him, aghast. "But, the Khorsky incident...."

It was more of a question than a statement, and he nodded gravely.

"You were there? I thought everyone responsible was either dead, in prison, or demoted."

He shrugged. "That's the official story, anyway. The reality is that I was promoted to captain soon after, and given command of the *Constitution*. My squadron may have done some stupid things, but they paled in comparison to IDF's response. If you knew half the things that went on behind closed doors ... well, suffice it to say they knew that I could be a big pain in their ass, and everyone knows you keep your enemies close."

From her face it was apparent that she almost didn't believe him. She looked at him askance. "So to shut you up, they didn't send you to prison, but promoted you? What did the Russians say?"

"Essentially, yes. And I have Abraham Haws to thank for it. He burst into Fleet Admiral Dawson's office during the secret court martial and laid out everything we knew about IDF, and basically threatened to go public unless they dropped the charges and gave us a ship. And so they did. As for what the Russians said, well, I guess IDF feared what I could say more than what the Russians would."

"What would you say? What would the Russians say?"

Granger's attention darted away towards the tactical station, where a fresh round of electrical arcing crackled as a technician swore. "We don't have time right now. Suffice it to say, the top brass at IDF have their heads so far up their asses that it's a wonder something like this fresh invasion didn't happen earlier."

She shook her head and squeezed her eyes shut. "Why are you telling me all this?"

"Several reasons. First, I want you to know how much Haws means to me, and what big boots you've got to fill."

"Is he dead?"

"No. But he could very well die soon." He took in a painful breath. Oddly enough, the truth felt liberating—good, even if his damned body didn't. "Second, if you're going to be my first officer, we have to trust each other. I'm laying it all out for you here. That Khorsky business is my deepest secret. I've got nothing to hide, and I expect the same from you. As such, I will both never bullshit you, nor will I pull punches. If you do your job good, I'll tell you. If you perform like a first-year ensign straight out of the academy, I'll call you on it. Understood?"

"Understood, sir." She paused, hesitating. "And how am I doing, in your opinion? I mean, since the crisis started."

He didn't answer for nearly ten seconds, letting her stew. When she began to look a little uncomfortable, he spoke.

"Admirable."

He still hadn't forgiven her for tearing apart his ship, but given that she'd almost put it back together again in less than a few hours, he could at least give her a second chance.

"Sir, I think you should know that I was about to write you up."

Now it was his turn to look at her askance. "What do you mean?"

"Back when you were tossing up obstacles to keep me from performing my mission. Getting in the way, subverting my authority. Admiral Yarbrough gave me clear operational authority, and told me to let her know if you were being difficult. I had a pretty nasty report all written up and ready to give her after the decommissioning ceremony."

"And now?"

She smiled. "I seem to have misplaced it in all the confusion."

"How fortunate."

There was an uncomfortable silence, during which the general sounds of frenzied activity in the background snapped their attention back to the emergency.

"Mag-rail status, Commander?"

She cleared her throat and swiveled the chair back around to face her console, which Granger only then noticed was Haws's station.

"I've diverted anyone not working on restoring fighters and the engines or making otherwise critical repairs to report to the gunnery chief for ordnance transfer. That includes most of the marines—Colonel Hanrahan wasn't happy about that, but he'll get over it. They should have the mag-rails reloaded within the hour. I've also directed them to transfer a double load, so that we can last for around twice as long as our first engagement before we need to do another ordnance transfer. They can store it in the hallways outside the guns. Not ideal, and not safe, but I think we've got bigger things to worry about than fleet Occupational Safety Services jumping on our asses."

"Good thinking." He nodded in approval. She was better than Haws. By far. Dammit. "And the fighters?"

"We lost thirty-two. The *Qantas* lost fifty-nine. Between the two wings we're now sitting at eighty-five, more than what we started with. We've also got about fifteen more about to come back online, so by the time we engage them again we'll be near a hundred." She paused. "As for the engines," she began, apparently anticipating his next question, "I'm sorry, you'll have to ask Commander Scott—she wouldn't answer when I called down there."

He stood up straight and stretched his back out, hiding the wince. "Excellent work, Commander. One more thing. What are your thoughts on the Swarm? Is this them? Have they really changed their technology this much in seventy-five years?

Their ships look nothing like the old ones, and that artificial singularity never showed up last time. Their hulls used to be vulnerable to lasers, which is why IDF has invested in petawatt class beams for all these decades. That's why most of our carriers are now sitting ducks—we're the only ship that still relies primarily on mass transfer weaponry."

She shrugged. "Who else could it be?"

"It's a big universe, Commander."

"True. But in this case, I think it is them."

She fingered several buttons on the terminal and motioned through several menus until she brought up what looked like a star map of the closest five hundred lightyears or so.

"Here, look at this."

"What is it?"

"It's my doctoral dissertation."

"Do we have time for this?" he asked, warily looking at the countdown timer which was keeping track of their approach to Earth. Over an hour remained until they began their deceleration burn, but there were still a whole lot of repairs to be made.

"You asked, sir. And yes, this will only take a moment." She pointed at a specific point on the map. "Part of my work was to see if I could determine a general location for the Swarm homeworld. Of course, that problem has been a hot topic in Swarm research for over half a century, and I didn't succeed." She tapped again on the map, drawing a circle around a few parsecs of space. "But I think I narrowed it down."

She drew a concentric circle around the first. "These systems all look like they were raided thousands of years ago.

Not many data points here, but we've found evidence of other civilizations. Other aliens. Just a handful. All very primitive. But there was hardly anything left—any artifacts we found point to an abrupt end, all roughly at the same time." She drew another circle around the first two. "These systems show similar signs of civilizational collapse, but hundreds of years later."

With her finger she drew a third, then a fourth, and a fifth circle. "In each of these zones, the destruction all happens at the same time. The theory was that the Swarm simply moved outward over time, conquering system by system."

Granger shrugged. "Sure looks that way, doesn't it?"

"It does. But it's happening systematically. They expand, clear out a region of space farther than they did the time before, and when they reach some pre-set distance, they stop, retreat and regroup, and essentially go into hibernation until the next time."

"What do you think it means?" It was an interesting theory, but Granger could not see any way it would help them in their current situation.

"At first, I agreed with all the other xenobiologists and anthropologists and thought they were simply systematically conquering their neighbors—expanding their territory slowly but inexorably. But do they start colonies? Do they take over planets? Do they exploit resources? No. They don't. They attack, they retreat, and they hibernate. Well, that last part's speculation—they may simply enter a sort of refractory period or regeneration cycle. They may very well stay awake and conscious—in fact, I think this current invasion proves that they spend their dormancy period developing new offensive technology."

"The point, Commander." Granger was getting impatient. They still had a lot of work ahead of them before their arrival at Earth.

"The point is that it's an evolutionary strategy. Somewhere, on some planet, they evolved from an animal that, every set period of time, swarmed outward from its habitat, cleared the space around them of competitors, such that when their offspring came of age there would be no competition for resources. The evolutionary trait has followed them to space, and I calculated the cycle period. Two hundred and eighty-nine years. Every two hundred and eighty-nine years, they expand their sphere of aggression by a distance factor of around fifty percent, wiping out any competitors within that space, spending the intervening years developing the new technology for the next cycle."

He stared at her, wondering if he missed the point.

"Did you hear me?" she asked.

It finally hit him.

"Did you say it happens every two hundred and eighty-nine years?"

She nodded, and shrugged. "With an uncertainty of plus or minus twenty years, but yes, that's what I said."

The answer hit him like a punch in the stomach. "Then what the hell are they doing out here just seventy-five years after their last cycle?"

"That, Captain, is a very good question."

CHAPTER FORTY-SEVEN

Near Earth
Bridge, ISS Constitution

The alarms were going off in Granger's head. It didn't make any sense—why would the Swarm come out of hibernation two hundred years early?

"Have there been deviations from the average cycle period before?"

"None. The largest variance was around twenty years, six cycles ago, but that's just noise in the data."

He stroked his chin and walked back towards his chair by the captain's console. "Could it have anything to do with the last time they invaded Earth? They just up and left halfway through the invasion. No one has ever figured out why."

"It's probably just that their cycle ended midway through the invasion. When the timer goes off, they turn around and go home, regardless of what they're doing."

He watched the timer tick down until their arrival at Earth.

Glancing at the long-range scanners, he saw that the alien fleet had yet to arrive there, though he wondered what they'd even be able to see this far out.

"Sorry, no," said Granger. "That's too easy of an explanation. Too simple. Too coincidental. Couldn't there have been something that would both explain their retreat seventy-five years ago, and that they're cutting their dormancy period short this time around?"

Proctor shrugged. "The conspiracy theorists would say that IDF lured them to Earth in the first place, to justify the military's existence and increase funding and support for its related industries."

He eyed her. "And you believe that?"

"Of course not. But as unified as Earth is, remember that some of the old nations want to reclaim their former glory, in their eyes."

Granger swore. "The Russians."

"Hey, don't put words in my mouth, Captain. All I'm saying is that the Russian Confederation didn't make out so badly in the last invasion. Nearly every other continent on Earth, and every other colony world got hit pretty hard."

It couldn't be. "That's just Russo-phobic nonsense, Commander. I'd have thought better of you. We've heard of these types of conspiracy theories for decades. Just because you've discovered that the Swarm has broken dormancy early doesn't lend any more credence to the crackpots."

"Fair enough," she said. "But just one more thing. Don't you think it a little odd that the Russian Science Federation just announced quantum teleportation technology a few years ago, and now the Swarm is back, flinging forced quantum singularities at us? From all our legacy data, they never had any sort of quantum technology—it was all gravimetric-field-based back then, like us. At least, their navigation was. Their improvements in that area would explain their new ability to sustain such high accelerations. But the singularities? That one came out of left field, and the only known users of quantum tech are a few small research groups at IDF Technical, and the Russian Science Federation. You do the math."

"Captain," said Lieutenant Diaz. Granger turned to face him, and noticed the man's face harden with whatever news he had. "*Valhalla Station* has engaged the Swarm, sir."

"Put it on the screen, maximum magnification." He knew they wouldn't be able to see much, just a lot of pixelated, blurred points of light swarming around the massive station.

"Aye, sir." The entire bridge crew looked up.

The alien fleet had stopped several hundred kilometers away, and were engaging what appeared to be a sizable IDF fleet—CENTCOM must have summoned at least two dozen heavy cruisers, light cruisers, and what looked like one of the super-carriers, probably the *ISS Justice*, Granger thought—its home base was Earth.

A flash of green. Then another. Followed by several more sustained bursts from the lead alien ship.

And it was gone—the super-carrier *Justice*. At least three thousand souls manning its gun crews, engine rooms, half a dozen flightdecks … all gone in a brilliant, pixelated flash of light. The massive ship fractured into two main pieces, and the aliens, not content with the destruction, blasted the remaining larger half until it too exploded into several dozen smaller pieces.

"Good god," breathed Commander Proctor, who was now standing next to Granger near the command console. "The *Justice* is the largest ship in the fleet, and it didn't last more than a minute against those monsters."

Granger stared at the screen, at the wreckage breaking apart and the alien ships blasting through it towards the remaining cruisers, which had started to mount a furious defense.

"If we survive this, heads are going to roll at IDF. Whoever ok'ed those smart-steel garbage hulls is going to be airlocked." He winced as another heavy cruiser erupted into a giant fireball, snuffed out by the vacuum. Tapping the comm, he yelled, "Rayna, do we have full engine power yet?"

Some flustered swearing in the background, then Commander Scott's harried voice. "Yes, sir. Eighty percent. That's all you're going to get, Cap'n, without going into dock."

"Fine." He turned to the nav crew. "Stop deceleration burn. I want another full thrust burn. Three g's. Hold that thrust for twenty minutes, then decel. How fast will that get us there?"

One of the techs ran the numbers. "Twenty-five minutes, sir, but at that speed we'll blaze right past the battle. It'll take us at least forty minutes to decelerate."

"Just do it. Three g's. GO!" He tapped the comm again. "All hands. Secure the ship for a full thrust, three g burn. And after that, return to battle stations. Red alert."

The navigation crew snapped into action, and before long they were all pushed into their seats as the ship once again leaped forward, the gravitational field struggling to keep up with the huge inertial forces acting on the ship and its contents.

"Sir, how in the world is this going to help? We'll get there faster, but only for a few brief seconds—" Granger held up a hand to silence his new XO. She was just like Haws in a way— he always used to bark his disapproval of orders he didn't understand, and, in spite of the breach of decorum, it comforted Granger.

"We're doing a drive-by. If we wait another hour to get there, there'll be nothing for us to do but bury the dead, Commander. At least this way we can take out one of their ships. Soften them up for whoever's left. And when we finally decelerate and swing back around, that's one less ship to worry about."

He strode over to the tactical station, nodding to the crew chief. Granger wasn't even sure this would work, but it was all he had. He mentally ran a few numbers, took a painful breath, and began. "Listen up. We only get one shot at this, so pay attention."

CHAPTER FORTY-EIGHT

Near Earth
Flightdeck, ISS Constitution

The four of them sat on a bench close to their fighters, ready for the inevitable moment that Commander Pierce would signal them to man their fighters and launch. Miller eyed the new pilot—the one who'd replaced Hotbox on their team. A young man from the *Qantas's* fighter wing. She didn't have time to catch his name, but he had introduced himself as Pluck.

Lieutenant Volz was murmuring instructions to Pluck while Dogtown held his lined face in his hands, whispering something to himself. All around the fighter bay, in the midst of the madness of the technicians and crew readying the last dozen or so fighters for launch, she saw the scene repeated over and over: pilots engaging in their rituals. One woman repeatedly kissed something hanging around her neck, which Jessica couldn't recognize from across the bay. A cross? A rabbit foot? Another young man next to her was tossing and catching a golfball over and over again. All of them preparing. Preparing for the performance of their lives. Or their deaths. Repeating meaningless rituals meant to calm and focus their minds.

She had nothing. Or did she? Her mind turned back to the picture sticking up out of the dashboard in her X-25. Little Zack-Zack, and Tom. All she had left of her husband.

What if she didn't return? Who would raise Zack? Could her parents handle it? Of course they could—they raised her, didn't they? But they were getting older, and should be enjoying their retirement, not doing her job for her.

She might not come back. The possibility stared her in the face, taunting her. Sucker-punching her in the gut.

Zack needed to know his mother was thinking about him at the end of her life. Even if he wouldn't appreciate it now, he would when he was older.

"Ballsy, here," she said, motioning to him. She twisted her wedding ring off her finger and held it out to him.

His eyebrows lifted. "Is now the right time, Fishtail? We haven't even kissed."

She ignored his joke. "Give it to my son. If I don't come back."

He stared at the ring, then back at her. "You're coming back. We're all coming back."

"Fine. But just in case, I want him to know I was thinking about him. That I'm doing this—all of this—for him." She held out the ring.

Ballsy swore, but took the offered ring. "Ok, but I'm giving this back to you when we get back." He slipped the ring onto his pinky—the only finger it would fit on.

"Thank you," she mouthed, for Commander Pierce was announcing something over a loudspeaker.

"All pilots, board your birds and stand by to launch."

And that was that. Everyone put away their golf balls, rabbit feet, crosses, rings, pictures of loved ones—things they'd been fiddling with to keep focused—and rushed to their fighters. Jessica climbed the ladder to her own bird and was about to jump into the cockpit.

"Fishtail!" She glanced to her right, where Ballsy was seated in his own cockpit. "I've got your back. Don't worry—you'll see the little guy again. I promise."

She nodded and smiled a tight-lipped acknowledgement.

But Ballsy wasn't God. Just some fighter jock with an oversized sense of self-worth.

The cockpit frame descended and locked into place, and she put on her headset. At least the kid meant well, and she appreciated it. Flipping on the comm, she signaled Volz. "Hey. Thanks."

"No problem, Fishtail. Now let's go kick some ass."

She rubbed the white groove on her finger left by the ring. "One ass-kicking, coming right up."

CHAPTER FORTY-NINE

Near Earth
Bridge, ISS Constitution

"When will we be in firing range?" Granger asked the weapons crew chief.

"In about twenty minutes, sir, but we'll only be in firing range for about a minute, and after that we'll be shooting past them at five kilometers a second."

"Wrong. We'll be in firing range for two minutes."

It took the crew chief a moment before it dawned on him. "You're going to turn the ship around?"

"Right after we pass them, yes. We'll flip a one-eighty, and resume blasting them with our mag-rails while we fly away from them. Ideally we'd only turn ninety, to give our starboard crews a direct line of sight, but we still need to decelerate, so one-eighty will have to do, and we only have a few rear guns, so just blazing by them without turning is out of the question."

"Understood, sir."

"And that's not all. You're going to concentrate all your fire at one spot on the lead ship. And you're going to start at double the regular firing range—I know we're less accurate that far out, but at least a few will find their mark, and it might distract them from pulverizing our fleet out there."

He pointed to a schematic of an alien ship that one of the tactical crew had brought up on his screen. "There," he said, tapping. "Concentrate all fire on this spot. Then, when we're at closest approach, fire our remaining nuke right at the hole we'll have made. As we fly away, your next target depends on what the nuke does. If the first ship is still intact, keep firing at it. If we disable or destroy it, choose a new target. Same drill—one spot on the other ship. Understood?"

"Aye, sir," said the chief, and the whole tactical crew saluted.

"Captain," said Proctor, sidling up to him. "What if they're generating a forced singularity when we fly by? Should we try to do anything about it?"

He turned to her, smiling. "And I assume you have a suggestion?"

She mirrored his smile. "I do."

CHAPTER FIFTY

Near Earth
Bridge, ISS Constitution

"It's not going to work," said Granger. He eyed the *Rainbow*, the small transport ship that had carried all the schoolchildren to the decommissioning ceremony but which now sat vacant, pushed to the rear of the main fighter deck. He wondered where all the children were—they must have been ushered further into the core of the ship—a much safer location than the giant bay filled with scuffed-up fighters, mechanics, grease, ordnance, missiles, fuel cylinder dollies, and pilots ready for the order to fly back out into battle.

Commander Proctor huffed, looking up at the shiny vessel. "It *will* work, sir. We'll link up the *Rainbow*'s autopilot to the *Constitution*'s nav computer, and we can handle the rest from the bridge. All they need to do down here is push it out the bay door when we're about to fly past. If a lone X-25 fighter will disrupt a forced singularity, then a corvette will have no trouble dissipating one."

"Push it out? And what if it hits one of our ships? What if the computers don't link up properly, and we lose control of it? It could fly right into one of our—" He trailed off, gritting his teeth. Truth be told, it was an excellent idea. But it wasn't his, dammit.

And his chest burned. Every breath was torture. The walk down to the fighter bay, though rather short, seemed alarmingly long as he wheezed.

"Fine." He motioned to the deck chief, and pointed at the *Rainbow*. "Chief, get her linked up to the *Constitution* and route the commands up to the bridge. Then position her right at the bay doors, and be prepared to shove her out with the hydraulic lift on my com—"

He didn't finish the sentence. Violent coughs erupted out of his throat, and taking his hand away from his mouth, he saw it was covered in blood.

Proctor's eyes widened. "Captain! Are you all right? You didn't tell me you were injured." She grabbed his arm as he descended into another fit of coughing.

He waved her off. "I'm fine," he finally managed to squeeze out in between coughs. Forcing himself to breathe long, slow breaths, he managed to calm the spasms. It was getting worse. If he were on Earth, he'd be in hospice care by now. Or, more likely, relaxing on some beach in Florida doped up on meds, living his last few weeks in the warm sun and sand.

But he was here. Earth was under attack, his ship was in mortal danger, and his people needed him. No time to convalesce, mope, or admit weakness. He straightened up and faced her, putting on a grim smile. "I'm fine," he repeated. "Just a previous condition acting up. But the doc says I'm clear for duty." He noticed the suspicious doubt lingering in her eyes. "I just talked to him an hour ago. He cleared me for duty, and by god I'm going to pull us through this if it's the last thing I do."

He hadn't meant to yell that last part, but as it was, several nearby technicians stopped to stare at him, their eyes widening slightly. He saw the fear in their faces. The uncertainty, and the confusion—he realized that down here, away from the bridge and all the firing crews, nobody likely knew much about what was going on.

Before he could say something to assuage them, Commander Proctor held onto his arm again and mumbled in his ear. "If you keep on your feet acting like some superhero, then it *will* be the last thing you do. Sir, you've got to see to your health—if you collapse in the middle of a critical operation—"

"I said," he interrupted sternly, indicating the matter was closed, "I'm fine. Come on, let's get back to the bridge." He glanced down at his watch. "We're nearly there."

CHAPTER FIFTY-ONE

Near Earth
Bridge, ISS Constitution

Back on the bridge, Granger nodded to the tactical crew chief, who nodded back, and apparently reading his mind, said, "All targeting solutions calculated, sir. We'll be in range in two minutes."

"Good. Navigation," he said, turning to the nav crew, "has the remote control of the *Rainbow* been passed up here yet?"

"Aye, sir."

"Good. If they've begun initiating their forced singularity weapon, and if I give the signal, you navigate that thing straight into the little bastard. Direct hit. Understood?"

"Aye, sir," the nav chief repeated.

He sat down in his chair. His feet ached, his back felt like it had been crushed by a parked starship, and his insides were on fire. *Ignore the pain. The ship comes first*, he thought, and turned to Proctor. "Commander, direct the fire crew."

"Yes, sir."

They all watched the countdown timer on the screen hovering next to the image—far sharper and less grainy than it had been before—of the battle still raging near the behemoth *Valhalla Station*. Now that the battle had drifted closer, the station had finally let loose with its formidable array of firepower, consisting mostly of high-powered lasers—which Granger now knew were ineffective against the alien hulls— but also several dozen mag-rails.

And, miraculously, at least half of the IDF cruisers were still intact.

But, appallingly, the other half were drifting and tumbling through space, broken and flaming, gorging debris and people into the void.

"Ten seconds," said Proctor. "Five. Four. Three. Two. One. Initiate mag-rail barrage on the lead ship."

On the screen, several streams of white-hot projectiles shot away from the ship, barely captured by the high frame-rate of the forward video cameras as momentary streaks.

Another thirty seconds passed before the mag-rail slugs started impacting on the alien ship, and the tactical crew chief shook his head. "As expected, at this distance the slugs just aren't finding their mark. Only about a third are hitting it, sir."

"Carry on. Keep firing at the target. Any gravimetric distortions?" he asked.

"None, sir," replied an officer at the science station.

Good. No forced singularity yet. He wondered what the target would be once they deployed their super-weapon. *Valhalla Station*? The largest of the heavy cruisers still intact?

The countdown timer had been reset to indicate the time

remaining until flyby. Two minutes. Granger was on the edge of his seat—nothing he could do now but watch the mag-rail fire find its target and hope for the best.

"Sir, incoming transmission from *Valhalla Station*," said the comm officer.

Granger pointed to his console. "Pipe it through."

Admiral Zingano's harried face appeared on his screen. There was absolute mayhem in the background behind him, as he was in the combat operations center. Before speaking to Granger, he turned to the side and spoke to someone offscreen. "Intensify point-defense screen on our port flank. Too many alien fighters are getting through and we've lost ten guns down there." He turned back to the screen. "Tim, I'm glad you're here, but what the hell are you doing on such a fast approach vector? You'll be in battle for less than a minute!"

The anger poured through the screen, but he was distracted. After issuing a few more commands to his combat crew, he turned back to the screen again. Granger cleared his throat. "It was our only option for getting here in time to have any effect, sir. If we'd waited to slow at a normal approach velocity, we'd have arrived far too late."

Zingano pressed his lips together in annoyance, and shook his head. "We're doing better than we might have hoped, though we've lost the *Justice*, the *Valiant*, the *Eclipse*, and the *Hemingway*, as well as a dozen other cruisers and god knows how many fighters and frigates." His eyes hardened for a moment. "And Tim, there's something else. Long-range scanners based on Europa have picked up the signal of another fleet, closing rapidly—even faster than this one. They'll be here in an hour."

Granger swore. "How many ships?"

"At least three more."

If they didn't find a way to make their weapons more effective against the alien ships, or repel their massive firepower with greater efficiency, then it was over. There was no way they'd stand up to seven of those monsters attacking Earth. "We're nearly there. Are we having any effect on the lead alien ship?"

Zingano glanced at his readout. "You're punching quite the hole in it. What are you going to do, hit it with a nuke?"

"Exactly."

He shrugged. "All of ours have been intercepted. Their targeting algorithms are even more advanced than seventy-five years ago. I—"

He cut off abruptly, snapping his head off to the side to listen to a report Granger couldn't quite hear.

"Sir!" Lieutenant Diaz looked up. "Detecting massive gravimetric distortions straight ahead. They're initiating the forced singularity, Captain."

CHAPTER FIFTY-TWO

Near Earth
Bridge, ISS Constitution

Granger thumbed the comm. "Chief, prepare to eject the *Rainbow* on my mark." He glanced at the navigation station. "You all ready?"

Ensign Prince nodded.

The countdown timer ticked away on the front viewscreen.

Twenty seconds.

Amidst the heat of the battle on the screen, they saw the tell-tale glimmer of the forced singularity. It grew quickly in intensity—whether from the increase in size, or the *Constitution*'s rapid approach, Granger couldn't tell.

Fifteen seconds.

"Commander, I want a full sensor suite focused on that singularity and the alien ships. I want to know everything about it. Everything."

Five seconds.

Proctor gave her signal. "Fire the nuke!"

Granger pointed to the navigation station. "Now. Eject the *Rainbow*. And be ready to rotate one-eighty."

On the screen, several things happened at once.

The nuclear missile shot away from the starboard side of the ship, streaking with incredible velocity toward the lead alien ship, where, in spite of the point-defense fire from the target, it made impact and detonated with an overwhelmingly bright blast.

When the screen desaturated from the nuclear explosion, they watched with held breath as the *Rainbow* plowed right into the glimmering singularity, and in the blink of an eye, both disappeared. Several bridge crew members fist pumped the air and cheered.

But from the wreckage of the lead alien ship came one of the remaining three, and it unloaded a ferocious barrage of shimmering green blasts towards *Valhalla Station*.

"Target that ship!" yelled Granger.

"Aye, sir," said the tactical crew chief.

But it was too little, too late. Whereas before the alien ships seemed content to hang back from the station to concentrate their attention on the fleet of IDF ships that had intercepted them, this ship now seemed intent on breaking the station. And to their dismay, one of the giant docking arms of the station completely snapped off, flashing fire and debris at the joint.

"Unload everything we've got, Lieutenant! Bring her down!"

"Sorry, sir," the tactical crew chief began, "We're running low on slugs. We need to reload."

Granger spun back to the screen. A second docking arm snapped off under the heavy barrage. "DAMMIT!" He pounded the armrest of his chair as one of the main sections of the station cracked in half, splintering into dozens of flaming pieces as that section's oxygen lines erupted into a fireball. One of the colossal flaming pieces drifted towards a derelict IDF cruiser, and the two collided in another explosion.

Granger turned back to his command station's screen to talk to Admiral Zingano, but the scene was a hectic display of smoke, sparks, and jumbled yelling and screaming. Zingano was nowhere to be seen on the screen, and in another moment it went to static.

"Nav, what's our decel rate?" he muttered, just above a whisper.

"Three g's, sir."

"Increase to five."

"But sir, our gravitational compensating field won't be able to keep up with a burn like—"

"You heard me. Five g's." He thumbed open his comm. "This is the captain. Prepare for severe gravitational and inertial disturbances. We're about to hit five g's. Grab on to something and hold on tight, people."

Proctor dashed for an empty seat at the science station. "Strap in, everybody!"

Within a moment, the ship began to shake, far worse than the throbbing caused by the forced singularity weapon. Seconds later, the ship seemed to lurch forward, throwing them all against their restraints, then backward again, then forward, as the ship's gravitational stabilizers struggled to calibrate themselves against the huge g-forces straining the ship.

"Ops, see if you can't stabilize that grav field," yelled Granger.

Proctor craned her head over to the ops station. "Increase the damping term in the harmonic oscillator kernel of the main grav program. Tie it directly to the output of the gravitational sensor array."

Within a few moments, the shaking and lurching lessened, but they all still had to hold on to their chairs and consoles.

"Passing out of weapons range now, sir," called out the tactical chief. "The second alien ship sustained moderate, but superficial damage."

It was maddening to know that with every second that ticked past, *Valhalla Station* and the fleet was being picked apart. Hundreds, thousands of lives were being lost.

And Granger could do nothing.

"Commander Proctor. What did our sensors pick up during our flyby?"

"I haven't had the chance to talk to the science team, sir." She turned to them. "Anything?"

One of the science officers cleared his throat. "We're still analyzing the data, sir, and I can't say anything definitive."

Granger rolled his eyes. *Scientists.* "Then say something speculative."

"Well, sir, best guess…. It's obvious that there is quantum coupling between the singularity and each of the alien ships participating in its generation. That's how the teleportation happens—they're essentially using quantum teleportation to transfer mass past the event horizon—"

"Wait," said Granger, interrupting, "it's a black hole. Why

the hell can we see it?"

"We're not seeing the black hole itself, sir. It's actually microscopic. And the event horizon is less than a hundredth of a millimeter across. We're just seeing the synchrotron radiation of the mass falling in as it orbits around."

"Ah. Go on, then."

The rumbling of the ship had started to intensify, but there was nothing they could do about it. The science officer continued, "Well, the link appears to go both ways. Obviously, it's quantum coupling—what happens to the singularity affects the power cores of the alien ships. At least, I assume they're using their power cores to generate the energy to transmit the quantum signal."

"And did we detect some change when the *Rainbow* hit the singularity?"

"That's what we're trying to figure out, sir. There was certainly a fluctuation in the link between the singularity and the ships. But at the moment of impact, the data is all washed out due to the spike in the gravitational waves coming off of it —when the *Rainbow* hit, that's a whole lot of mass to get absorbed all at once, and it resulted in, essentially, a very miniature supernova. In fact, that's what's going on when they launch or teleport the singularity at their target. The amount of mass falling in overwhelms the black hole, bounces off the singularity at the core, and explodes outward with extraordinary energy."

So that was the fate of Lunar Base. They were essentially caught up in a miniature supernova explosion. Good god.

"Well, keep at it. We need some answers."

"Aye, sir," the science officer said, turning back to the data on his screen.

A distant rumble preceded a violent lurch that would have launched everyone out of their seats were their restraints not fastened. As the rumbling increased, a loud droning whine coursed through the ship. "Sir, our grav stabilizers can't handle this. We're about to lose gravity, and if we keep it up we may lose q-jump capability too—"

Granger thumped his armrest and swore to himself. "Of course," he muttered. He glanced at his console and saw that they probably only had enough stored energy for one q-jump. A second would require another hour or so of charging. "Cut the thrust to three g's," he said to the nav crew, before adding, "and prepare for q-jump."

"Sir?" Ensign Prince looked up, surprised. "To where?"

"Where the hell do you think?"

CHAPTER FIFTY-THREE

Near Earth
Bridge, ISS Constitution

"Brilliant," Commander Proctor said, tapping at her own console, which surprised Granger. It wasn't a particularly brilliant maneuver, just one that was not often done due to the stresses involved in q-jumping so close to the gravity well of Earth, and definitely not while engaged in a deceleration burn. The strain on the *Constitution* would be considerable, but nothing she couldn't handle. Proctor continued, "And we'll have enough energy stored up for a second jump if we cut power to the main engines and—"

"We're not cutting power to the mains, Commander. We're going to q-jump and continue decelerating until we're right back in the thick of things. Draw their fire off the rest of the fleet, since our armor seems to be the only thing that can take a beating and come out the other end alive."

Proctor glanced up at him. "But, sir, our gun crews report

that we've run through our loaded ordnance. It'll take another half hour to get fully loaded again."

"*Every* mag-rail is depleted?"

She glanced at her screen to confirm. "Mostly, yes. Crews five, twenty, and forty-three through forty-five still have about half a magazine each, but the rest are already engaged in reload."

Granger shrugged. "Fine. You go to battle with the army you have, Commander, and our people need us."

A few minutes later, the calculations were complete, and Granger prepared to give the order to jump. "All hands, prepare for battle. You've performed admirably twice so far. Let's show them what we're made of this time. Anticipate heavy incoming fire. Damage crews be on alert and make main power and mag-rails your priority. All fighters, prepare to launch."

Before signaling the q-jump, he tapped the comm. "Commander Pierce, this is Granger. Your boys ready?"

"Ready for action, sir. We'll give them an ass-whooping they won't soon forget," came the young CAG's reply. Granger knew the young man was probably still reeling from the knowledge of his father's certain death, but he was handling it admirably. Professional and unflappable—just how they were trained to be.

"Good. Are the *Qantas*'s fighters integrated into the squadrons?"

"As best we could, sir. There's still some lingering communications and computer system integration, but we'll just have to do the best we can."

"Good man. Focus your attention on the Swarm fighters.

Let us take care of the capital ships, but stand by for updates. Granger out."

With that, he signaled to Ensign Prince to initiate the q-jump, and within a few seconds the familiar queasy, vaguely off-balanced feeling typical of q-jumps washed over him before he steadied himself on his chair.

"Time to weapons range?" he asked, as he watched the view of the continuing battle raging near the wreckage of *Valhalla Station* subtly change, indicating their change in position.

"Thirty seconds."

"Hold fire until we're right in the middle of it. Then let loose on that second ship we were targeting earlier. Fighters, prepare to launch in"—he glanced at his readout, looking for their arrival time—"two minutes."

On the screen, the battle still raged, but things were looking far more grim than they were just ten minutes ago when they flew past the first time. Several more IDF capital ships had broken up into dozens of smaller pieces, and as they watched, another small cruiser took a direct blast from the deadly green directed-energy weapon and erupted into a blinding explosion as its power core went critical. The blast caught dozens of fighters in its wake, sending them careening into other vessels or off into deep space. Wreckage hurtled through the field of the battle, and it looked as if the remaining IDF ships were rallying for a sustained assault on the alien ship the *Constitution* had damaged on its previous flyby.

"What's the comm chatter like?" he asked the communications officer.

"Admiral Jones on the *Trident* has taken command of the fleet, sir—all comm traffic from *Valhalla Station* is silent. He's ordering all craft to close in on the alien ship we damaged and concentrate fire on it."

"Great minds think alike," Granger said wryly. "When we arrive, position the *Constitution* between the alien ship and as many IDF vessels as you can." He turned to the tactical station. "And stay on the lookout for that singularity. I want to know the second they start generating it."

"Aye, sir. Ten seconds until we engage."

"Speed?"

"Down to one thousand kph and falling."

Proctor frowned. "We're still coming in too fast."

Ensign Prince nodded. "We'll overshoot by about fifty kilometers. It'll take a few more minutes to swing back around."

"Open fire," said Granger. "Launch fighters. Commander Pierce, engage the alien fighters. Draw their fire away from the cruisers. See if you can't lure them towards the other two alien ships to act as a defensive screen they'll have to target and fire through."

"Aye, sir," came several voices at once.

And with that, they entered into close engagement combat for the second time in a day. The battle near Lunar Base already seemed like ages ago, as if they were all battle-hardened veterans. He chuckled to himself at the absurdity. Yesterday he was about to retire the oldest ship in the fleet and take a desk job in an IDF that hadn't seen so much as a border dispute in over seventy years, and now they were all veterans who knew more dead comrades than living.

The ship rumbled. Green lit up the viewscreen as an alien beam slammed into the forward section.

"Evasive maneuvers. Starboard thrusters, engage at point five," yelled Proctor. "Emergency crews to port mag-rails. Get guns twenty through forty reloaded now!"

Granger nodded. His new XO was getting a handle on combat. Hell, for that matter, they all were.

The ship shuddered again with another sustained blast. "Heavy damage in the forward section, port side! They've cut through the hull!"

Damn. Ten meters of solid tungsten, cut through like a filleted fish. He wondered how the remaining IDF ships had lasted so long.

As if in answer, the nearest heavy cruiser flared in a blinding flash. Debris and bodies came streaming out of the fissures in the ship as it broke in two.

"That was the *Trident,* sir," said the comm officer.

Admiral Jones was dead. He glanced at his command readout at the roster of available IDF ships and realized there were no admirals left. Not even a commodore. And of all the remaining captains, he had the longest tenure, which in the absence of any standing order transferring command, meant that he was it.

"Open a channel to the fleet," he said with a nod to the comm station.

"Open, sir."

"This is Captain Granger. I'm taking operational command of the fleet. Any cruisers with offensive nuclear capabilities, contact me immediately. All capital ships, focus your fire on the lead. All corvettes and frigates, swarm around the other two.

Aim for their weapons installations. Keep at least five hundred meters between each ship to avoid collateral damage in case of catastrophic loss. All fighter squadrons, engage the alien fighters and draw them away from our cruisers...."

On the screen, another light cruiser erupted into a spherical white blast, punctuated by the nightmarish green alien energy beam. He grimly added, "And if your vessel is in imminent danger of loss, you're hereby ordered to execute Omega Protocols."

Proctor glanced over at him, her face grim. "Has it come to that?"

He simply nodded, without responding. Omega Protocols —he'd just ordered the fleet captains to be suicide runners.

"Sir, the four new alien ships are nearly here. Two minutes until they're in weapons range."

CHAPTER FIFTY-FOUR

Near Earth
Bridge, ISS Constitution

Two minutes. They seemed to be finally holding their own against the original three alien ships—at least, a third of the IDF fleet was still firing and hadn't been lost yet. But four more alien ships meant their very certain and quick deaths.

"We just lost the *Furious* and the *Minnesota*, sir. Those were our only two heavy cruisers with nuclear missiles still in service." The tactical officer sounded grim and distant. Granger looked around at the bridge crew—they looked like dead men and women, like they had given up and knew their deaths were certain and imminent.

The ship shuddered with another direct blast from the alien's devastating energy weapon. "Sir! Hull breach on deck twenty, forward section!"

"Seal bulkheads!" yelled Proctor. "Get emergency crews up there!"

Another explosion rumbled through the ship, and then another much closer which caused the bridge to lurch, dislodging more material from the jagged crack across the ceiling and starboard wall.

And inevitably, the tell-tale throbbing and rhythmic shuddering began. Not of explosions or the impact of the energy beams, but a harbinger of something far worse.

"Sir, they're initiating the singularity!"

On the screen, again, the now familiar white shimmering light appeared in the midst of the three alien ships. The green beams ceased as the three ships apparently paused to redirect all their attention and energy to the generation of the singularity.

And there could only be one target. *Valhalla Station* was ruined, tumbling apart in pieces. The *Furious* and the *Minnesota* were destroyed, and the only remaining heavy cruisers were belching flame and debris. The smattering of light cruisers darting around the alien ships, unleashing whatever weapons they still had, were no great threat. The *Constitution* was the largest target around.

"We need to hit that thing with something really big," said Proctor.

"Well said, Commander." Granger raised his eyebrow at his XO's way with words. He scanned his command console, looking for the most damaged cruiser—one that might be near destruction anyway. Jabbing the screen with a finger, he thumbed open the comm.

"Captain Bryan, your engines are going critical. What's your status?"

He watched the light cruiser tumble out of control. Debris

was streaming from its sides. It was a wonder anyone was still alive over there. A voice crackled faintly over the comm. "Tim? Is that you?"

Granger winced. "It's me, Gordon." Gordon Bryan was one of his good friends from his first assignment aboard the *ISS Warrior*. That old ship—another one in the Legacy Fleet and basically a carbon copy of the *Constitution*, lay in dry dock at Europa Station around Jupiter, but Granger still kept in touch with many of his old friends from his time there.

"Not going so well, is it?"

"No, it's not." Granger glanced at the timer on the screen that indicated roughly how long they had until the singularity was expected to launch. Less than two minutes. "Look, Gordon, our readings indicate you're about to lose engine containment."

"Yeah, turns out that battle's a bitch. Who knew?" His friend chuckled, but then grew serious. "Look, Tim, I know what you're going to ask me to do. But our navigation's out. We're goners."

Explosions and yells came out of the speakers. "Gordon?" Granger leaned forward. No response. He sighed. "Gordon? You still there?"

A cough, and a rasp. "Yeah, still here."

Granger studied the tactical arrangement of the battle on his screen. The *Missouri*, Captain Bryan's ship, was very close, and directly between them and the growing singularity. "Gordon, we're going to push you in. That'll disrupt the singularity, and give us more time to take these bastards out. If we don't, the *Constitution* is toast. And it's looking like we're the only armor out here that can put up with that—"

"Yeah, yeah, I know, you want me to take a bullet for you." A pause, and a fit of coughing over the speakers. Damn—Gordon sounded worse than Granger, who suppressed coughing of his own. "Sounds like a plan. Push us in. We've only got another few minutes anyway."

Granger motioned over at navigation, and murmured, "Move us in close, rest the hulls together, and give them a momentum transfer in the direction of the singularity."

"Aye, sir."

Granger looked at the comm speaker, imagining his old friend on the other side, most likely burned, or bleeding. "Gordon, we're coming in close now." He paused, searching for words appropriate to the occasion. Nothing particularly eloquent came. "Thank you, sir. It's been an honor."

"Likewise, Tim. Say goodbye to Julie for me, if you come out the other side of this alive." The ship lurched as it gently collided with the *Missouri*, and began to push against it. The other ship slowly, but surely, tumbled away, moving steadily toward the singularity. "Tell her I love her. Tell her sorry. I wanted to come back and work things out with her but—"

Granger nodded. His friend was rambling. Probably a little delirious from loss of blood or combat stress, and talking about things that Granger wasn't familiar with, but it didn't matter. "I will, Gordon. God bless."

"Tell her I wanted to make it right. Tell her I wanted to—"

The speaker cut off in a hiss of static, and Granger's stomach clenched as he noticed the green flash on the screen.

"No," he breathed, watching as one of the alien ships lanced the *Missouri* with its green beam, and the light cruiser exploded in a fiery white blast. It was so close that the

Constitution was caught in its wake, pelted with debris, and the Old Bird shook and lurched.

Commander Proctor approached him from behind. "Sir, we need something with higher velocity, or else they'll just blast it before it reaches the target."

He nodded. Numbly, as if in slow motion, he reached for the comm again. "Commander Pierce, bridge."

"Captain?" came Pierce's voice.

"Order one of our fighters into the singularity."

"Sir?"

"You heard me."

Pierce protested. "But, sir, I can't—"

"You *will*, Commander. Do it now. That's an order. Granger out."

He turned to Proctor, shaking his head. The horrified look on her face told him all he needed to know.

"God help me, Shelby."

CHAPTER FIFTY-FIVE

Near Earth
X-25 Fighter Cockpit

"Ballsy! I—there's—" Miller broke off, struggling to maintain control as she weaved through the knot of alien bogeys. This time there were more of them. Many, many more. Hundreds. Possibly in the thousands. She began to understand why they'd picked up the name *Swarm* all those years ago. "There's too many! I can't—"

"Just hold on! Pull hard to your left on my mark and corkscrew z minus two. Ready ... GO!"

Trusting his tactics, she pulled sharply to the left and was thrown violently to her right into the restraints. Struggling against the g-forces, she keyed in the corkscrew. Plunging through the plane of attack and wincing from several rounds that hit the body of her X-25, she exhaled in relief as Ballsy shot upward through the middle of her corkscrew, blasting about half a dozen bogeys into brief fireballs.

"Woo hoo!" he yelled into the comm, and she grinned. Reaching forward to touch the picture propped up on her dash, she swung the fighter around and came up behind Dogtown and Pluck, who'd picked up several bogeys on their tail. With a few quick depressions of the trigger, she unleashed a stutter of rounds into each craft, sending them flaming, tumbling end over end, until they broke apart on the hull of the alien ship just a few hundred meters away.

"Well now you're just showing off, Fishtail."

She took a moment to survey the battle. In spite of their squad's successes, things looked desperately grim. As she watched, another IDF heavy cruiser broke in two as a devastating green energy beam darted out from the nearest alien vessel and sliced right into its core. Debris and fire coursed out of the blast zone. She felt sick when she realized what some of the debris was—the unmistakable tangle of bodies and limbs. One flew by her cockpit viewport as she raced ahead of the exploding cruiser, cartwheeling head over heels out into the deadness of space.

"Fishtail! Pay attention!" Ballsy's voice broke her focus on the body, and she snapped back into action.

Nearly too late.

A pair of bogeys was bearing down on her, and she flinched at the jolt of rounds colliding with her wings.

"FISHTAIL!"

She swerved, and plunged, and banked hard to the right—anything to lose the two craft spewing fire at her.

And to her surprise, they exploded. An X-25 fighter burst out of their debris cloud. "Ballsy?" she asked.

"That was all Pluck this time. That little mother-plucker."

If her stomach wasn't already up in her throat she would have chuckled at the poor joke, but that was too close of a call for comfort.

The cockpit walls all around her pulsed, throbbing with regular intensity. She knew what that meant.

A voice crackled over her comm. "This is the CAG." Pierce paused, as if unsure of himself. "Pluck. You're hereby ordered to make an Omega-Protocol run at the singularity. Ram it full speed. That's an order."

Silence and static came over the headset. She couldn't believe what she was hearing. A moment later, Pluck's young, confident voice answered. "Aye, sir."

Pierce's voice was broken, and raw. "Thank you, Lieutenant. You're a great man, and you'll be remembered in honor."

Fishtail watched out her viewport as Pluck veered off towards the shimmering white light, dodging a few bogeys that veered towards him, guns firing.

And she screamed.

Pluck's fighter exploded as a deadly green beam lanced out from the nearest alien ship, slicing the little craft in two.

Fighting back a tear, she set her sights on another alien fighter and blasted it to pieces, using far more ordnance than was necessary as she pummeled it until there was nothing left.

"Fishtail, you're up," came Pierce's voice again.

She closed her eyes momentarily. This was it.

Somehow, in that moment, her only thought was that she did not envy Commander Pierce's position in the slightest. To make decisions like he'd just made was unimaginable. Realizing she was thinking this, she also noticed that she was remarkably calm.

It was time. It was her time.

"Yes, sir."

"Thank you, Jessica."

It was her time.

Forgive me, Zack, she thought, touching the picture on the dash. She wanted more than anything to be there for him. But first, he needed to live. He needed a planet to live on. His world needed saving.

Gritting her teeth, she pushed the controls forward and darted away at maximum acceleration.

"Fishtail," came Ballsy's uncharacteristically quiet voice. "I've got your back. I'll escort you in."

"Just promise to pull away in time," she replied, dodging a green beam that shot out from the alien ship nearby.

"Right on." He swooped in behind her and blasted a pair of bogeys that had her in their sights. "Let's get this done."

CHAPTER FIFTY-SIX

Near Earth
Bridge, ISS Constitution

A silent pall had fallen over the bridge as every head turned toward the screen. A lone fighter had peeled off from the melee of combat and was screaming towards the shimmering singularity, now nearly as large as the one had been over Lunar Base before it launched at the surface.

Granger stood up. If a pilot was going to willingly sacrifice himself for his fellows, the least he could do was stand to acknowledge it. "Commander Proctor. Give me his name. Rank. Hometown. Tell us who it is."

The XO tapped buttons on her screen before clearing her throat. "Lieutenant Jessica Miller. Callsign Fishtail. From Sacramento, California. Age twenty-four, newly married, and was scheduled to transfer to the *ISS Clyburne* after our decommissioning to serve aboard the same ship as her husband." Proctor looked up, her face obviously pained. "The

Clyburne was one of the carriers destroyed defending Lunar Base."

Granger nodded, and bent over to tap the comm. "Fishtail, this is the CO."

"Hell of a view from out here, sir," came the static-laced voice. The bridge watched as the fighter, tiny against the backdrop of the remaining IDF and alien ships still blasting away at each other, swerved and dodged the wreckage of dead ships and the intense energy beams as the aliens tried to knock out her little craft before she hit the singularity.

But the fighter was too fast and nimble for them.

"I'm sure it is, Jessica. Godspeed, Lieutenant. And thank you." He saluted. The rest of the bridge crew, those not occupied with immediate combat duties, likewise stood and mirrored him.

"Ah, hell, sir, you would have done the same for us if you were out here."

The distance between the fighter and the singularity narrowed to just a few hundred meters, and closed fast. Lieutenant Miller continued, "Besides, this is how I always wanted to go out." Her voice quavered slightly, betraying her attempted show of bravado. "Taking out a shitload of Cumrat ships." She was silent for a moment, before whispering, barely loud enough for Granger to hear, "I'm sorry, Zack-Zack. I'm sorry."

And, too soon, the fighter closed in on the shimmering light. "Oh god—" Miller's voice murmured, right as her ship plowed into the singularity, which a moment later erupted into a massive explosion that engulfed the nearest alien ship, and the wreckage of the *Missouri*.

When the blast subsided, the alien vessel was spewing flame from the side nearest the destroyed singularity.

Granger spun around to tactical. "Whatever we've got left, send it into that blast zone on that ship," he yelled, pointing frantically to the screen.

"There's nothing left, sir. All our mag-rails are either destroyed, or empty of—"

"Then lasers! Anything! Just pound that blast zone with whatever we've got!"

A moment later, all the remaining undamaged laser turrets lit up and unleashed a brilliant barrage of ultra-high-energy pulses at the gaping wounds on the alien ship, vaporizing all the debris in their paths, penetrating deep into the core of the vessel which then spewed even more fire and debris.

Moments later, after what seemed like minutes but could only have been a dozen seconds, the entire alien ship lurched, and exploded in a blinding flash as its core went critical and split into several steaming chunks.

"Two down, two to go," murmured Proctor.

Granger sat down, staring steely-eyed towards the screen at the remaining two alien ships. "Two down, and it only took half our fleet going down in flame to do it."

Two down. Two left. Granger shook his head. The odds looked grim. The *Constitution* was hobbling along, punctured and wounded. The remains of the fleet, which at the beginning of the battle had numbered over forty ships, now crept along at just over ten. And the massive *Valhalla Station*, the centerpiece of IDF's headquarters and Earth's primary defense, floated in pieces, smoldering and steaming, debris still occasionally blasting off into space from the explosions erupting on its wrecked surface.

The odds looked beyond grim. They looked impossible.

"Sir," the tactical officer turned to face Granger with a tired look on his face. "The other four alien ships have arrived."

CHAPTER FIFTY-SEVEN

Omaha, North America, Earth
Operations Center, IDF Spaceport

Vice President Isaacson, his chief of staff, and a handful of senators and cabinet officials sat off to the side in the operations center of Omaha Spaceport as the officers worked frantically to scramble the fighters and what other last minute defenses could be mustered. They'd been given that area of the center as a communications hub to coordinate with the rest of the civilian government still in New York and Washington, and CENTCOM headquarters in Miami.

But truth be told, there wasn't much for Isaacson and the other officials to actually do—the United Earth government had already dispersed from the central location in New York, scattering throughout the world to ensure a functioning government would survive any attack targeting the capitals, and CENTCOM was quite busy repelling the invasion. As it was, Vice President Isaacson sat back, stone faced, watching the updates and video feeds scroll by on the wall of viewscreens nearby.

It wasn't supposed to happen this way.

A voice in his ear mumbled, "A word, Mr. Vice President." He turned to see the sallow face of Yuri Volodin. What now? Hadn't the bumbling fool done enough already?

"What is it?"

"Do you know President Avery's current location?"

Isaacson shook his head. "Classified. It's part of the contingency plans for an invasion—she gets whisked away immediately to a secure location."

Yuri regarded him with a cold expression. "You didn't answer my question. Of course it's classified. The question is, do you know where she is?"

A pit was forming in Isaacson's stomach. This whole scheme had gone too far. Millions were dying, and if things didn't turn around, billions more would follow. And now Yuri was still focused on killing Avery? After his odd insistence that they avoid the Miami area, where ostensibly they'd be the safest given its extensive defenses, Isaacson had become suspicious of Volodin. What were the man's true motives? He'd acted quite surprised at the treachery of the Swarm, but now seemed to be taking it in stride, keeping his focus on overthrowing or killing the President.

"Yes."

"Where? Miami?"

"Is that important?" Isaacson snarled, keeping his whisper low enough to not be heard by the nearest senators, all of whom were talking frantically on their personal comm devices anyway. "After this, there's no way she's staying in power. When we repel the invasion and pick up the pieces, people will be calling for her head for allowing this to happen. Her and all the other proponents of the Eagleton Commission."

Volodin smiled. Cold and deliberate. "But that might not happen for months. We need to move fast. We may only have a few days. Tell me where she is."

"What in high heaven are you going to do with that information, Yuri? Order a Russian strike force to take her out? They'd never get within a hundred kilometers of her."

"Of course not. Don't be a fool. But if the Swarm were somehow ... encouraged ... to move in her direction, it would play to our benefit."

The words ran like ice through Isaacson's spine. Was he still communicating with the Swarm? How?

And suddenly their earlier conversation made a little more sense. Was it possible? Was Volodin being influenced by the Swarm from afar?

Or worse, was he ... compromised? Was he *wiser*, and *smarter*? Was he completely controlled by the Swarm?

My God, what have I done?

The smart-steel quantum modulation codes. The defense network frequencies. Dammit—the Russians had all of them now, and so did the Swarm.

He needed to figure out a way to ensure Volodin wasn't under the Swarm's influence. Somehow.

He nodded. "Good point. Let me see what I can do—I don't know her coordinates, but I may be able to convince one of our officers to tap into her personal comm channel and we can triangulate from the source." He stood up and motioned for Yuri to stay where he was. Across the room Admiral

Gregory was barking out orders. He'd be too busy to handle something like this. But his eyes rested on a commander coordinating responses across the various stations scattered across the room. Isaacson approached him.

"Commander, I need your help."

"Sir?" The lanky man paused between stations.

Isaacson leaned in close to the Commander's ear. "We have a possible security breach. Don't look around. Don't look at the group of senators and dignitaries behind me. In fact, nod a few times and point up at the screen as if you're telling me something helpful."

For the barest moment the Commander's eyes widened and Isaacson almost saw him glance back to Volodin and the senators, but to the man's credit he nodded and pointed up at the screen. "What's this all about, Mr. Vice President?"

"Tell me, Commander, can you do a meta-space scan of this room?"

"Of this room?" said the Commander, blankly, obviously trying to keep the surprise out of his voice.

"You heard me. Scan for meta-space signals originating from this room."

"But how is that even possible, sir?"

Isaacson glanced back at Volodin, and winked. "I don't know. But humor me."

CHAPTER FIFTY-EIGHT

Near Earth
Bridge, ISS Constitution

The odds went from impossible, to … Granger squeezed his head between his hands, trying to think through the growing pain. What came after impossible? Especially when he was fresh out of ideas and pushed into a corner, with his body breaking down at a rate that rivaled the battered old ship around him?

"I'm open to suggestions," he said, glancing at Proctor, and around at the rest of the bridge crew.

Ensign Prince turned around. "Ram them."

"Ram them?" Granger raised an eyebrow. "Suicide run?"

"Their armor is strong, but not as strong as ours. Maybe we can cripple them one by one, and—" He trailed off, realizing his idea sounded foolish and desperate now that he said it out loud. "Sorry, sir."

"No, Ensign, you're right. We may get to the point where

we will all have to do exactly what Lieutenant Miller just did. We may have to sacrifice the *Constitution*. But not yet." He turned back to Proctor. "Anyone else?"

"Sir!" Lieutenant Diaz had stood up, tapping the controls on his console furiously. "It's the aliens. It's…." He trailed off.

"What is it, Lieutenant?" Granger turned to the screen to see for himself.

The two remaining ships were leaving. Plowing through the debris field, darting away from the handful of IDF ships that still limped along, firing feeble blasts at the fleeing ships.

"Are they retreating?" asked Proctor.

Granger shook his head. "No. They're heading towards Earth." He looked at the distant globe far below. *Valhalla Station* had been in an orbit about double that of a geosynchronous orbit, so the surface was still a good fifty thousand kilometers away, but the continents, and even several large cities were clearly visible.

Lieutenant Diaz nodded. "Confirmed. And the four new ships haven't even slowed down. They flew past twenty seconds ago and never even fired a shot at any of us." He tapped a few more buttons. "And they're heading"—he looked up at Granger—"straight towards Earth. Western hemisphere."

They were relentless. The aliens were not going to even stop to mop up the remains of the fleet that had met them at *Valhalla Station*, but were going straight for the prize. Right to the endgame.

"Engine status?"

The engineering officer on duty shook his head. "We lost main engine power during the battle, sir. Got hit pretty hard back there. I can give you ten percent thrust. If that."

Granger frowned. "How fast does that get us down to low Earth orbit?"

"We've got Earth's gravity working for us here, but even so, all we can manage is one-point-two g's. We can't match the aliens—in fact, they're already almost there...."

In desperation, Granger thumbed the comm. "Rayna, bridge. Please tell me the caps have had enough time to recharge for another q-jump."

A few moments of shouting and clanking sounded over the speakers before Commander Scott's voice fluttered through the bridge. "Well, Cap'n, I got good news and bad news."

"Fine. What's the good news?"

"I can get you down to low Earth orbit pretty quickly. We've built up enough charge for a short q-jump."

"Brilliant." He hesitated. "And, the bad news?"

She didn't answer for a few seconds, and when she did, it sounded like she was trying to hold back tears. The *Constitution* was hers as much as it was his, but his chief engineer had always had a more emotional attachment to her, like she was her baby. "We got hit pretty hard in that battle, sir. Cracked the containment vessel clean in half. We're not spewing radiation … yet. But we will be once we make this jump, sir, and when we do, it'll be her last."

The words sank into the bridge crew. This would be the last journey of the *Constitution*. Granger had been holding out hope the last two weeks that somehow they'd be able to put off decommissioning. That something would unexpectedly come up. Some clerical or administrative issue would be discovered that would buy the *Constitution* an extra month. An extra week.

The aliens returned, and it bought the Old Bird an extra day.

"Understood, Rayna. Make preparations to execute jump. Get your people out of there—once that thing loses containment, I want the core ejected before it goes critical."

"Got it, Cap'n," she replied—Granger could hear the hint of a sniffle. "It'll be a few minutes. If we don't take a few precautions we'll just explode in q-space, half of our molecules showing up and the other half staying here. I'll let you know. Scott out."

Granger turned to Proctor. "Are the weapons crews reloading?"

"Already on it, sir." She'd been issuing orders during his conversation with Commander Scott, and he nodded his approval. "And we should check on the escape pods. Get a few people from ops to make sure they're all operable—some may have been damaged during the fight."

"Aye, sir."

"And get a repair crew on the lasers that can be fixed up in the next ten minutes. Looks like those bastards are vulnerable to them, but only if we've punched through their armor first." He turned to tactical. "Incorporate that into your firing patterns. Puncture with the mag-rails, then boil the shit out of them with the lasers through the holes we punch."

The seconds ticked by inexorably, slowly, and every moment felt like he was abandoning some North American city to a hopeless, cruel, fiery fate. Surely the alien ships had arrived by now, and he doubted there were any ships left to defend their planet—everything had been sent to *Valhalla Station*. The aliens had free rein over the entire surface. There were a few orbital defense platforms, sure, and the surface defenses were nothing to sniff at, but the planetary defense command had no chance against the forced singularity weapon. Nothing did, except mass. Lots of it.

It was up to *Constitution*, and *Constitution* alone.

Unless….

"This is Captain Granger," he said, thumbing the comm open to a wide signal. "All remaining ships in fighting condition, report in." He'd forgotten about the remnants of the fleet—all of the remaining vessels were severely damaged, most drifting listlessly. But there may have been one or two with q-jump capabilities. Any help was better than none.

A voice crackled over the comm. "Captain French reporting in, commanding the *ISS Picayune*. We're limping, Granger, but we've got some fight in us yet."

Granger nodded. Good—the *Picayune* was just a light cruiser, but perhaps hiding in the shadow of the *Constitution* she could pelt the enemy with enough mag-rail slugs to make shielding her worth it.

Another voice sounded out. "This is Captain Wei. *ISS Xinhua*, reporting for battle, Captain. We've lost main thrusters, and all mag-rails. But we can q-jump in with you, and have nearly all laser turrets operational, and half a fighter wing we can bring to bear."

"Good to hear it, Captain." He scanned his command board, and, seeing the status of the remaining ships, realized he probably wouldn't be hearing from anyone else. The rest were too damaged to help. And given that their captains weren't responding, their bridges were probably destroyed anyway.

"Captain Granger! Long time no see!"

A third voice boomed out of the speakers. Granger glanced at his board again to see which ship was the source, but none of the ships which had survived the battle were signaling.

"Who's this?" he said, standing up.

"You old bastard, don't you remember your own roommate at the academy?"

"Pickens? Is that you? I thought you retired!" he replied with a broadening smile.

"Yeah. Funny that—I just recalled myself. Looked like we could use a little help, and they only mothballed the *Congress* a year ago. I made a call to Admiral Zingano before *Valhalla* blew, asked if I could have a skeleton crew to fly to the rescue, and the rest is ancient history. Ancient being four hours ago."

Granger's jaw dropped slightly. "You recommissioned the *Congress* in under four hours? She's space worthy?"

"Hell, she wasn't exactly space worthy when I commanded her. These Legacy Fleet ships are basically just hollowed-out asteroids with a few guns bolted to the sides. But their systems are so simple that all we did was blow off the dust, execute a hard restart of the engines, and off we went. Given the emergency, I didn't pay much attention to the finer details like, well, oxygen regenerators and food and shit. But I figured we were just going to die in a few hours, so what the hell, right?" He laughed darkly, which made Granger chuckle along with him, in spite of the dire situation.

"The Legacy Fleet. All back together, huh?" Granger beamed. "All we need is the *Warrior*, the *Chesapeake,* and the *Independence*, and we've got the band back together. It only took a hundred years and two alien invasions."

"Shit, at this rate we'll resurrect the *Victory.*" She was the first ship to fall to the aliens during the first invasion, and a giant memorial stood to her in the middle of Salt Lake City, near where she'd crashed.

"Where are you, Bill?" Granger didn't see the other ship on his console—if she was anywhere near, he'd see her, since, as one of the *Constitution*'s twins, she'd be detectable from hundreds of thousands of kilometers around.

"Still in dry dock, of course. Sitting on our supports just outside of Omaha."

"You're still on the ground in *Omaha?*"

"We just shooed the last of the tourists out a few hours ago and got emergency responders to clear a ten-kilometer radius around us just in case."

Granger frowned. "In case of what?"

"In case we blow up Omaha by q-jumping directly out of dry dock, of course."

CHAPTER FIFTY_NINE

Near Earth
Bridge, ISS Constitution

Things were dire. But just a shade less dire than an hour ago. With the *ISS Congress* about to join them in their showdown with the aliens in low Earth orbit, there would finally be two hardened targets to present to the invaders instead of just one. The *Congress* didn't have a ton of mag-rail slugs, but it had enough for at least ten minutes of battle. Which, Granger thought grimly, would be just about right if things went how he expected.

"Proctor, Zheng, have we analyzed the data intel from the last singularity explosion yet?"

Lieutenant Zheng nodded excitedly. "It's not just quantum coupling, sir. It's quantum entanglement. I can't believe I didn't realize it earlier, given how they seem to be able to teleport the thing underneath the surface of a planet—they're not launching it at all, and the quantum efficiency of the inter-

atomic exchange is just phenomenal. I wouldn't be surprised if
—"

"Lieutenant," Granger interrupted with a stern glare. "Save
the science lesson for another time. Cut to the chase."

Only slightly perturbed—as Zheng was one of the
longest-serving members of the *Constitution*'s crew and was
used to Granger's prickly style—he continued. "The alien ships
—they not only have to couple their reactors with the
singularity during its growth, they're also connected with each
other. And that connection is more than just a weak bond. It's
actually quite strong, though it decreases linearly with distance
—which is why in all instances we've witnessed its creation the
alien ships have been huddled tightly into a group."

"And when the singularity explodes, it sends energy back
along the link?" Granger was standing, and now pacing
excitedly. "Is that how we can take them out?"

"Not too fast, sir. It's important to understand exactly
what's going on when a mass hits one of these singularities.
We've observed that when one of our mag-rail slugs passes the
Schwartzchild radius—that's the event horizon—nothing
happens, except the blasted thing grows bigger. But when a
sufficiently massive object—many times more massive than the
singularity itself—say, Lunar Base, or the *Rainbow*—makes
contact with the singularity, something very interesting
happens. In fact, Yanukov Polenski theorized last century that
when enough mass fell into a small black hole at a sufficiently
elevated rate, the effect was that all the mass approaches
relativistic speeds within a few microns of the center, bounces
off each other, and locally creates perturbations in the
gravitational field, which rapidly and catastrophically grow until

the mass and energy is all ejected at once, gravity be damned."

Granger was getting impatient. *Scientists.* "Right. That's what we've been witnessing. The singularity destroys itself when we hit it with anything bigger than a fighter."

"Exactly. But the question is what happens to the ships that are still linked to it. From this data,"—he tapped his screen—"I can't be one hundred percent sure, but I think we see quantum feedback transmitted into the cores of the other ships. The nearest one that was damaged, it looked like it was roughed up from the outside—which it was, but the greater damage was on the interior. They lost core containment for several seconds. That's probably why their laser dampening field failed—they had no power for the crucial few seconds after that blast, so when we hit the damage zones with lasers, there was nothing to stop the beams from cutting right into the core."

Granger stroked his chin and stopped pacing. "Lieutenant, do you think if we hit it with something bigger—say, a light cruiser or a medium-sized asteroid, or a missile or torpedo from the surface—could we destroy the ships outright?"

Zheng shrugged. "No idea. Makes sense—may as well try. What else have we got?"

"We've got the *Congress.* Between us two, and the smattering of ships IDF can scramble up last minute, we just might pull it off."

"Against six alien ships?" Proctor motioned towards the screen, where, magnified, they saw the ominous, massive alien vessels slow as they entered low Earth orbit. A swarm of fighters had flown up to meet them and in response the advancing ships disgorged what seemed like thousands of their own fighters—reminiscent of the old vids from the first Swarm War—and now there was an intense fighter battle raging. But with nothing to stop the main ships, there was nothing to prevent them from repeating the destruction of Lunar Base all over the planet.

Starting, apparently, with Miami. The Florida peninsula sprawled out below them, and the massive city occupying the southern tip looked suddenly small and vulnerable against the threat approaching from above.

"Rayna," Granger said, tapping his comm, "you all ready down there?"

"Almost, Cap'n. Just leaving now. I'll transfer remote control to the bridge and run things from down there. Give me a few more minutes."

He drummed his fingers on his armrest. Impatience gnawed at him. Not impatience. Urgency. Millions were about to die unless they did something. Anything.

Proctor apparently noticed his fidgeting. "Nervous?"

He cleared his throat, and coughed a few more times. "Commander, I've been nervous for fifteen years. Ever since I saw firsthand what my own government, what my own fleet, was willing to sacrifice and ignore and lie about all in the name of stability and progress."

She nodded. "The Khorsky incident?"

He only stared at the screen, watching the alien ships grow smaller against the vast backdrop of the blue globe below. "The Russians had been building up their military in the Khorsky Sector for years, in violation of treaty. But did the higher ups tell us? Did they warn us? No. What the hell was I supposed to think? Every indicator pointed to a resurgent

Swarm. And then, when I detected massive fleet movements towards Britannia, what was I supposed to do? Sit by and idly watch the Swarm invade?"

"But it was the Russian fleet on a training exercise," she said. If she was judging him, there was no indication in her voice.

"It was the Russian fleet, on a training exercise," he repeated. "But in newly designed ships. Newly designed fighters. Completely new. Like nothing we'd seen before. What the hell was I supposed to think?"

"You could have signaled fleet intel and asked for guidance —"

"Everything was jammed. Nothing in or out. But I knew that, whatever they were, they couldn't have been there without IDF's knowledge. And permission. If it was the Russians building an unauthorized new fleet, then why were we letting them? If it was the Swarm embedded firmly within our space, preparing an attack, why the hell were we letting them? But the bureaucrats behind their desks at IDF were too busy angling for promotions and service medals to care." Granger looked from the screen back to Proctor. "So I forced the issue. I ordered my carrier, and Abe's frigate, into a confrontation. Intercepted them."

"And people died."

She had kept her tone neutral. He nodded. "People died. We q-jumped right into their path, caught them with their pants down, and they fired. We launched our fighters. They launched theirs, and by the time IDF showed up with the Russian ambassador, we had a full-on orbital battle going on over Vitaly Three." He turned back to the screen, looking for the telltale sign of any forced singularities. "I was escorted out of the Khorsky Sector by our flagship, and faced a whole table of admirals back at *Valhalla Station*. But did I get a commendation for uncovering the fact that the Russians had violated treaty? That they were rapidly building up their forces? Developing new offensive technologies? New directed-energy weapons? New inertial cancelers? All outside of the purview of IDF, which they are supposedly full participatory members of? No. They threatened me with court-martial. In essence: shut up, or you'll be locked up until you rot."

Proctor shuffled uncomfortably. "Maybe there were negotiations happening behind the scenes. Maybe IDF knew about their fleet and treaty violations all along, and you stumbling onto the situation might have made things worse. Set back the secret diplomacy."

"Bull. Last time I checked, we live in a democracy. That's what the Senate is for—not that I trust the politicians, but the way I see it is if they really had no idea what was going on, then I did them a favor, and if they did know what the Russians were up to, then they deserved to be exposed."

The old memories were making him angry, boiling up inside of him. That was good. It meant he was still alive. Dead men couldn't fight. Only living men, fuming at injustice and enraged at the loss of their fellows, fought, and won wars.

"Cap'n, she's ready," said Commander Scott, greasy in her blackened coveralls. She'd stepped onto the bridge while he was staring at the screen.

"Very good." He tapped the comm again. "Commander Pierce. Are the fighter squadrons ready for one last run?"

"More than ready, sir." The CAG sounded firm, but

distant. The experience of choosing who would die was obviously weighing on him. But no time to grieve, no time to help the man come to terms with the harsh, unforgiving realities of battle. You either buck up and perform your duty, or you die. And sometimes you die anyway. Pierce continued, "And we've picked up a few dozen more fighters from some of the destroyed heavy cruisers and the super-carrier. We're actually past full complement right now—one hundred and twenty fighters at your disposal, sir."

Granger raised an eyebrow. That was some grim math, there. They'd started the day with eighty-two fighters, lost who knows how many dozens of fighters in the ensuing two battles, and ended the day with forty more than they started. "Very good, Commander. Granger out." He turned to the gun crews. "Are we reloaded?"

"Aye, sir," came the response.

Granger cleared his throat, and stood up. Time for one last speech. He tapped the comm.

"This is the captain. We're about to reengage with the enemy."

He hesitated, swore, and shook his head. To hell with speeches. "Go kick their asses. Granger out."

Proctor raised an eyebrow at him. "Short and sweet. I like it."

Facing the screen, and pointing towards navigation, he swept his finger towards the front of the bridge as he gave the order to q-jump. "Ensign, initiate q—"

His knees buckled, and his vision blurred before he fell. He heard sounds come out of his mouth, but couldn't understand the words.

The last thing he saw before his vision went dark was Proctor kneeling over him, shaking his chest, yelling words he couldn't hear.

CHAPTER SIXTY

Near Earth
Bridge, ISS Constitution

The doctor was saying something, and from his face it looked urgent. But for the life of him, Granger couldn't understand a word he was saying.

Could he hear? He closed his eyes and focused on the sounds, and just the fact he was focusing on sounds made him realize he could indeed hear. He opened his eyes again and looked bewilderedly at the doctor, who finally stopped yelling and reached in his bag for something. Moments later he pushed a metasyringe full of some liquid against his arm. The liquid disappeared, and the doctor produced another one and likewise injected him with the contents.

"What the hell is that?" he tried to say. But the sounds he heard come out of his mouth were unintelligible.

Grabbing another few tools, the doctor fixed an electronic device on his forehead, which throbbed with a warm, pulsing sensation, while simultaneously rubbing another instrument against the back of his head.

After what seemed like several minutes, Granger sat up and looked around. Commander Proctor was no longer there, but back at the command station talking with tactical. The doctor was kneeling next to him, holding his arm. "Take it easy, Captain. Don't get up."

"What happened?" he said, and this time he could understand himself, though his words were slightly slurred.

The doctor leaned in close, speaking so that only the two of them could hear. "The metastasis in your brain is pressing up against an area of the frontal lobe responsible for language processing. It's getting bigger, Tim, at an alarming rate."

Granger rubbed his temples. The doctor continued, "I've given you something to deaden the pain—otherwise you'd have a splitting headache right now. And I've used hypersonics to relieve the pressure the tumor is placing on the brain and administered meta-steroidal agents to the affected region to make it more elastic and resilient. That'll help some—you should retain language skills for another few days."

Granger swore. At least he would probably only need another few hours. Enough time to kick the aliens' asses out of the solar system. He planted his fists on the floor and raised himself up to a kneeling position. The doctor moved to stop him, but Granger waved him off. With a wave of dizziness, he stood up.

"Status?" he croaked.

Proctor wheeled around. "Oh, thank god. How is he?" she said to the doctor.

"I said, status!" Granger barked.

"All departments ready for the q-jump command, sir. Every mag-rail reloaded—we even got another one operational while you were down."

"How long was I out?"

"Just ten minutes," she replied. "Looks like you hit your head harder than you thought." She nodded to the doctor. "Will he be all right?"

The doctor shuffled, as if uncomfortable. "Actually, Commander, I'm placing you in charge of the *Constitution*. The captain is unfit for further duty. I—"

"Bullshit," Granger interrupted, taking a threatening step towards the doctor. "I told you, doc, that I'll step aside as soon as the immediate emergency has passed, but not a second earlier. Now get your ass off the bridge before I order the marines to drag you off in irons."

The doctor shook his head. "No. When it comes to your health and fitness for duty, my authority trumps yours, sir. I hereby remove you from duty and order you to sickbay." He turned to Proctor. "Commander, you are now acting CO."

Granger took another step towards the doctor, seething. "You can't do this," he whispered through gritted teeth.

The doctor tried to remain emotionless. "Your judgement is impaired, sir. I'd be remiss in my duties and endangering the lives of everyone on board if I allowed you to continue as CO."

With an aggressive finger jabbing at the viewscreen, Granger yelled: "Those Cumrat bastards out there are the ones endangering our ship, not her captain! Can't you understand that, you imbecilic quack?" He immediately regretted the words, but there was no taking them back as he was standing toe to toe with the doctor, yelling in his face, as the rest of the bridge crew stared tensely in silence, collectively holding their breath.

"Captain," the doctor whispered, "don't make me escort you off the bridge by force."

"If Haws were up here, he'd beat the snot out of you, you know that?" Granger spat.

"Captain," the doctor sighed heavily. "Commander Haws is dead."

CHAPTER SIXTY-ONE

Low Earth Orbit
Bridge, ISS Constitution

Granger stumbled backward, stunned. He'd been preparing himself mentally for that eventuality, of course, but he hadn't expected it to happen so fast. So soon. There just wasn't enough time. No time.

The doctor continued, "And unless you want the same fate for us all, I suggest you follow me to sickbay."

Still too stunned for words, Granger speechlessly nodded. The doctor turned and made for the bridge's sliding doors. Granger followed, trying to hide the sway in his step and his eroding sense of balance from the bridge crew.

"Commander," he said to Proctor as he walked out the door. He wanted to save his ship. He wanted to give one last piece of advice, one more insight or strategic move she could make that would shift the odds of the battle, but nothing came.

"Beat the shit out of them."

Her face was like stone, but she straightened her back and saluted. "Aye, sir." He turned to leave for good. Her voice followed him out the door. "Thank you, sir."

The walk to sickbay was the longest he'd ever taken. He knew it was only three minutes away, but since he had to pick his path through debris and wreckage and dodge the occasional damage control team dashing through the hallway, it seemed like it was half an hour later that he sat down on an examination bed in sickbay, right next to another bed with a blanket-draped figure lying on top.

He knew, instinctively, who it was. The doctor said something Granger didn't pay attention to, then ducked out of the room, leaving Granger alone with his thoughts, and the body of his best friend.

"Damn it all, Abe," he mumbled, standing next to the bed. "Look where we've ended up. I always thought I'd be the one to go first. Thought nothing could take you down. Thought you'd stare death in the face, and that death would shit its pants, turn tail, and run screaming to get away from you, you crazy old bastard." He stared at the unmoving form, silently listening to the rumble of distant explosions. "Now look at you."

They were in a small examination room within sickbay, and he could hear the bustle outside in the central care area as the doctors and nurses rushed from patient to critical patient, trying to save the lives of the trauma and severe burn victims. He had a vague sense of the damage from the previous battle —he knew they were hit hard, but he hadn't yet had time to review the casualties or damage reports, much less tour the most heavily hit areas. The sounds from next door confirmed to him that they were in a bad way.

He turned to the medical station next to the bed, and brought up his charts. Scrolling through the various test results and scan images, he settled on a picture of his lungs. Riddled through with black and mottled-red tumors, the healthy tissue was lost in the sea of cancer and necrotic flesh. It was a wonder he was still alive, much less walking around. "Wyatt said we could have prevented this. But I delayed. I procrastinated. I never came in for my scans. And now, this. Stage ten thousand cancer. And you know why I didn't get those scans?" He looked back at the blanket-draped figure. "I was scared of dying. Terrified. Didn't want to face it. Didn't want to acknowledge it might happen—that I'd be forced to retire, confined to a hospital bed and get bed sores all over my ass. And then, boom. Nothing. No thoughts. No feeling. No existing. Just … nothing."

The ship rumbled. They'd entered battle—he knew.

And he knew there was no chance they'd survive. Zero. None.

And for the first time in decades, staring from the tumor-plagued picture of his lungs to the draped figure of his dead friend, feeling the violent, distant blasts that he knew all too well meant the aliens were hitting them with the unstoppable, deadly, green energy beam, he sobbed, and sat down on his bed, utterly exhausted.

Dammit. What the hell am I doing? he thought, bitterly. *Get off your ass and stop blubbering like a child, you moron,* he swore at himself. He raked his fingertips across his face and gripped his hair in frustration.

Getting old was a bitch. Dying was a bitch.

He inhaled deeply—*damn the pain!* He jumped off the bed and ripped the blanket off his friend, revealing the cold, blue figure of Abraham Haws. His eyes were closed. His temple dented.

"Damn you! Abe! Damn you! Where the hell are you when I need you!" He pounded twice on his friend's chest, then rested his hand on the stiff shoulder, gripping it tight.

The deck rumbled, even more violently than before, and he heard distant explosions. Without a doubt, he knew, the ship had been breached again by the aliens' energy beam.

His people were dying. And he was sitting on his ass.

Bent low to his friend's ear, he whispered hoarsely, "I won't let them. I promise, you'll be the last one I'll bury. You're the last one they'll get."

And without another word, wiping his eyes and squaring his chin, he strode out into the main care area. The doctor intercepted him. "Oh no, you don't, sir."

"Doctor," he said, taking the man by the shoulder and looking him in the eye, "I'm afraid you don't understand the gravity of our situation—"

"Look, Captain, I've already told you, it doesn't matter how grave it is, you can't be commanding the ship in your state. I just won't—"

"Shut your damn mouth and listen to me, Armand. I'm not trying to get command back. I'm trying to save the life of everyone in sickbay. This battle here? This is it. This ship is going down, and it's going down fast. Minutes, not hours."

The doctor's eyes narrowed as he processed what Granger was saying, and he started to shake his head as if in disbelief. Granger continued, "It's true. We don't stand a snowball's chance in hell against that alien fleet. We're dead in twenty minutes. And there's no escape—the engines are damaged beyond repair." He pointed to all the patients lying in beds and on tables. "We've got to get these people to escape pods. When the evac order comes from the bridge we won't have nearly enough time to save them all. But if we start now, we might."

"You're sure?"

"Dead sure." The irony of his reply was not lost on him.

The doctor regarded him once more, then spun around to his staff, who had all paused to eavesdrop. "Get everyone here to the escape pods. Five patients and one medical staff per pod. Move!"

Every doctor and nurse sprang into action, organizing the wounded into groups for the pods—the critical patients were distributed evenly to all the pods such that they could continue receiving more intense care from a doctor or nurse, and the less seriously wounded filled in from there. Doctor Wyatt oversaw the operation, grabbing what supplies he thought he needed for any eventuality—Granger heard him mutter something about surviving in the wild in case all the major cities were destroyed. Would it come to that? Of course it would, he knew, if the *Constitution* failed. If he failed.

And in all the bustle and confusion, Granger quietly slipped out the door.

CHAPTER SIXTY-TWO

Low Earth Orbit
X-25 Fighter Cockpit

For the third time that long day, Lieutenant Volz wove in and out, through and under and around the thousands of alien fighters that had come pouring out of the intruding ships, which had seemingly been holding back their swarming hordes until the very end.

And half his squad was gone—Fishtail and Pluck both lost in the previous engagement, and Hotbox in the one before that. "Dogtown, pull up hard. I'll knock those bogeys off your tail!"

He squeezed off a few shots, and the two alien fighters erupted in a cloud of debris, leaving Dogtown free to swing around and blast his way through a few bogeys angling for one of the laser turrets on the *Constitution*.

In spite of the thousands of ships disgorged by the alien cruisers, things didn't seem quite so hopeless this time, at least in the fighter battle. Hundreds, possibly up to a thousand IDF fighters had risen up from the surface to join them, mobilized to defend Earth. They may have been without capital ship support, but they were making the aliens pay a punishing price for their intrusion into low-Earth orbit.

"This is Commander Pierce. All *Constitution* fighter squadrons, join with Eagle Wing from Fort Walton and focus all firepower on the alien ship at twenty mark two."

Volz muttered under his breath—he saw how badly the *Constitution* was being pounded by the alien fleet and knew if they pulled off to assault the alien cruiser the Old Bird's time would be even shorter. "Come on, Ballsy," said Dogtown, "let's get over there and put the little bastard out of its misery."

He gunned his thrusters, and darted away from the *Constitution* in a blaze of ion-drive fire. On his port side, he saw another cloud of fighters rise up from the Florida peninsula. Eagle Wing. Just in time to join the assault on the alien cruiser Pierce had indicated. They numbered some five or six dozen Y-52's, and before he had time to catch his breath, the battle was back on.

"This is Commander Kruger of Eagle Wing. Hello, boys! We'll tackle the bow if you guys will handle the stern. Let's take this bitch out!"

They swarmed over the alien cruiser, pelting it with hundreds, thousands of streams of fire, ignoring the hordes of bogeys that had diverted from the main fighter battle to scare them off.

An explosion out his starboard viewport made him wince. Damn—that was one of the *Qantas's* fighters. Caught in a crossfire.

They were being torn apart. By focusing all their attention on the alien cruiser, the fighters were being picked off one by one.

But it was working. Judging by the way the massive ship started to list to starboard, the cumulative effect of all their fire was having a devastating effect on it. "Keep it up, boys!" came Commander Pierce's voice over his headset.

And in a piercing explosion, it was over. The shockwave of the alien ship blasting into two pieces caught him in its wake, and for a moment he thought it was the end, but his fighter's containment held, and he darted away out of the blast field before getting punctured by high-velocity debris.

"Oh, no...." Commander Kruger, of Eagle Wing, moaned through the speaker. "No. No. No."

Ballsy looked around, seeing a swarm of alien fighters on his scopes, but that was normal.

Then he saw it.

The familiar shimmering white globe that had begun to form between the invading ships had disappeared. And judging from the massive brown and black cloud over the southern tip of Florida, he knew exactly where it had gone.

Pierce's voice shouted over the comm. "All fighters! Get your asses to the ship at forty-two mark five! We can't let another singularity through!"

Dear lord. The cloud was enormous. It spread and mushroomed higher and higher, looking like the old footage of the first Swarm War, when the aliens struck multiple cities with thermonuclear warheads.

But this was far bigger. Far more devastating. Destruction on an unthinkable scale.

It was hell on Earth.

"Roger," he said. "Let's get the hell over there, Dogtown."

How many had just died? How many lives snuffed out in an instant? How many more were screaming, terrified, as the blast zone continued to expand outward, ripping apart neighborhoods and communities and towns?

He shook his head. No. He couldn't think about that. Not yet.

Squeezing off a few shots at some passing bogeys, he veered towards the next alien cruiser. On his status screen, he saw that they'd lost over forty fighters in that last assault, and they were down to less than eighty.

The odds were not in their favor.

CHAPTER SIXTY-THREE

Low Earth Orbit
Engineering Section, ISS Constitution

Granger stumbled down the hallway. He'd wanted nothing more than to take Haws with him into one of the soon-to-be departing escape pods, and hopefully arrange for a proper burial once they were on Earth, but it was not to be.

As it was, he was huffing and sputtering for lack of air just to make it down ten decks. The damn Swarm energy beam had cut clear through the main lift. Stopping every deck for a breath, he cursed himself for not getting a secondary lift installed like his XO had demanded five years ago. He thought it unnecessary at the time, but was now regretting his obstinacy. How had Haws put up with him all these years?

Hell, they'd put up with each other—the other man was no picture of perfection himself.

"Are we going to die, Captain?"

Granger nearly stumbled over someone crouched near an

open door on a landing. No, he wasn't crouched, he was just short.

"Cornelius?"

"We're going to die out here, aren't we?" His small face looked pained and he spoke softly. A far cry from the incorrigible boy back at Lunar Base.

I am, he thought, but he said, "You will do no such thing."

"But the ship keeps shaking. I can hear explosions. They … they say the aliens are going to blow up the ship!"

"Over my dead body. Son, I'm going to get you off this ship, get you safely back to Earth, and then I'm going to kick their asses. Got it?" He remembered the boy had liked short, vulgar speeches, and sure enough, his face broke into a small smile. "Look, Dexter, don't worry. You'll grow up and race your motorcycles. But first we have to get you and your classmates off the ship. Where's your teacher?"

Dexter pointed through the open door, down a hallway where Granger saw the teacher trying to keep twenty other schoolchildren calm inside another small conference room. He motioned the woman out into the corridor. "Get the children and follow me. We've got to get you all into escape pods."

A minute later Granger, Dexter, the teacher, the *Rainbow*'s captain, and twenty children were rushing down the hall. Granger pushed a button on a control panel along the wall, exposing two escape pods. He ushered the teacher into one with ten children, and the *Rainbow*'s captain into the second with the ten others.

Dexter was the last to climb in. He looked a little less scared than a minute ago, but his face was still drained of color. "Later, Captain. Go kick their asses."

Granger winked at him. "Watch your mouth. And"—he nodded—"I will."

The hatch closed and he ensured the pods' engines fired before continuing down the hall towards the stairwell. With a deep, painful sigh, he started the long descent, wincing with each rumble and explosion as the ship sustained more direct hits from the Swarm invasion force. Proctor had better be giving them a pounding in return.

He stopped—it was deck fifteen, and he knew that beyond the door at the opposite end of the hallway from the stairwell was *Afterburners* and the observation deck. Huge windows spanned the length of the exterior wall. It was one of the very few places on the ship not guarded by ten meters of solid tungsten armor—here, it was only two meters, and was recessed behind the giant doors to the fighter bay such that, while still affording an excellent view, the windows were not as exposed as they might have been in other areas of the hull.

Hesitating, he made his decision, and jogged the length of the hallway, just to catch a quick view. Get a feel for the lay of the field of battle before he made it to his destination.

The doors slid aside, opening his view up to the wall of windows that looked down on the battle raging outside.

Earth was there. Close, and immediate. It filled up nearly the entire view from the windows.

And the battle raged. Somehow, IDF had managed to scramble up another handful of ships. Not as large as the fleet at *Valhalla Station* had been, but formidable nonetheless. Nearby, less than a kilometer away, floated one of the alien ships, and it was taking a beating from the *Constitution's* mag-rail batteries.

But it, and one of its fellows was walloping the *Constitution* in return, lancing it with the now familiar deadly green energy beam. A fighter screamed past the window, and Granger jumped as it exploded when another green beam shot straight through it and slammed into the hull just a hundred yards to stern. The explosion nearly threw him off his feet, and he steadied himself against the wall.

He counted. One, two, three, four.... Four. Somehow, against all hope, Proctor had managed to take out two whole alien capital ships by herself. Well, probably with the help of Captain Pickens on the *Congress*.

Searching the field of battle for the *Congress*, he almost thought it had already been destroyed. It was nowhere to be seen. Just four alien ships, a handful of IDF heavy and light cruisers, along with a small fleet of frigates and gunships, and a swarm of fighters, both IDF and Swarm. But no *Congress*.

He caught his breath when he saw her. She drifted out from behind the shadow of one of the alien ships, nearly engulfed in flames shooting out of what looked like a hundred holes dotting her hull.

"No...."

Another green beam lanced out from the alien ship nearest it and ripped into the forward section of the *Congress*'s hull. The old ship spewed more debris and flame. It lurched.

Moments later, one of its massive rear thrusters exploded, sending the ship into a tailspin as it descended towards the Earth. The faint glow of compressed air lit up like a shell around it as it hurtled through the upper atmosphere, tumbling out of control.

More green beams blasted out from the alien ships

towards the *Constitution* and the ship rocked violently.

It was nearly time. He turned and bolted back down the hallway, and took the stairs two at a time at a speed that would have tired him out thirty years ago.

At last, he rounded the final turn and stepped out onto the landing in front of his destination. Two marines stood at attention as he approached. "Sir!"

"As you were." He stepped forward.

They didn't move.

"I'm sorry, sir. No one can go in there. Radiation levels are too high."

"I know, son. Stand aside. In fact,"—he looked back up the stairwell—"you're dismissed. Go help the injured to escape pods. The battle's nearly over."

The marines looked nervously at the door, then back to him. "Don't worry," Granger went on, "I'll lock it from the inside. No one will get in."

"But, sir, you'll die in there."

He smiled. And it was a genuine smile. "A captain's got to go down with his ship, son. Once you're all evacuated, there's something I have to do. Go." He pointed back up the stairs, where he could hear the frantic sounds of pounding footfalls and agonized shouting as the injured were dragged out of the damaged sections just above them.

The two marines looked at each other, back at him, and then ran up the stairs, leaving Granger alone outside the doors.

Did he really want to do this? The radiation would kill him within half an hour. He could just wait until the ship was deserted and carry out his plan from the bridge.

No. He was a dead man anyway. He'd made his decision.

There was nothing to fear from the radiation. Nothing could hurt him now. Not even the bloody Swarm. It was remarkable —once he had taken his life into his own hands, once he had decided to face his mortality, he was invincible.

With a smile—his first real smile in weeks—he passed his credentials over the ID reader. The doors slid aside with a groan, and he stepped forward into the warm flood of radiation that bathed engineering.

CHAPTER SIXTY-FOUR

Low Earth Orbit
Engineering, ISS Constitution

It was strange—he couldn't feel the deadly bite of the radiation. There was no indication whatsoever that he was absorbing many dozens of times the accepted yearly dose of radiation every second. But almost as soon as he stepped into engineering, his head lightened, his vision stabilized, and his purpose and final mission became crystal clear.

He dashed across the room to bring up the ship's status schematic, and immediately saw that the situation was dire. Decompression on nearly a dozen decks. Systems failing. Main power gone. Most mag-rails inoperable. Life support on the fritz.

The *Constitution*'s time had come.

And so had his. It was the Old Bird's time to shine. Theirs, together.

His hand hovered over the comm button, ready to

message Commander Proctor his intentions, but at the last moment thought better of it. She might try to dissuade him, wasting precious seconds she didn't have. No, if he knew her, she'd already ordered most personnel to escape pods. He clicked over to general standing orders, and confirmed his suspicions. There was a general evacuation in effect. All hands to escape pods except for the bridge crew. They would leave last, of course.

A pulsing sensation throbbed through the vast bay. A sensation he recognized very well by that point. In confirmation, he brought up the sensor readings, and nodded. There it was. A forced singularity was forming just three kilometers off the starboard bow, in the middle of the four remaining alien ships.

He scanned the rest of the field of battle and saw the remains of all the ships that had been mustered for this final, desperate fight. They were almost all in pieces, billowing smoke and debris. The few that survived hobbled along, pockmarked and broken, pelting the four remaining alien vessels with whatever paltry, ineffective weaponry they had left.

And the *Congress* continued its flaming descent through the atmosphere, with a fiery tail like a comet.

"Goodbye, Bill," he murmured. "I'm sure you and Proctor made a good team."

Too many goodbyes.

Checking the main engine status, he winced when he saw that five of the six main thrusters were almost completely destroyed. Luckily, the sixth seemed operational. Barely.

The pulsing intensified, indicating the growing size of the singularity. He checked the time. Assuming a similar growth rate to the previous ones, he had less than three minutes.

With a glance at the escape pod status screen he confirmed that nearly all the main pods had launched, leaving the handful reserved for the bridge crew, and soon those, too, began to zip away from the broken and beaten ship.

No, not beaten.

That left one pod. The main command pod, reserved for the CO and a few key bridge officers. He tapped a button on the screen and confirmed it was still operational, but not launched. Had she gone in one of the others?

In answer to his unspoken question, Proctor's voice sounded over the speakers. "If anyone's still here, this is the final warning. Evacuate immediately. The ship will not last more than a few minutes. CO out."

And a moment later, the indicator for the command escape pod turned red, indicating it too had blasted away.

Granger was alone. Just he and the dead. A fit of coughing overcame him, and his hand once again came away dripping red, and a wry, gallows-humor grin tugged at his face—a dead man piloting a dead ship full of the fallen, to save those who still lived.

He pulled up the navigational controls and nodded in approval when he saw that Proctor had set the ship on autopilot, on a heading that would take it directly into the singularity.

But it would not be enough. That was his suspicion, his fear. The aliens would not stand by and permit them to disrupt another singularity, and in confirmation, the ship rocked and shuddered as one of the alien ships laid into the *Constitution* with a full barrage of energy beams. He pulled up the tactical display and watched the four ships, with the singularity in their midst, pull away from him, eluding the autopilot, which, after all, could only move towards a specific point in space—not follow a randomly changing location.

"Oh no you don't. I see you, you bastards."

CHAPTER SIXTY-FIVE

Low Earth Orbit
Command Escape Pod

Commander Proctor settled into one of the cramped seats on the escape pod, gritting her teeth against pain—she'd twisted her ankle during the last violent barrage of fire from the aliens.

"Heading?" asked Ensign Prince, who squeezed into the limited nav controls—escape pods weren't built for maneuverability, rather escape, but they could at least guide the craft towards a target.

Proctor racked her brain, trying to think of the most appropriate destination. If her last gambit didn't succeed and the *Constitution* failed to disrupt the alien ships by slamming into the singularity, then Earth was doomed, and in a sense it mattered very little where they landed. In that scenario, it might make the most sense to steer towards a lightly populated wilderness area in an attempt to evade the alien's destruction and live to fight another day.

But if the plan succeeded, IDF would regroup, and this surely would not be the last wave of Swarm vessels. If Earth survived the day, it would need to prepare itself for the unavoidable reprisal that would soon follow.

"Omaha. CENTCOM HQ was destroyed in the singularity explosion under Miami. Omaha is the auxiliary HQ, and is where IDF will regroup, most likely."

"Aye, sir. Setting course for Omaha."

The atmosphere started blazing around them as the compression shock wave enveloped the pod, and the little craft shook violently. The things were not designed with comfort in mind, only survival.

"Sir! They're firing on the *Constitution*!"

Proctor craned her neck to look out the tiny viewport. Sure enough, the alien ship was pounding the Old Bird with a heavy barrage of its energy weapon, blasting chunks off into space. The fresh punctures briefly belched fire before the deadening vacuum of space quenched the flames.

"It's not going to help, you bastards," she muttered to herself, smiling darkly.

But then her heart sank as she watched the formation of alien ships pull away, with the singularity following them in their midst. They passed over and to starboard of the *Constitution*, moving out of the targeted heading she'd entered into the autopilot.

"Shit," she breathed.

So it was over.

Within a minute, the aliens would teleport the singularity down underneath yet another North American city—most likely Los Angeles, as that was the closest obvious target below them—and after that would continue raining down destruction upon city after city, remorselessly and mercilessly vaporizing human civilization from the map.

And from there the destruction would spread. The Veracruz Sector was most likely already lost, but dozens of other sectors and scores of worlds would follow. And without Earth, without the center of humanity's strength, how could they even think of prevailing against such a deadly and persistent enemy?

"Uh, sir?"

"What now?" she snapped.

Lieutenant Diaz pointed out the viewport. "The *Constitution*. She's changing course."

She jumped to her feet and stared out the window. Sure enough, in a wide arc, the Old Bird soared through the debris field, aiming straight for the shimmering singularity, even as the aliens tried to evade her.

"Impossible." She brought up the sensor display on her tiny console. "I thought you told me no life signs remained on board!"

"That's what the internal sensors said, sir!"

"Then how the hell is that thing changing course?" she hollered, pointing out the window.

The comm beeped softly, and Proctor almost missed the sound in the commotion and the shaking of re-entry. She stared at the amber light indicating the signal. Finally, she tapped it to accept the incoming transmission, still eyeing the old ship out the window suspiciously.

A familiar voice sounded over the speaker, and somehow,

she wasn't surprised in the slightest to hear it. "Commander Proctor. Job well done."

Her voice caught. "Sir, I—"

She didn't know what to say.

"I hope this fireworks display will be worth it—I'm sure giving away the farm here."

Lieutenant Diaz murmured, "He's closing fast. Less than a kilometer now."

"Thank you, sir," said Proctor. "For everything."

"Ah hell, don't get all weepy on me, Commander. The captain goes down with his ship—you know that."

"I'm sorry I tried to take her away from you, Tim."

A silence.

"No. You helped me find her again."

The pulsing light from the singularity intensified, and Proctor knew the aliens were preparing to teleport it to below the surface, deep underneath Los Angeles. Waves of gravitational energy buffeted the escape pod.

The tip of the *Constitution* was close to the singularity, and it started to visibly stretch as the space distorted all around it.

Granger's voice sounded out again, this time distorted by heavy static, but defiant. "Take that, you bastards—"

And several things happened simultaneously.

With a blinding flash, the *Constitution* plunged into the singularity, disappearing in a violent flare. For a split second, the invisible quantum tethers that had connected the singularity with the reactor cores inside the alien ships became visible, shimmering with an unearthly green glow, and in the next moment, all four ships erupted in massive explosions.

Proctor shielded her eyes with a hand. The viewport

dimmed automatically under the intense radiation, but it was still too dazzlingly bright to look at.

When she opened her eyes, the remains of the four deadly alien vessels were smoldering shells, husks of twisted metal and armor, debris and smoke and the alien's organic liquid spewing out into the void. They were gone. Defeated.

The singularity was gone.

The *Constitution* was gone.

Granger was gone.

"The old bastard did it," she murmured.

Somehow, against all odds, he did it. Against overwhelming firepower. Against unthinkable odds.

With an unthinkable sacrifice.

They did it.

She shuddered, angling her head so her two fellow bridge crew members wouldn't see her face as it contorted. When she first boarded the *Constitution*, she thought of her assignment as a chore. An unpleasant little detail that needed doing in order to check a box, to advance her to the next stage of her career, hopefully on to newer and more prestigious ships, where she could travel the galaxy to see hundreds of new worlds. And Granger was the cantankerous old fart that was deliberately standing in her way. Intentionally making her life difficult.

But with the emergency, he changed. He transformed into a leader. And even when humiliated by the doctor's not-so-discrete intervention, he still managed to foresee the inevitable, decide on a plan, and do what needed to be done.

And saved them all.

She touched the viewport, pressing her hand against the spot where the Old Bird had disappeared, taking Granger with it.

Something far off to the side caught her eye. She almost missed it in the atmosphere blazing past the viewport, but the sight of another explosion was unmistakable.

Out of nowhere, a ship snapped out of the ether and into existence, just a handful of kilometers from the destruction of the four ships.

"Impossible…." Proctor stood up again and pressed her nose to the viewport.

It was impossible. The singularity should have chewed up anything caught in its wake.

But there she was. Even more broken and hobbled than she'd looked just moments ago:

The *Constitution*, blazing fire and debris, hurtling down towards the atmosphere.

CHAPTER SIXTY_SIX

Low Earth Orbit
Command Escape Pod

"GET A SENSOR LOCK!" she bellowed at Lieutenant Diaz. "Get a lock, dammit! I want to know if anything's alive over there!"

Her fingers danced across the tiny computer console screen, bringing the emergency thrusters online and pushing them to their limit. "Get us out of the atmosphere!"

"But, sir—"

"NOW!"

"But, sir, we may have descended too far into Earth's gravity well. These things weren't designed to enter orbit." Ensign Prince's face was flushed—he knew what was at stake, Proctor could tell, as his eyes flitted back out the viewport towards the *Constitution*, which itself was falling precipitously towards the atmosphere.

She seethed. "Try. Try, dammit!"

"Trying, sir," he replied, frantically working the controls, desperately trying to arrest their descent and enter orbit.

"Sir," Lieutenant Diaz began, shaking his head in disbelief, "picking up one life sign in engineering. Very faint."

He's alive.

"Ensign Prince, if you don't get us over to that ship in the next two minutes, I'm going to toss you out when we hit the stratosphere."

Ensign Prince's face went white, apparently not picking up on her gallows humor. "I think I can get us over there and intercept her trajectory, but we'll never break our own descent, sir."

"Fine. Get us over there."

She held her breath as the escape pod drifted ever closer towards the *Constitution,* which itself began billowing red and orange compressed atmosphere all around it.

"Are we going to be able to re-dock with the escape pod port through that compression shock front?" Lieutenant Diaz eyed the fiery air streaming past the *Constitution* warily.

"If not, it'll be a hell of a story, won't it?"

And in another thirty seconds, they were there. As soon as the pod hit the compression shock front, the entire craft shook violently, buffeted by the hyper-compressed, ultra-heated air. But the next moment, with another burst of the thrusters, they were in. Nuzzled safely into the port. But safety was relative.

Proctor fingered the controls to open the airlock. Lieutenant Diaz protested and pointed at his console's screen. "Sir, the seal is damaged. We're partially open to vacuum."

"Screw it. I'm going in. You should have enough air if you close the door fast behind me."

"And you, sir?"

She flashed a dark grin. "Guess I'll have to hold my breath." She stood and stepped to the door. "Ready?" They both nodded. She wrenched the lever, and the door burst outward towards the compromised airlock as a rush of air from the escape pod flooded past her.

She sprang out into the airlock and pushed the escape pod's hatch closed with a grunt. She felt the air grow thin as she dashed the two meters across the airlock and opened the hatch into the ship. Another blast of air nearly knocked her over, but gripping the door frame, she pulled herself into the corridor beyond, fighting the air rushing inexorably against her.

With a balled-up fist, she bashed the door controls, which closed the hatch behind her, and the violent wind whipping past calmed considerably.

But it didn't stop. She glanced down the hallway where the wind was going, understanding that there must be a hull breach in that direction.

Turning into the wind, she limped down the debris-littered corridor. She nearly tripped over a figure huddled against the wall, and reached down to feel his neck. At her touch, the figure slumped backward onto the floor—most of the man's face had burned away, along with his clothing and most of his skin. She shuddered, straightened herself, and resumed her sprint to engineering.

She recognized the fighter bay up ahead, which meant that engineering was only three more decks down. The temperature was rising, but, oddly enough, the ride through the atmosphere was strangely smooth. Apparently the buffeting of re-entry was no match for the sheer mass of the *Constitution*.

The Earth's surface, though, would be less forgiving.

Sprinting two steps at a time down the staircase, she felt her lungs scream for air and her sprained ankle protest—she didn't know how much time she had, but the sooner they could get out, the better.

Rounding a loop to another landing, she saw something odd out of the corner of her eye. She'd seen a few more bodies on her mad dash through the ruined ship, but except for the burned man crouched against the wall, they were all laying prostrate.

Down this hallway, which she recognized ended in the *Afterburners* bar on the observation deck, she saw a figure seated in a chair in front of the huge windows that looked out at the maelstrom of atmospheric fire beyond, slumped to the side as if asleep. Was it another body? But why in the world would a body be propped up in a chair in front of the observation deck's windows?

"Captain!"

There was no response. No indication he heard her. Swearing, she half bolted, half limped down the corridor, grabbed his shoulders, and gently shook him.

No response. His head was lolled back and his eyes closed. She felt for a pulse at his carotid, and found it, but it was deathly faint.

"Captain!" she repeated, but he didn't stir.

She eyed the window. The surface of the Earth was looming up closer now. They'd broken through to the stratosphere, and were descending rapidly like a fireball through the sky—the trail of fire stretched away from the window, and she could just glimpse below them the telltale white salt flats of western Utah, and to the northeast, the Great Salt Lake.

Stooping over, she pulled Granger forward and draped him across her shoulders. She'd never carried a man before in her life—just her sister when she was younger when they'd play in the back yard.

With a grunt, she lifted.

He was surprisingly light. Still heavy as a sack of potatoes, but bearable. She'd never noticed what a thin, haggard, rail of a man he was.

She struggled down the hallway, her ankle screaming in pain, racking her brain to remember the location of the nearest escape pods. Would they even be there? Wouldn't they have launched during the evacuation? Only one way to know. At the stairwell landing, she held on to the railing as she descended the remaining level to engineering. The door to the giant bay stood wide open.

Hadn't Commander Scott warned them about lethal levels of radiation? She glanced at the rad warning lights, but they were dark. Normal radiation levels. Odd.

Struggling across the engineering bay, she finally found the airlock that led to the escape pods for engineering.

She checked the control panel outside the door.

They were all gone. Every single pod.

"I think I tried that already," came a murmur from near her shoulder.

"Sir!"

She bent forward and let him down as gently as she could, but he still slid off the last two feet and landed with a grunt on the floor. "Sorry!"

He vaguely waved her off. "Fine. I'm, I'm fine."

"What happened? How did you get up to the observation deck? I found you in *Afterburners!*"

His eyes narrowed, and he shook his head. "Can't remember. But"—he stared at the escape pods—"I know I tried those."

She grit her teeth. There really was only one option. "Then I'll have to guide her down and make a landing."

He closed his eyes. "Sounds like a plan, Commander." He laid his head back down on the deck. "I'm afraid I won't be much help. I'm … I'm tired…."

She dashed across the bay to the computer stations where she could bring up the navigational controls. The indicators showed they were coming in fast. Very, very fast. Somehow, they had to arrest their speed, and come in at a shallower angle. Ships like the *Constitution* weren't designed with aerodynamic landings in mind, but she knew that at least *some* attention was paid to that remote possibility. There were aerilons and flaps that could extend and help guide the descent, and if she could get some engine thrust there was the chance they could make a somewhat controlled landing.

Her fingers danced on the console. All engines were dead. No, wait, engine six was still online. Barely. Applying power to it, slowly so as not the burn out the thruster, she managed to increase the thrust to nearly ten percent. She flipped the thruster into angled mode, which slightly rotated the nozzle direction downward. Between that, the flaps and aerilons, the navigation computer was telling her the ship's speed was slowly decreasing.

But it wasn't enough. They were still coming in at over five hundred meters per second. Supersonic. The atmospheric drag was doing a wonderful job slowing them down, but it wasn't doing it nearly fast enough.

On the monitor, she eyed the Great Salt Lake below them, and on a whim, she retracted the port aerilons and leveled out the one thruster. As expected, the *Constitution* arced to port, beginning a giant spiral down towards the lake.

If she could just make a few loops....

The ship angled towards the north, then west, then swept towards the south, dipping ever lower, until finally, at still well over three hundred meters per second, they hit the water.

The ship lurched. She was thrown into the air, halfway up to the ceiling five meters overhead, and came back down with a crash, feeling her wrist snap under her as she landed.

Grunting against pain, she pulled herself back up to the console and watched the external view on the monitor. The *Constitution* glided like an angry, burning swan over the surface of the vast lake, still moving at just under supersonic speed and sending up giant waves in her wake. But the water was slowing her down quickly. Soon, the ship emerged up onto land, crashing over a superhighway that, thankfully, had been cleared of traffic, then burst through a series of embankments and sailed through onto the wide park-like meridian of the transportation line leading away from the spaceport several kilometers to the west.

They were going to make it. The excitement rose in her chest, into her throat. Daring a glance at the speed indicator, she saw they were under fifty meters per second.

She groaned as she saw the view up ahead. Office towers and skyscrapers. Busy city streets. But even as she watched, the streets cleared as drivers veered off down side streets, pedestrians bolted for cover, and emergency craft flew in front of the *Constitution,* blaring their sirens to warn people of its approach.

They clipped a building, then another, and a third. She had no idea if they survived, but the rattling and rumbling was diminishing, until, finally, the ship ground to a halt. The monitor showed the view ahead of her, and she nearly laughed. Up ahead, just a few dozen meters from where the *Constitution* had come to rest, stood one of the monuments to the *ISS Victory,* towering over the interplanetary business district of south Salt Lake City.

She craned her head back to Granger. "Did it, sir."

He grunted, but fell silent, and lay unmoving on the floor. She dashed over to him, and saw new injuries sustained during the descent.

We're not going to lose you now. Not after all that, she thought.

Not after all that. And especially now that she was noticing some of the details around her. There were strange modifications made to several of the consoles in engineering that she hadn't noticed before. Maybe Commander Scott had made them sometime in the last few hours, but she thought that unlikely. The whole situation was odd, and unnerving. The alterations in engineering, the lack of radiation, the fact that Granger was seated in a chair in *Afterburners* on the observation deck, unconscious. Not to mention the Old Bird's reappearance after being swallowed by the singularity.

We're not going to lose you now, 'cause you got some explaining to do.

CHAPTER SIXTY-SEVEN

Omaha, North America, Earth
Operations Center, IDF Spaceport

Vice President Isaacson kept nodding at Yuri from across the room, hoping that the ambassador's suspicions would not be aroused by how long he was taking. He would have supposed a basic meta-space scan would be a simple matter, but it had been over half an hour since he'd been standing over the communications specialist the Commander had assigned to the job.

And in that half hour the pit grew in his stomach as he saw hell blazing over all the viewscreens on the massive wall. Image after terrifying image of giant gray mushroom clouds from the mysterious Swarm weapon. Miami—thank God Yuri had convinced him not to go there—Mobile, Houston, Phoenix—all gone. At one point he'd been tempted to order a shuttle to take him further north, but the alien fleet stayed well to the south of Omaha, orbiting relentlessly westward along the sunbelt of North America.

Tens of millions lost. If Avery was alive, there was not a chance on Earth she'd stay in office longer than a week. Assuming Earth was still there.

And then, miraculously, the alien ships exploded. No one in the operations center had any explanation, other than furious cheering and shouting and high-fiving. For the moment, no one had any time for explanations. Only relief.

"Mr. Vice President?" He looked down at the communications specialist.

"Yes?"

"I've completed the scan."

"Yes?" He leaned in closer, glancing to the left and right to make sure their conversation was not heard. But in the midst of the celebration it would have been miraculous for anyone to eavesdrop.

"I integrated the scanning over half an hour. If there was any signal during that time, I would have seen it. Sorry, sir, there was nothing."

Another wave of relief passed over Isaacson. He glanced back at the Russian ambassador, who gave him a questioning look. He responded with a shrug, indicating he had no idea where President Avery was, even as he mumbled, "you're absolutely sure? Not one meta-space signal from Omaha in the last half hour?"

"Oh, sure, there was tons of meta-space traffic coming through Omaha—we're the de-facto command and control center for all of IDF now that CENTCOM Miami is gone. We've been in contact with ships and worlds all over United Earth space. But coming from this room? Nothing."

"You're absolutely sure?" he repeated. "What's the resolution? How finely can you pinpoint a signal?"

"A few meters. It's basically just a radio signal converted into a meta-space carrier wave. We can detect the remnant radio wave as it bleeds off the receiver. It's not a strong signal, but still easy enough to pick up and distinguish."

Isaacson nodded. "Good. Thank you, Ensign," he added, glancing at the officer's insignia and unsure of what to call him.

The vague scowl on the officer's face told him he got it wrong, but it didn't matter. Earth was safe. For now. And Yuri was still just Yuri Volodin—not Yuri Volodin the Swarm-influenced agent masterminding Earth's fall. He, Vice President Isaacson, was safe, and in control.

And soon, he could drop the "Vice."

CHAPTER SIXTY-EIGHT

Omaha, North America, Earth
Sally Danforth Veterans Memorial Medical Center

"That's what I'm telling you, Commander. I have absolutely no memory from the time I entered engineering until now."

He was sitting up in bed, trying to enjoy some chicken soup, but his XO, Shelby Proctor, was pestering him for more information.

She needed to relax. They'd won. Against overwhelming odds, they'd won.

Sure, the aliens would be back. But give a man a few moments to enjoy his victory for hell's sake, and at least let him eat his soup! Besides, his head was splitting from the headache he'd had since he woke up. Probably from the damn tumor, or maybe from where he'd bashed it when she'd made her miraculous crash landing.

"Nothing? But surely, sir, you remember talking to me

when I came to get you?"

He shook his head, trying hard to remember. Maybe....

"Yeah, could be. It's all a blur, really."

He glanced out the window—they were back in Omaha, and in the distance, on the horizon, stood the giant support pillars against which had once rested the *ISS Congress*. Other, smaller vessels sat in dry dock, some in various phases of construction.

"Where's the *Congress?*" he asked. "Where did Bill end up?"

She pursed her lips. "Atlantic Ocean. They came in hard and plunged deep into the water about a hundred kilometers off the Azores. But they were all dead long before that."

Granger nodded. A noble sacrifice. At least Bill got to go down in a blaze of glory with his ship. Not like Granger. He'd live for another day. Maybe a week. Maybe a month. But he was still on his way out. Maybe the doc would let him get hospice down on Perdido Key on the Gulf Coast, right on the beach with a margarita in one hand and a cigar in the other. Go out in style.

"I want you to find Abe's body, and get him a proper burial. And I want to be there."

She inclined her head. "Of course. But, sir, you've got to remember. You've got to think. Ask the doctor for something to jog your memory—a cortical stimulant or something. You've *got* to remember." Her voice was urgent, and persistent.

"*Got?* I've *got* to? Tell me, Commander. Don't beat around the bush. What the hell is going on? I can't get any answers out of the IDF debriefer that keeps coming by. Just asks me questions. Same questions as you."

She stared him in the eye, squinting, as if she were wary or distrustful. How odd.

"Ok. This is classified, and they haven't decided to tell you yet, but to hell with them, I'm going to tell you. Court martial or no. You've earned that, at least." She stood up and closed the door to the hospital room, and returned to his bed, leaning in close.

"That serious?" he joked, spooning another mouthful of soup.

"Sir, how long do you think you were gone? After you collided with that singularity?"

"I don't know, maybe a few seconds? That's what Ensign Prince told me when he visited earlier. Told me the *Constitution* disappeared, then reappeared moments later. Like it had q-jumped just a few kilometers away."

She nodded, "Ok, so right away I see something wrong. That's impossible—no q-jumping closer than at least a few thousand ship-lengths. The quantum field just doesn't allow it."

He shrugged, slurping another spoonful. "Fine. But it's a frickin' singularity. All rules of physics break down around them."

"No, they don't break down. They just asymptote to a more general, higher-energy variation of the same law. The forces unify. Symmetry unbreaks, or some physics shit that Zheng was trying to tell me."

"What's your point, Commander?" He was getting a little impatient. And tired—all he wanted to do was sleep for another day. On top of the three he'd already slept.

She leaned in closer. "Sir, the computer records on board the *Constitution* indeed show it was gone for approximately ten point five seconds."

She paused, and glanced over her shoulder to make sure the door was closed. "All except for one record. Doc Wyatt left the audio recording running in sickbay—that's how he decided to dictate his patient notes in the flood of casualties he was dealing with. Just kept a running, continuous log. He figured he'd sort it all out later."

She paused again.

"And?" he said, expectantly, spooning more soup.

"And, that recording was left on. For over *three and a half days*."

The spoon stayed poised in the air halfway to his mouth.

"Say again?"

"Three and a half days."

"All silence?"

"Mostly static. Except for a few snippets right at the beginning." She paused, apparently deciding how much to tell him. "Voices. In Russian. Just a few snippets, like I said."

A chill ran up his spine.

"What were they saying?"

"Something about reviving someone. We can't tell much beyond that—the recording descends into static, and stays that way for over eighty-five hours. Eighty-five hours of static, until the last fifteen minutes where the two of us crash land the *Constitution* down into the Great Salt Lake, leaving a trail of destruction straight down into the center of South Salt Lake City."

The spoon dropped to the floor with a clatter. "Well...." He trailed off, shaking his head slowly. "Shit."

"Shit's right," she replied, sitting down on the foot of his bed.

Granger set his soup bowl down on his thigh. "Shelby, do you know what pissed me off so much about the Khorsky incident? I mean, besides the obvious complacency, incompetence, and collusion displayed by our own leaders?"

She seemed taken aback by the sudden change of subject. "What's that?"

"In those few minutes we were engaging the Russians, and before IDF showed up to break up the fight, I saw something. Another ship. Right beside one of the Russian dreadnoughts. I swore it looked like a Swarm ship, or, at least what one might have looked like sixty years on. But it q-jumped the hell out of there when we showed up. I called Yarbrough and Zingano out on it, but...." He shrugged, picked up his soup bowl again and struggled to reach to the floor for his spoon. "Well, we all know how that ended up. And to think, after all these years, they really *were* somehow in contact with the Swarm. My god, Shelby, we're looking at a galactic conspiracy here."

Someone knocked on the door, and entered. It was the attending physician.

"Captain Granger? I have your test results." He glanced at Proctor. "You'll have to leave, ma'am."

The doctor sat down and shuffled some papers, looking quite nervous. Doctors always sit down when they're the bearer of bad news.

But Granger, still shocked at Proctor's revelation, didn't have the words to speak, so he motioned for the doctor to continue, and for Proctor to stay.

The doctor watched her sit back down, and shrugged. "You're the picture of health, Mr. Granger. I pulled your chart that Dr. Wyatt was keeping for you on the *Constitution*, and there is absolutely no trace of the cancer he claims you had."

"Claims?"

"Well, given your current condition, I simply see no conceivable way you could have had stage four lung cancer just seventy-two hours ago. He said it had metastasized into your brain, your liver, your pancreas. Said you were the walking dead. I don't know what led him to make such a wildly fabricated diagnosis, but the fact remains, Mr. Granger, you are cancer-free, and free to go."

The bowl of soup joined the spoon on the floor, breaking into several pieces with a crash. Proctor shot him a look, which he wasn't sure spoke of suspicion, or relief.

"Well … shit," he repeated.

CHAPTER SIXTY-NINE

New Orleans, North America, Earth
Farnsworth Memorial Gardens

The funeral was short, without any clergy, and featured booze passed around amongst the mourners—just like Haws would have liked it. To his chagrin Granger had to give one final speech, but he kept it short, as was his custom: "A damn fine officer, and a damn fine friend. Abraham Haws." He held up the bottle he'd been nursing, and those with drinks did likewise, and before the funeral even really got started it was over.

Granger stooped to gather a fistful of earth and tossed it on the IDF flag-draped casket suspended over the hole. He turned to leave, and out of the corner of his eye, he saw the two fleet intel security guards that had been shadowing him since he left the hospital two days ago move as if to follow him.

Wonderful. Save the world, and all it earns you is suspicion and surveillance. Par for the course for IDF, Granger thought, grimly. It was a wonder Earth still existed after not one, but two alien invasions, given the level of rampant bureaucracy and mistrust and general incompetency.

But the guards stopped and turned away before Granger even took a step away from the grave. The rest of the crowd was dispersing—mostly old comrades of Haws and a few fleet dignitaries. One of the top brass, Fleet Admiral Zingano, who had just apparently dismissed the two security officers, approached Granger. His arm was in a sling and half his face bandaged—injuries earned at the doomed *Valhalla Station*. Miraculously the command section remained intact, albeit thoroughly and violently damaged.

"Tim. Good to see you."

"Admiral." He took a few steps towards his ground taxi waiting on the street.

"Tim, we need to talk."

Granger stopped, still looking towards the taxi, his back to the Admiral. "The answer is no."

"I haven't even asked you yet."

"I know what you're going to ask." He turned to face the other man. "I've resigned. I'm not coming back. The *Constitution* is dead. She's my ship, and I'll not serve on another —I'm too old. That duty belongs to younger men."

Zingano snorted. "Bull. Tim, we need you. Like it or not, you're now the most decorated and battle-tested veteran in the fleet. You're the only captain to have faced the aliens at the helm of a starship and lived to tell about it. You and Proctor. I can't just let you retire."

"Like hell you can't."

Admiral Zingano looked down at the grave, and nudged some more dirt in with the toe of his boot. "He was a spitfire, recalcitrant, rebellious old bastard, wasn't he?" Zingano smiled. "Just like you."

"On a charm offensive, I see," remarked Granger.

Zingano sighed. "I'll give you a new ship. You won't have to wait for the *Constitution* to be refurbished."

Granger had turned to leave again, but now paused mid-step. "Did you just say you're refurbishing the Old Bird?"

"I did."

The *Constitution*. Alive again. Rising from what he had been sure was her grave.

"Then I want her. That's the only way you get me back."

Zingano smiled—apparently he knew exactly how to get Granger back. "She's yours. But, Tim, she won't be ready for at least six months. I've drafted an army of engineers and workmen to restore her as fast as humanly possible, but it's a big job."

Granger started walking toward his ground car again. "Then I'll see you in six months."

"I'll give you another one in the meantime."

Granger chuckled. "I don't want some modern, slick, paper-thin-hulled monstrosity that IDF seems keen on churning out these days."

"No, not one of the modern super-carriers or cruisers—in fact, IDF is scrapping that design and is in a frenzy to build a whole fleet of solid metal behemoths like the *Constitution*. No, I've got something better for you."

"I'm listening."

"The *ISS Warrior*. One of the remaining ships of the old

Legacy Fleet. She's been mothballed over at Europa Station ever since her decommissioning nearly forty years ago, and we intended to use her for scrap. But you know how IDF bureaucracy works. They run paperwork at the speed of thick chicken shit. As a result, she's still there. Stripped some, but otherwise intact. I've had a team of a thousand workers there for the past five days getting her ready, and she needs a captain."

Granger closed his eyes. Since the cancer had left, and seeing pictures of the wreck of his old ship, he'd wanted nothing more than to retire to a warm, white sand Florida beach with an open bar and free massages courtesy of IDF's generous retirement package. Another tour? Another ship? Another crew?

"Your planet needs you, Tim. I need you. Miami's gone. Houston's gone. Phoenix is gone, and the aliens are coming back. We've already detected activity in their space, and it looks like they may be on the move soon. You, at the helm of a Legacy Fleet ship, are the best weapon in our arsenal."

Granger took a turn kicking dirt into Haws's grave.

"Fine. But I want my old crew. Every single person that'll have me as their captain."

"Done."

"And I want Proctor."

Zingano started. "Shelby? Sorry, no. She'll be commanding the *Chesapeake*, the other Legacy Fleet ship we're restoring. After you, she's the most battle-hardened veteran we've got, and I need her at the helm of—"

"Then my answer is no." Granger turned to leave, but didn't walk away just yet.

A long pause. *A game of chicken,* Granger mused. Who would give in first?

"I'll ask her, and give her the option. But it's her choice—I'm not going to dangle a command in front of her and then snatch it away just to send her back to some old crank," he replied with a wry grin.

"And I won't blame her for turning me down. But I can't imagine going into battle without her."

He walked back to his taxi, and noticed the fleet security guards pull up behind him in their own vehicle. Granger waved Admiral Zingano down. "Call off the intel goons or the deal's off."

Zingano hobbled towards Granger's taxi, his free arm making an over exaggerated motion to compensate for the limp and the other useless arm in the sling. "Sorry, IDF intel insists. Says you're still a possible security risk given the circumstances surrounding the *Constitution's* disappearance."

Granger chuckled. "You're giving me a starship, but think I'm a security risk?" His face turned serious. "Cut the shit."

Zingano pointed towards the horizon. "Tim, half of Florida is under water. Mobile is a steaming watery pit. Houston is a crater. At least fifty million people have died, and in the meantime you somehow disappeared in a quantum singularity for three and a half days in the middle of the battle for Earth. Intel is right to be a little cautious with you, in spite of your well-deserved war hero status."

Granger only stared at him icily, daring him not to call the guards off.

Zingano shrugged, and motioned for the guards to leave. "I'll pull what strings I can at fleet intel, but the order came from high up."

    "How high?"

    Zingano turned to leave.

    "The top," he called behind him.

CHAPTER SEVENTY

Sacramento, North America, Earth
Miller Residence

Lieutenant Tyler Volz glanced back down at his datapad and confirmed the address. And the picture of the house on his screen matched the modest building in front of him, a nondescript house on the outskirts of Sacramento.

He inhaled, paused, then approached the door. Toys littered the front steps, along with chalk drawings on the walkway, and a small, red tricycle.

Dammit, Fishtail, why did you ask me to do this?

He knocked. He'd thought about calling ahead to make sure they were home, but reconsidered when he realized he would have nothing to say over the comm. *Hello, Mr. and Mrs. Miller, can I drop by later to tell you your daughter died? Ok, thanks.* He shuddered—how do you talk to a computer screen and tell someone their daughter is gone? And wasn't there a special corps that was responsible for notifying next of kin, showing up in person to console the survivors? He knew the answer: of course there was, but being overwhelmed with the deaths of hundreds of thousands of servicemen and servicewomen, they'd be backlogged for years.

His hand paused mid-knock. It occurred to him that he still had no idea what to say, even in person.

Dammit. Someone was coming.

The door opened.

Mrs. Miller. Fishtail's mom. He recognized her from the contact file on his datapad. The blood left her face when she saw his uniform.

"No," she whispered.

Volz cleared his throat and clutched the small package he'd brought with him. "Mrs. Miller? May I come in?"

A small boy peered from behind her legs. Zack.

It was like a dream. He somehow wandered into the house after her—had she invited him? She must have, because she was leading him to the kitchen, where a man with graying hair was sitting at the table. Mr. Miller?

Fishtail's mother stood standing by the sink, looking out the window. Mr. Miller remained motionless and silent at the table, his eyes bleary and puffy and red and staring at the table, his lips pressed tightly together.

Volz shuffled uncomfortably. He'd never comforted anyone in his life. What the hell was he doing here? He shifted on his feet again.

No. They needed confidence from him. They needed assurance that their daughter had died a hero. That there was a point to all of it. That her sacrifice had not been in vain.

Dammit, why hadn't they trained him for this?

"Mr. and Mrs. Miller, I'm Lieutenant Tyler Volz. I served with your daughter aboard the *Constitution*. I'm here because...."

He swallowed hard. "I'm here because she asked me to come. To give you this in case something happened to her." He extended a hand to Mr. Miller, who accepted the offer.

The man held the ring in his fingers, looking down at it. He shook, and closed his eyes.

"She wanted me to give it to Zack, but I thought it'd be safer with you for now. But I brought this for him instead." He presented the small package he'd been clutching to the little boy who was playing with a toy car on the floor. "Open it," he said.

The boy accepted the package eagerly, and tried to open it, but couldn't figure out the ribbon. So Volz ripped the paper off for him.

A perfect model of the X-25 fighter his mother had died in. He squealed with delight, and immediately began playing with it, balancing it high above his head, clenched in his little hand, letting it soar.

After some moments of silence, punctuated by the sounds of the boy playing, Zack abruptly stood up and faced Volz. "Is Momma and Dad gone?"

Volz nodded. "Yes."

"Where is she?"

"I—I don't know."

It was true. He had no idea where Fishtail was. Nothing remained from the collision with the singularity. For all he knew, given Granger's reappearance, she could be on the other side of the universe, or hiding just behind the moon.

"Is she flying?"

"I—I don't know." He couldn't tell him the truth, but by the look he gave the boy's grandparents, he confirmed it. "She's flying really high, Zack."

"I want to fly too."

The boy continued to play with the toy fighter, and Volz turned to the parents. "She sacrificed herself. She saved the *Constitution*. She saved Earth. Gave the Old Bird enough time to take out the rest of the invasion fleet. Your daughter is ... was ... is, a hero." He stumbled over his words, unsure of what to say.

Mrs. Miller turned away from the sink and faced Volz. Tears streaked her pained face, but she forced a smile. "Thank you for coming, Lieutenant."

Minutes later, he stood outside on the sidewalk, facing the house again. It had started to rain.

"Goodbye, Fishtail," he murmured, and got back in the taxi.

CHAPTER SEVENTY-ONE

Europa, Jupiter, Sol System
Europa Shipyards

Miraculously, in the aftermath of the devastation on Earth, Lunar Base, and the Veracruz Sector, much of the usual red tape vanished. Granger would have expected a transfer to a new ship to take weeks, and the requisitions for new supplies and ordnance, plus all the crew rotating into their new assignments would have taken months. But it was less than twenty-four hours after the funeral that his shuttle entered Jupiter orbit after a q-jump and set a course for Europa.

"I expect it'll take some work to get her into shape, Cap'n, but we'll get her there. You'll see." Rayna Scott had accompanied him on the shuttle, along with Ensign Prince and Lieutenant Diaz, to help lead the work crews that were still in a frenzy getting the *Warrior* in shape for service. "My grandpa served on the *Warrior*, you know. Was the assistant chief engineer. Boy, he'd love to see me now, taking over his old engines for him."

"I'm sure he'd be proud," replied Granger, craning his head towards the viewport to get a good look at Europa Station. The huge spaceport now filled the window, turning slowly as their shuttle orbited, angling past a handful of starships in various stages of construction in the shipyards.

"Looks like they're already changing the design of these, sir," said Diaz, pointing to the nearest half-built cruiser. "They're not even bothering to strip off the smart-steel. They're just plating right over it with thicker armor."

"Like they should have done years ago," mumbled Granger, still looking out the window. Any moment now....

And there it was. The nearest construction arm of the station swept past, revealing one of the *Constitution*'s twins. The *ISS Warrior*, with hundreds of umbilicals stretched towards her from the construction pylon.

"Beautiful, isn't she?" said Ensign Prince.

Granger snorted. "Ugly as hell. But she'll be good to us if we're good to her, just like the Old Bird."

Once docked, a marine greeted them at the airlock and escorted them to the bridge. Hundreds of workers scurried the halls, working faster and harder than Granger had ever seen unionized crews move in his life.

The doors to the bridge slid aside, revealing a familiar sight.

"Captain on the bridge!" said the marine.

A head popped up from underneath the command console. She clutched a bundle of wires and cable, and smiled broadly. "Nice of you to finally drop in!"

Granger's jaw dropped.

"You came? What about the *Chesapeake*? I was sure you'd take your own command—"

She chuckled. "Don't flatter yourself, Tim. I will be commanding the *Chesapeake*."

Granger deflated somewhat. "Oh." He glanced around the bridge, watching the work crew install a new tactical station. "I suppose you're just here to see us off?"

"Of course not. The *Chesapeake* won't be ready for another two months—they stripped her something fierce, sir. Thought I'd take the best of both worlds—be the XO on the *Warrior* before being the CO on the *Chesapeake*. And besides, I can't even imagine spending two months overseeing repair of a starship when there's a war going on. Can you?"

Granger shook his head grimly. "Looks like we're in it for the long haul. Fleet intel has detected another fleet—this one heading for the Francia Sector."

"Bailing out the Francia Sector? Nothing ever changes, doesn't it?"

The irreverent remark caught him off guard, and he chuckled. "Right."

She bent back down underneath the command console. "Well, sir? What are you waiting for? Let's get to work."

He nodded, and tossed his shoulder bag onto the seat of his chair.

It was good to be home. Well, not home, but at least a pleasant rest stop on the way there.

Still nodding, he rubbed his hands. "Let's get to work."

Thank you for reading *Constitution*.

The story continues in:

Warrior

Victory

Independence

Defiance

Liberty

Sign up to find out when the next book of *The Legacy Fleet Trilogy*, is released: smarturl.it/nickwebblist

Contact information:

www.nickwebbwrites.com

facebook.com/authornickwebb

authornickwebb@gmail.com

DISCARD

60964706R00200

Made in the USA
Columbia, SC
19 June 2019